PRIESTS

THE GUISE AND GUYS BEHIND THE COLLAR

a novel

1

TO

MY BROTHER PRIESTS

**WHO RUN THE RACE
AND FIGHT THE GOOD FIGHT**

A special note of gratitude to Charlotte Miller and Christopher Madigan for their patient and professional guidance.

Contents

FOREWORD

A valid argument could be made that this book should never be written. But, then, an equally valid argument could contradict that stance. I am obviously opting for the latter. In fact, the book needs to be written; the curtain needs to rise on a cast of characters largely misunderstood for centuries. They have been placed on pedestals by some and vilified by others, but never really understood. Some see them as enigmatic, some as hypocritical; saints or sinners; humble servants or self-serving egotists; starry-eyed idealists or simple fools; intellectuals or dolts. Some view them as courageous reformers but others as mindless conformists; some as having the common touch and others as condescending martinets.

Almost all of these perceptions have some validity. I know these guys; in fact, I'm one of them—I am a Catholic priest. A priest is a real person, with the same personality quirks, same likelihood of dysfunctional family history, same temptations, same ability to hurt or be hurt, same baggage, same aches and pains, same need to love and be loved, same human joys and desires as anyone else. But here's the kicker: somewhere along the line he has fallen in love with God and has without any personal merit of his own received a call to serve Him, to proclaim Him, and—if you will excuse the presumption—to be like Jesus. But all this high-minded stuff doesn't take away the humanity; he remains just a person, sans halo or horns.

For over 54 years I have sought to understand the chasm that exists between the beauty of the call that I received to be a priest and the reality of the flawed individual who had the temerity to answer it. I have watched the world sizing up my struggle and those of my brother priests. Throughout this book the priestly characters are based on the priests whom I've known, watched, taught, counseled, shared the good and the bad, endured, imitated, directed, buried, and loved. Some made my heart soar; others made my heart wince in shame. Yeah, a priest is just a guy who receives a call through no merit of his own.

While the priests, bishops, deacons, laity and general population herein are all fictional, any resemblance to you or anyone you know is both coincidental and probable. In fact, if my characters don't remind you of some of the people you know, both those with and without collars, I've missed the mark. In truth, every priest character in this novel has both virtues and vices with which I can empathize; I bet you can too.

CHAPTER ONE

MONSIGNOR CLEMENT J. DONNELLY

Ann Margaret Sullivan Donnelly was about to give birth to her second son at St. John Hospital. Little Timmy fidgeted in the waiting room next to his small-boned father, Al, and his adoring grandparents. The date on the ominous funeral home calendar was November 23, 1934; the clocked ticked the seconds loudly in the room long quiet from exhausted pleasantries. Long past his bedtime, Timmy's hopes for a baby brother were now accompanied by his whining as he watched the silver beads of his grandmother's rosary slip through her fingers and her lips move in mute prayer. It had been several hours since the doctor had whispered that problems had arisen; the baby had failed to turn in the womb. Timmy had never seen his father so quiet or so strange. The doctor returned to the waiting room and there was more whispered conversation with Al before returning through those doors where Margaret lay in pain and prayer.

Suddenly Timmy's father took him by the hand and rushed down the hall. Timmy was glad for the exercise. The father arrived at his destination, and hurriedly knelt before the statue of the Sorrowful Mother, barely visible in the dimly lit chapel. He pulled Timmy down beside him. And, for the first time, Timmy saw his daddy cry and then sob loudly. Timmy was frightened as his father hugged him, really hard, too hard. "Oh, God, don't let Maggie and the baby die. Please, Mary, help them. I'll do anything you ask. I'll give you anything you want." Timmy felt his father's tears against his own cheek and, sensing his dad's anxiety, began to cry also and to pray in his own childish prattle the prayers Margaret had attempted to teach him.

Al heard the swish of skirts and the rattle of rosary beads behind him and he looked up to see Sister Mary Assumpta, who brought him the news that the doctor had succeeded in turning the baby and that the delivery was proceeding normally. All the fear and anxiety burst forth from Al in a mixture of tears and laughter. Timmy knew that things were now all right.

Clem weighed eight pounds and four ounces, was hearty and evidently just too lazy to turn in the womb. It was the feast of St. Clement and Al had not forgotten his promises in the chapel. He was determined to devote this child to God from birth. Timmy thought Clem was strangely inept and far from fun, hardly the playmate he had been promised.

By the time Clem was five, he idolized his older brother. Regardless of how much Timmy teased him, beat him, or swiped his toys, Clem just loved him more. By the time Timmy reached high school he had morphed into Tim, a rough and tumble, good-hearted football player for Catholic High School. He had no greater fan than Clem, whose laziness in the womb was only exceeded by his total disinterest and ineptitude in sports. As many times as Tim tried to teach him to throw and catch any shape or kind of ball, he succeeded only in establishing that Clem would never be an athlete. Clem was content to watch Tim and vicariously experience athletic triumph through the brother he loved. Tim had his own cheering squad in Clem, who was genuinely happy for his brother's talents. Envy simply did not interest Clem.

Clem found his niche in his sophomore year at Catholic High when he tried out for a part in the school play, *Our Town*. He snagged the part of the stage manager and was surprised by the praise and acclaim of his fellow students. His next triumph was on the debate team, where he was named captain. For Clem public speaking was easy and simply felt "right." And, just as the girls had swarmed around Tim with his success on the gridiron, now they found Clem, who seemed to love everyone, but particularly the girls. When Tim left for the University of Oklahoma at Norman, Clem felt the loss of his brother but the void was filled by several "steady" girlfriends. Clem's grades were above average but he never extended himself. His good manners, ease with adults, and ready smile made him popular with peers and teachers alike.

Carole Kennedy was particularly attracted to Clem, and he found her easy to be with, pleasant to kiss, and attractive enough. They fulfilled each other's need for dates on Friday nights, occasional dances, and even a few shared illegally purchased beers. It was a simple time to be a teenager; few engaged in sexual intercourse and almost no one had even thought of drug use. The demands of peer pressure were small, and the family was still the central focus of life.

And Clem loved his family. His mother, Margaret, was the source of abundant love for all the others, generally expressed through her many talents in the kitchen. Clem rarely walked through the back door after school without being greeted with wonderful aromas that promised a great dinner and the presence of a mother who loved him no less than she had that night he was born at St. John's. Al, his dad, was the family rock and almost as demonstrative as one, rarely showing his affection for his sons. Oh, the love for his sons was always there, but it was a time when men did not speak of such things.

There was no doubt concerning the Catholicity of the Donnelly family and it was not the most popular thing to be in Oklahoma in the '50s. There were still tirades on the radio by fundamentalist preachers against "papists," and the KKK had planted enough bigotry that distrust and suspicion lingered in the minds of many. The Donnellys simply elected to ignore it and live the Catholic life. It was who they were. Missing Mass on Sunday was never an option; it never even entered their minds. Both Tim and Clem served Mass at St. Catherine's Church from the fourth grade until they graduated from high school. They attended almost all the parish activities: forty hours devotions, missions, retreats, sodalities, men's club, Knights of Columbus, Catholic Youth Organization, endless potlucks, and parish fairs.

But church attendance does not guarantee sanctity, and the reality of sin was always clearly defined in the sermons that the Irish pastor delivered. Clem had always felt the beauty of the Mass. He was in awe of the Eucharist, and the parish priests were honored in his family, their human faults overlooked. Clem had little trouble in respecting his parents; he had no reason not to. He became aware of his sexual urges when he was about eleven, did his best to repress them, but occasionally fell to the demands of his increasingly insistent testosterone. His behavior filled his adolescent mind with shame and became fodder for frequent confessions during his high school years.

By the end of his junior year, Clem's high school guidance counselor started reviewing options for his college years and possible professions. Due to his speaking abilities, law, business, and even acting were suggested. As none particularly interested him, he settled on a liberal arts trajectory that might provide some leeway in selecting a more definite course later. His pastor and one the priests at Catholic High School had both suggested the priesthood to him, but Clem didn't think himself morally fit for that and was really interested in making a ton of money, building a mansion, and marrying a really pretty girl who would provide him with equally pretty children.

Due primarily to his excellence in public speaking and acting in high school plays, Clem received a partial scholarship at Regis, a Jesuit college in Denver, Colorado. Although Clem wanted to attend the University of Oklahoma with his brother Tim, his father insisted that Regis would open more doors for him and that the scholarship should not be wasted. Additionally, Al reflected once more upon his promise to the Blessed Virgin and thought that a Catholic university would be still another way of keeping that promise.

No one else in Clem's class chose to attend Regis and so when it came time to leave for his first year, Clem felt quite alone. There were no parents, no brothers, no girlfriends, and no buddies to fill his life. He was determined to make it on his own and turned on all the charm he could muster to fit into his new environment. But it was far more difficult than he had imagined. He was no longer surrounded by friends from childhood, with whom he had gone to grade and high school, friends who shared the same background and the same dreams. He particularly missed his close friend from childhood on, Greg Owens.

It was that sense of alone-ness that caused Clem to attend daily Mass, seeking solace where he had always found it: in the Mass, the Eucharist, and all the trappings of Catholic worship. In the church he knew he was loved; there he felt at home; there his heart was always at peace; there he was not alone. There he could kneel before the life-sized crucifix in the vestibule of the university church and feel "right." At one of the side altars, an elderly priest celebrated Mass daily. He was so enfeebled that a Jesuit novice not only humbly supported him physically but occasionally had to remind him where he was in the liturgy. Nevertheless, the priest's piety and devotion were obvious. Clem was entranced by the priest's dedication and love; it was clear he possessed something precious. Clem wondered if he could have it too.

By the end of his freshman year, Clem told his parents and his pastor that he wanted to become a priest. Al immediately reflected upon that night almost twenty years before and the promises he had made in the chapel; he knew in his heart that God had responded to his prayer. Margaret cried the tears of joy that only a mother who loves God, the Church, and her son deeply could begin to understand. Tim, now entering his senior year at the University of Oklahoma and engaged to a beautiful, dark Jewish girl from Dallas, laughed and hugged his brother: "Now I know why God wouldn't ever let you catch the damn ball; He wanted you to win souls, not football games."

The studies and the discipline in the seminary were both intense. The stately old buildings seem to mirror the minds of the professors. As with all faculties, the quality of the teachers was mixed, all the way from senile priests whom the archbishop sent to teach in the seminary because they did not fit in parish life to the near genius, Rome-educated professors that made both dogmatic and moral theology come alive in the hearts and minds of the seminarians. While Clem's mind was being formed, his soul was being shaped into that of a priest. And, as they always had been, the most precious moments of formation for Clem came to him as he knelt before the Eucharist in the chapel of the seminary and let God touch his heart. He was at peace there.

On May 15, 1960, Clem was seated in St. Mary's Cathedral waiting to be ordained. His thoughts ranged from excitement about what was about to happen, to feelings of guilt about sins, though confessed and forgiven, he had never been able to overcome, to inadequacy and self-doubt about his ability to be a holy priest of Jesus Christ, to the love he had for the Church and the sacraments, to a collage of feelings he had for his family seated in the front row.

And then Clem heard his name as he was called into the sanctuary to be ordained a priest. As he prostrated himself, the cold marble of the sanctuary floor somehow seemed to jolt him into an awareness of the presence of God and let him know that God's power would provide the qualities he felt that he lacked. Clem was at peace; he knew that he was exactly where he should be, doing exactly what God wanted him to do.

As he stood next to the bishop and for the first time said the words of consecration, Clem perceived the power that had been experienced by priests for almost two thousand years. He felt somehow disembodied, part of something cosmic, something rooted in eternity. As he distributed the Eucharist to his parents, Tim and his wife Esther, and family and friends he had known all his life, he sensed God's love for them and felt humble to be a part of that love.

At the end of the Mass, it was time for Clem to give his first priestly blessing to his family. Al could not look at his priestly son and humbly bowed his head, remembering once more those now fulfilled promises made to Mary on the day of his son's birth. Margaret was radiant and looked at now "Father" Clem with the assuring love that she had always given him. Tim's eyes filled with tears for his brother as his folded hands unclasped momentarily to give Clem a private "thumbs up" for scoring the ultimate touchdown. Tim's reaction touched Clem so deeply that he had to leave the sanctuary abruptly and make a hurried exit into the sacristy, where all the emotions he had bottled up burst forth in sobs. The responses that love evokes are often difficult to understand, and love's beauty is at times painful.

Father Clem's first assignment was to St. Francis Xavier Church as an associate to an elderly pastor who was both kind and deeply spiritual. He welcomed Clem warmly and showed him to the spartan bedroom that would be his for the next two years. It was a simple agrarian parish with parishioners who made few demands of their priests, and who were content to attend Mass on Sundays and holydays and to send their children to the small parish elementary school.

Clem embraced his early priesthood with excitement and vigor. In fact, with far more excitement and vigor than was required in the small parish. He loved teaching religion to the children in grade school, working with the teenagers in the Catholic Youth Organization, counseling young married couples struggling with their marriages and children, but most of all, he loved the sacraments.

In the '60s the laity still came to confession regularly and while some did so in a routine manner and without much thought, others were moving in their repentance and sincerity. Clem learned a great deal about the spiritual struggles of the people he was ordained to serve and he listened attentively as their sins, grief, frustration, sorrow, shame, and relief filtered through the black cloth that divided his cubicle from where the penitent knelt. He knew that Jesus was healing and forgiving through him and the feeling was humbling but gratifying.

On the First Fridays of each month, Clem visited the houses of all the shut-ins and the convalescent homes in the parish. He was always struck by the humility and appreciation of the sick, and the gratitude and respect of their families. They obviously loved the priesthood and loved him as a priest of Jesus Christ. The crucifixes above the beds of the sick and the trust in their eyes let Clem know that they possessed spiritual treasures from God that he was still hoping to attain.

But it was the celebration of Mass and preaching that were the center of Clem's life. He loved both. The mystery of the Eucharist which became present in his hands as he said those same words that Jesus proclaimed at the Last Supper, the sense of exaltation that he always felt when he elevated the Blessed Sacrament, the goodness of the laity as they knelt to receive the Body of Christ made sense of everything in Clem's life. And he could see God's hand in his natural speaking ability as he preached at Mass. Preaching was always an exciting challenge, an opportunity to connect with the minds and hearts of the people about the only thing that really mattered, God's love. He loved being a priest.

Clem had been at St. Francis for about two years when his old flame from high school, Carole Kennedy Meade, arrived for a visit with her older sister. He had lost contact with Carole after he entered the seminary nine years before and he rarely thought of her. Carole had been married to Bob Meade, a man fifteen years her senior, but divorced him and stopped practicing her faith. It was quite unexpected when Clem received a call from Carole's sister, Diane, a member of the parish, inviting him to come to dinner; there was no mention of her sister's visit.

When Clem arrived at the home, Carole answered the door and greeted him with a hug and a smile. He was happy to see an old friend with whom he had shared so many adventures in high school. Diane appeared, offered him a beer, told him she had to finish cooking the dinner and disappeared into the kitchen. It was then that Clem began to realize that he had been set up. He felt really uncomfortable. Carole sat next to him on the couch, put her arm around him, her other hand on his thigh, and moved in to kiss him. He turned away, got up rapidly, and started talking nervously about their shared high school experiences. Diane finally reappeared. The dinner was served and the mood was awkward. Clem made his excuses and left as soon as he could politely do so.

He felt betrayed by both Diane and Carole. The motivation for the dinner invitation was all too obvious. Carole was out to snag her old boyfriend, and Clem's vows of celibacy and the Church meant nothing to her. In an ironic manner, the experience was good for Clem as it made him question himself regarding his vows of celibacy. That Carole was his for the asking was clear. But far clearer to Clem was how much he loved Christ, the Church, and the priesthood. As he did each evening, he visited the Blessed Sacrament before he retired. There in the chapel that he knew he was complete, there that he knew he was loved in the only way that made any difference to him. He never saw Carole again, but heard later that she entered into two other unsuccessful marriages. The experience that evening was helpful to him in the years to come when other women confused his kindness for something more and made advances; he was now aware of the signs that could endanger his ultimate love for Christ and His Church.

After another year, Clem's bishop sent him to a slightly larger parish to assist a pastor with both health and alcohol problems. There he was able to see what happens to a priest when he loses his focus upon Jesus Christ and seeks the bottle as his refuge. The pastor was manipulative, unpredictable, and angry with everyone, including himself. He gave Clem little direction but much sarcasm and scorn. Clem found himself doing almost all of the parish work, making excuses for the pastor's increasing absence at church meetings, and hurriedly filling in for morning Masses when the pastor was "too ill" to celebrate Mass.

Towards the end of his second year at the parish, a deputation of the laity went to see the bishop about their pastor's obvious problems. When the assignments for the year were released by the chancery office, the pastor was granted a "sick leave," and Clem was assigned his own pastorate in a small parish. While those last two years were trying, lonely, and even disheartening for Clem, they forced him to focus on what made a good priest and what could stifle the greatness of the priesthood within the soul. From the first pastor he assisted Clem had learned the importance of simple kindness and humility in a priest; from his second he had learned dangers to avoid.

The year was 1965 and the Second Vatican Council was in its last session. The impact of the Council was yet to have any effect upon Clem's diocese or certainly his own new parish. The people were kind and welcoming, happy to have a bright, energetic young priest of thirty-one who gave great homilies and cared about his people. He had learned what the laity of a parish really wanted: a priest who sought his own holiness and that of the flock he served, who administered the sacraments devoutly, who preached well and sincerely, who really loved his parishioners and knew he was there to serve them, and who wasn't afraid of work. He knew that if a priest was all that, the people would love him, respect him, listen to his counsel, come to him in time of need, and love the Church—as well as forgive his very human failings.

Clem would remain pastor of that church for ten years. It was a difficult time for the Church in the United States. No one knew exactly what to expect from Vatican II, and almost everyone expected either too little or too much, which resulted in much disillusionment and confusion among clergy and laity alike. Clem was hurt as he saw close priest friends leave the priesthood and that frightened him. He tried to convince some to reconsider; he pleaded, argued, wrote letters, made phone calls, but they left. They seemed angry, as if the Church had somehow left them, rather than they had left the priesthood. Few that abandoned the priesthood even remained in the Church.

Throughout the upheaval among the clergy, Clem was never seriously tempted to leave the priesthood. The priesthood was his life. He knew that Jesus had given us the Church and existed within it and its members. Not to be able to celebrate Mass, not to be able to preach, not to be able to minister in the name of Jesus, not to be able to forgive sins in Jesus' name was simply unthinkable. He lived to celebrate, preach, minister, and forgive; it was his identity.

Every priest at that time experienced the anger and confusion of the laity. Altars were turned around, altar rails were removed, Latin was replaced by the vernacular, shared responsibility of the laity was stressed, and the parish priest was often the one to bear the frustration of the laity. Nothing had changed in the Church for four hundred years, and now the stability that Catholics had prized seemed to be threatened by a whirlwind of change. Clem constantly counseled patience, humility, trust in the Church's authority, and emphasized the essence of the sacraments rather than manner in which they were administered. Clem received tongue lashings from angry parishioners who wanted things to remain the same but also from those who wanted changes far beyond the intentions of the Council. Clem and every other pastor went through hell, and keeping their parishes on track demanded deep faith and diplomatic skills inspired by the Holy Spirit.

Clem knew that if he were to survive the storm, he had to get to his knees in front of the Blessed Sacrament and pray for the Church, his parish, and his own priesthood. The Divine Office was also a life preserver cast into the angry seas, as the Psalms constantly reminded Clem that his refuge was in the Lord. He knew the Church would survive; Jesus had promised that it would. He felt like the captain of a ship who sought refuge from the storm in his cabin as he prayed to God for guidance. He knew that the Lord would eventually bring calmer seas, and as time passed He did. The squalls would continue to emerge from time to time during Clem's priesthood, but he always knew where to seek refuge and who was really in charge. He had faith.

Throughout Clem's priesthood, each bishop he served would always find a bigger parish and greater responsibilities for him to shoulder at the diocesan level. He was genuinely convinced of the need for authority and knew that while bishops were fallible they also had the guidance of the Holy Spirit. In an age in which "blind obedience" was ridiculed in almost every facet of life, he was always willing to do whatever the bishop asked. Perhaps it was this quality in Clem that made him trusted by the bishops he served and which led to his becoming vicar general for the diocese, at only forty years of age. He would hold this position for a diocesan record of thirty-two years and through the tenures of three bishops.

Clem shouldered the responsibilities of being second in charge of the diocese while simultaneously pastoring one of its larger parishes. Clem's responsibility was to chair the diocesan clergy personnel board, which meant, practically speaking, that he was to see that the bishop's desires regarding his priests, their conduct and assignments, were properly administered. Needless to say, that did not always endear Clem to his brother priests. While he sought to advise the bishop in ways helpful to both the parishes and the clergy and sought to approach his brother priests with kindness and understanding, he was in the position of making hard decisions that did not always simultaneously benefit both priest and parish.

Some of the more difficult cases that Clem had to administer involved Father Adam Coors, Father Joseph Mulalley, Father Joshua Constantine, and Father Christian Mangan and his father. Clem agonized over each case, prayed long and hard, sought advice, lost sleep, and finally made the steps that were demanded.

The stress, the long hours, the hospital calls in the middle of the night, the funerals with the accompanying grief of loved ones, the weddings with the demands of often unreasonable brides and their mothers, the counseling sessions with mixed results, the ever increasing demands of the diocese and the parishes he served, personnel problems for both the diocese and the parish, and his own declining health began to take their toll on Clem. He was now seventy-two, had been ordained for almost forty-seven years, had lost his parents and seen his beloved Tim die at forty-eight of pancreatic cancer.

At 9:15 one evening, Clem had just returned from a difficult parish council meeting, trying to discern whether a new wing should be added to the parish school. As always, there were the pro and the con, sometimes reasonably discussed, sometimes not. He was absolutely drained as he sank into his recliner, wondering if he had the energy left to finish his Divine Office, brush his teeth, and get ready for bed.

He stared at the ceiling as he began his daily examination of conscience. He thought of the many blessings that had been his over the years: faith, family, friends, vocation, assignments, the love of the people he served, the tens of thousands of Masses he had celebrated, the hundreds of thousands of confessions he must have heard, his love of preaching, and most of all, the constant presence of Jesus in his life.

He wondered why he had been so blessed. He knew the problems of some of his brother priests and their struggles which did not always end happily. He thought of some of his close friends in the priesthood who had died, two by their own hands. The problems and the triumphs of Vatican II. A country that had experienced dramatic moral decline during his years as priest. Widespread abortion and contraception. The pain caused by the scandal of pedophilia. The loneliness which is a part of celibate life. His own sins and temptations which had never ceased. Nominal Catholics who did little to sustain or nourish their faith. The beauty of those afire with the life of the Holy Spirit. The beauty of a child receiving First Communion. The collage of jumbled memories both painful and pleasant drifted through his weary mind. His hands relaxed from holding the Divine Office and his head nodded to the side.

Clem's newly ordained young assistant, Father Alain Moreau, tapped on the door jamb before entering Clem's room. He had come to seek the advice of the older priest whom he respected for his wisdom and balance. Something strange about the position of Clem's head prompted Alain to look more closely. Clem was not breathing. His hands lay palms up on either side of the open breviary resting in his lap, and Alain was startled when he noticed those familiar words from night prayer: "Into thy hand, O Lord, I commend my spirit." The pledge was now completed.

The funeral took place four days later. The church was filled, as would be the case with the funeral of any priest who had loved his parishioners and served them well.

The bishop spoke eloquently but overly long, as might be expected when eulogizing his vicar general. Even the priests whom Clem had been forced to reprimand or change from one parish to another were present with at least a grudging respect for one of their own who had fought the good fight and done it with integrity.

In the third row was a teenage boy Clem had baptized, given his First Communion, counseled when his parents were having marital problems, and had served Mass for Clem for eight years. There were tears the in boy's eyes as he remembered Clem's kindness, his joy in his priesthood, the unselfishness with which he had always addressed his family's needs. And the boy thought to himself, "Maybe I could be like that."

CHAPTER TWO

FATHER ADAM COORS

Adam was the fourth child born to Gene and Ferris Coors in a small town offering little opportunity for advancement. The population was less than 200, and it would have been difficult to locate where even that many lived. The year was 1950 and the baby boomer phase was in full swing. Gene had returned from the war in 1945, rapidly marrying his old sweetheart Ferris and turning out a child a year. Supporting his family was difficult for Gene, who had gone to work at a local shoe factory. Ferris had come from a farming family and brought into her marriage emotional baggage she had inherited from her unstable upbringing.

Gene and Ferris attended a little mission church staffed by a priest from a neighboring parish. Each Sunday they would get the children together, lecture them on how to behave at Mass, and drag them into church in their hand-me-down clothes. The children were for the most part clean in appearance; Ferris looked perpetually haggard and Gene sullen. Should any of the children "act up" at Mass, they would receive a swift swat on the rear from their dad; they rarely acted up and appeared a bit cowed.

By the time Adam entered the first grade at the consolidated school twenty miles north, Ferris had given birth to one other child and showed signs of being emotionally distraught. Having five children under twelve had taken its toll. The children learned to take care of one another and even to take care of Ferris. Gene grew increasingly sullen, saw little purpose in life, and had become a functioning alcoholic. The children were amazingly resilient and generally well-behaved, but had no adult to love them or give them much in the way of emotional support. They grew up thinking that was how life worked.

The young priest who came to the mission church was energetic, laughed a lot, paid attention to the children, stayed after Mass to teach them their catechism, and always had something encouraging to say to each of them. Compared to what the Coors children had at home, he was great. He would even treat them to hamburgers from time to time, but it was the personal attention that the Coors children so sorely lacked at home that endeared Father Smith to them.

Adam was in the third grade when he returned home to find that Ferris had left. While the older brother and two sisters seemed sad at the loss of their mother, they were also somewhat relieved that they would no longer have to cope with her. The baby of the family had long since learned to depend upon his siblings for care and seemed almost totally unconcerned by Ferris' absence. Adam, however, felt betrayed and abandoned. As he had a compassionate heart, he had always snuggled up to his mom, even when she was mentally somewhere else. Gene felt no need to explain Ferris' absence to his children. "Your mother doesn't live here anymore; she won't be comin' back" seemed sufficient to Gene. "Just do what I say and we'll get along fine without her. She wasn't much use anyway."

Adam was the only one in the family who cared. He knew that it was useless to share his feelings with his father or his siblings. He would be ridiculed. He felt very alone and angry. He walked down the street, alternately using the swear words he had heard when his father had too much to drink and then asking God to bring his mother back to him.

On the following Sunday during catechism class, Father Smith noticed that the Coors children looked more forlorn and disheveled than usual and that Adam obviously was having a really hard time. He asked the class to write down adjectives that they might use to describe Jesus and instructed Adam to come with him. Together they sat on the cracked cement steps that led to the little mission church, and he gently took Adam's small hand and held it as he spoke.

"Adam, I want you to tell me why you are so sad today."

The boy wiped his runny eyes and nose with the back of his free hand. He felt embarrassed to say that his mother had left the family. Maybe his dad wouldn't want him to tell and he would get in trouble. But he felt so alone, and finally someone seemed to care about him and why he hurt so badly.

"Mom's gone."

"I saw that she was not with you at Mass. Are you okay?"

"Why did she have to leave, Father? It's not fair. Nobody else cares. She was the only one who loved me. Why did Jesus let her go?"

A wise priest knows that there are often no ready answers to tragedy, death, absence of a loved one, or life's turning upside down. "I don't know the answers to your questions, Adam, but I want you to know something really well. Look at me and listen carefully. You are not alone. Wherever your mother is, she still loves you and would never have left you unless she had to. Her heart has you in the center of it right now. And there is someone else who loves you too–and you know who that is, don't you?"

"You mean Jesus, don't you, Father? But he is not here. He can't hold me and tell me he loves me."

"But he is here, Adam. He is here in me. I'm his priest; he lives in me, and he loves you through me. He speaks to you in the Bible we study after Mass; he comes inside you every Sunday when you go to Communion. You are never, never alone."

It was a lot for a third-grader to wrap his mind around. Father finally let Adam's hand go and placed his arm around his shoulder and gave him a reassuring hug. He offered a handkerchief to Adam. "Wipe your nose. We're going back in now, and you're going to be fine because you know that God is with you and cares about you. Okay?"

"Okay."

"We'll see if the Dairy Queen has any burgers left after class." For the first time since he found that his mother had left, Adam smiled.

As the years went by, Adam saw each of his siblings leave as soon as they graduated from high school. He could hardly blame them; there were no emotional family ties and no decent jobs available. Gene's alcoholism had progressed and his chain smoking had led to emphysema and the loss of his job. A close bond had developed between Adam and his younger brother Jake, and Adam had to protect his brother from their father, who had a tendency to become abusive when he drank heavily. One evening Adam had to physically threaten his father with a knife when he had thrown Jake to the floor and was pummeling him with one hard blow after another. A few days later, when Gene had fallen asleep in his recliner, the boys left the house and never returned. Like mother, like sons.

Adam had never forgotten the kindness of the young priest, who was now a pastor in a city fifty miles away. The boys hitch-hiked and arrived at Father Smith's rectory door about 2 a.m. Father Smith heard the doorbell, threw on his robe, and opened the front door to find two very tired and frightened boys. He took them to the kitchen, fed them, and let them tell their story. The priest knew the family history well enough to know what they were saying was true. He told them they could sleep in the guestroom and they would talk in the morning.

The next morning Father Smith drove to visit Gene, who thought the boys had probably just gone to school and didn't seem very concerned about their absence. The priest confronted Gene with his alcoholism as well as his neglect and abuse of his boys. Gene responded that he'd had a hard life himself and didn't much care what happened to his sons, who were old enough to take care of themselves. Father Smith returned to his rectory and found a good home where Adam and Jake could spend the remainder of their school years. An older couple took them in, tried to show them love, and provided for their basic needs.

Perhaps it was due to the example of Father Smith that Adam realized in his senior year of high school he wanted to become a priest. He still felt ashamed of his background and unloved. He did, however, often remember what Father Smith had told him on the steps of the little church after his mother had left. He knew that he wasn't really alone and that he was loved. He wanted to do for others what Father Smith had done for him; he wanted to give them hope and love; he wanted to save them, just as Father had saved Jake and him.

The next eight years in the diocesan seminary were challenging for Adam. He was not like most of the other young men, young men who had come from good homes with loving parents. He continued to feel embarrassed, alone, edgy, and even still a little angry about his background. Apart from his spiritual directors, he did not share his personal history with anyone, and made up stories to tell his fellow seminarians about why his "parents" were so much older than those of his classmates.

As the day of his ordination approached and his classmates' families helped to prepare for their First Mass celebrations, his sense of aloneness grew. Father Smith's parish was hosting his event, but there was no family involvement at all. His two older sisters had left the faith and sent word that they would not be able to attend. His older brother now lived across the country and could not afford to attend. Jake was still working his way through graduate school and planned to take the bus and arrive on the morning of the ordination. Adam tried to fabricate the joy that he knew should be in his heart, but there was little there.

As he blessed the couple who had cared for him during his last year in high school, he felt appreciation for them and the gentle kindness they had shown, but that was all: there was no deep sense of love or tenderness. The highlight of the ordination for Adam was when Father Smith dressed him in the priest's stole and chasuble. He looked into the teary eyes of his priest-mentor and saw a glimpse of what true unselfish love must really be. He remembered what the priest had told him on the steps of the mission church about God loving him through the priest himself. Adam prayed that he could be such a loving priest.

Father Adam began his priesthood with hope, determination, and the vigor of youth. He sought to become an effective priest by constant work and activity. He was honest about his spiritual journey in his homilies to the extent that the congregation was at times uncomfortable. It was obvious to them that the priesthood was not an easy road for him. The pastors under whom he served always liked Adam as he never backed away from responsibility or challenge, but there was never much conversation at the rectory dinner table, and Adam's replies often seemed tinged with sadness and even a little veiled anger.

Adam was faithful to his prayer life, although it did not seem to fill his heart. The Divine Office was often simply a burden. The emptiness he felt at prayer created a perceived chasm between God and himself. There were those moments when the Holy Spirit touched him but they were rare. Feeling unloved, he found it difficult to love. How he longed to know the love of God. How he longed to experience any love from anyone, even within himself. He determined to work harder, serve better; surely the emptiness would disappear.

He would have loved to be accepted within so many of the good parish families he served. As he watched loving parents bring their children to church and saw the closeness they shared, he reflected upon how different his own family had been. The young families seemed too busy to share their lives with Adam, and he felt uncomfortable about intruding upon their unity. He knew that he was to serve like Christ, but he wanted to be so much more.

What little there had been of his family had seemed to dissolve. The older couple who had cared for him after he left his father had never emotionally bonded with him; they did their "Christian duty" for two homeless boys and that was it. Gene was found dead in his home several years after the boys left. There was still no word concerning Ferris. His older siblings showed no interest in continuing anything connected to their past. There were occasional phone calls from Jake, mostly when he needed a "loan" from Adam.

Some priests are able to fill the void in their lives through their ministry, their prayer life, families, hobbies, or friendships with other priests. None of those worked for Adam. After ten years in the priesthood, he became increasingly depressed and felt that he had no one to turn to. He was ashamed to tell his priest/mentor Father Smith how unhappy he had become; he didn't want to disappoint the only person who had ever loved him unselfishly.

There was no deliberate intention on Adam's part to use alcohol as a crutch for his loneliness and depression. After he received his own little parish, it was easy to relax in the evening in front of the television and have a few beers or maybe a vodka or two. Having seen what alcohol did to his father's life, he became even more depressed that he saw the same thing happening in him that had happened to the man who had hurt him so deeply.

As his solitary drinking increased, his attention to parish duties began to slip, and his parishioners began to notice that their young pastor no longer had the drive and the verve he had possessed when he was first assigned. His homilies were shorter and somehow less uplifting; calls to the rectory were unanswered and messages unreturned; counseling sessions were perfunctory and distracted, parish meetings unattended, suggestions rebuffed, sick calls almost non-existent, and he was often late and occasionally even absent for Mass. The laity is generally more perceptive than most priests, including Adam, realize. After some months of this, parishioners started to voice their concerns (some charitably, some not) to the pastors in neighboring parishes. The bishop was finally made aware of the situation and sent his vicar general, Msgr. Clement Donnelly, to talk with Adam.

Confronting his brother priests about their problems was never one of Clem's favorite things to do He was never comfortable with using authority or causing his brother priests pain, and suspected that this meeting would be very uncomfortable, possibly even tumultuous, and expected a lack of candor and truthfulness. After all, if a priest has given in to alcoholism, he has become accustomed to lying.

When Clem rang the door of the rectory, there was no answer. He tried again, and then again. Adam's car was in the carport. This time Clem placed his finger on the doorbell and left it there. The door swung open abruptly, and there was poor Adam, glassy eyed, obviously angry at being bothered by whoever was ringing the bell, and not at all pleased to see that it was the vicar general.

"Hey, Adam, it's Clem. May I come in?"

"Well, I was just getting ready to leave."

"I need to talk with you, Adam. Now."

The living room was in disarray. The television was tuned to a soap opera. The venetian blinds were closed. An almost empty bottle of vodka sat on the table next to a recliner. The room was dim. Cluttered papers filled the couch and lay about the floor.

Adam was not so far gone that he couldn't see that the evidence of his problem surrounding him and he could read the reaction on Clem's face. He knew that there was no use protesting his innocence. He was profoundly embarrassed and deeply saddened as he and Clem sat down and looked into one another's eyes.

Adam's eyes watered as he nervously rubbed his hands over his thighs. "I know what you see, Monsignor. I see the same thing. I couldn't take it. I couldn't take the loneliness. The emptiness. Not belonging. I've let down everybody that means anything to me. I let down God, the Church, the bishop, my parish. God, I hate myself; I hate what I have become."

Clem was relieved at Adam's repentance, his openness, and that he did not have to engage in a heated argument involving accusations and denials. As Father Smith had done so many years earlier, Clem took Adam's hand in his. At this action, those memories flooded back, and Adam broke down sobbing.

"I'm so glad you're here, Monsignor. I don't know what I would have done if this had continued. Each day was worse than the one before."

The sincerity of Adam's remorse was obvious. Clem did his best to assure him that his priesthood was not at an end, that his fall was understandable in light of his background, and the bishop would be eager to help him.

Almost every priest who requires correction from his superiors travels through the five steps of grief: depression, anger, denial, bargaining, and finally acceptance. Adam had spent most of his life in the first two stages and they had enveloped his personality as his drinking had increased. There was little room for denial due to the circumstances in which Clem had found him.

When it came to the solution for Adam's problem, the bargaining phase began. Clem told him to pack his bags, that it would necessary for him to leave the parish with him, and that he would be sent to an out-of-state rehabilitation facility specifically designed for clergy. Adam's stomach turned cold as he imagined the humiliation that leaving the parish abruptly would certainly provoke. He had tried so hard, overcome so many obstacles, prayed, sacrificed . . . and now he saw it all disappearing. As he had lost one mother, now he was losing another, the Church. They had both given him life, and he had loved them both. Did he have to go through that nightmare again?

He attempted to convince Clem that he could remain sober and once again become the kind of priest the parishioners needed to serve them. "If only the bishop would give me another chance . . ."

Clem was not buying it; he had seen the same problem too often, beginning with the second pastor under whom he had served so many years ago. He knew that the parish would continue to suffer if Adam were to remain and that action had to be taken. There had already been enough scandal and enough harm to the parish.

"Adam, both you and I know that you can't handle the sickness you have and that you are hurting the very people you love. Arrangements have already been made for you to enter the rehabilitation center, and they will be expecting you tomorrow afternoon. You need to come with me now. You'll stay with me at my rectory tonight. I'll fix us a steak. You'll get a good night's rest, and I'll put you on the plane in the morning. This is what has to happen."

He could see that there was no chance of Clem's relenting. Further bargaining for more time, another chance, would be useless. And he was so tired, tired of fighting it all: the temptations, the feelings of futility and uselessness and abandonment. As he had so many years ago on the steps of the little mission church, he wiped his tears with the back of his hand. Were the tears prompted by self-pity, anger, relief, or simple grief at seeing the priesthood he had wanted so badly crash and burn? Whatever their cause, the tears burst forth again. Clem placed a compassionate, fraternal hand on his shoulder, and Adam turned away—as always, unable to accept love.

The first of the six months in the center may well have been the most difficult of Adam's life. He had never shared his feelings well. The early years had given him little reason to trust what others might do with exposed feelings, secrets, fears, his heart. He had no desire to undress emotionally in front of others; he expected to be standing in the harsh draft of their judgment. He empathized with the first Adam's need for a fig leaf.

Ever so gradually, as the second month began, he became less afraid of being judged and petal by petal he opened his inner life to the others on the same journey to sobriety and recovery. He learned he was not unique. The others had also used alcohol and/or drugs as a crutch with increasing, damaging regularity. The healing had finally begun.

Adam was both eager and afraid to return to his parish: eager to return to the only thing that had meaning for him, but afraid that he might not be strong enough to be the kind of priest he yearned to be.

CHAPTER THREE

FATHER JOEL TAYLOR

The afternoon Clem loaded Adam and his belongings into his car and drove him to his rectory for the evening, he also called Father Joel Taylor. Joel was between assignments and, therefore, a convenient replacement for Adam. Adam and Joel were about the same age but dissimilar in almost every other aspect. Whereas Adam was unsure of himself and hesitant about relationships with others, Joel was never unsure about anything and enjoyed being in the middle of whatever was happening.

Joel's father was an attorney, known for winning his cases. He possessed a towering intellect and an ego to match. His attitude was cynical and condescending, and his three sons and one daughter often seemed to be on trial for his affection. The Taylor home was never a very peaceful one and was frequently the scene of verbal jousting, with the father using every courtroom trick he knew to bully his children and wife. Joel grew up knowing that every encounter with his dad should have begun with "En garde!" and an epee for a tongue. It was thrust and parry against an opponent who surrendered ground to no one. Joel unfortunately learned how to play that game all too well. His siblings had learned early on in their lives that they would never win an argument with their dad and retreated into a position of sullen, quiet disrespect.

Joel's mother had become cowed by her husband during the first year of their marriage. She sought her solace in the Church and her children. She attended Mass almost daily and prayed that somehow her children might escape inheriting the overbearing attitude of their father. Her prayers were largely answered, with Joel being the exception.

From the first grade on, Joel's extraordinary intelligence was recognized by his teachers; he made sure of that. He excelled not only in his studies but also in the manipulation of his teachers and classmates. He was quick to ridicule the shortcomings of others, as he had seen his father do to all the members of his family. He knew he was sharper than others and was quick to lord it over them.

Joel's pastor was one of the few people he respected. Monsignor Carroll was in his sixties when Joel entered St. Joseph's Elementary School. He was from Ireland, had a great mien of silver hair, carried himself like a prince, and wore his monsignori cassock everywhere. He presented a striking figure as he strolled the parish grounds with his beautifully groomed collie by his side. Even Joel's father had a certain grudging respect for Monsignor, and Joel had witnessed his pastor best his dad in verbal conflict, a singular accomplishment.

Msgr. Carroll dutifully distributed the report cards to all the children each grading period, with appropriate comments to each student. The words for Joel were of course always complimentary concerning his straight A's, perfect conduct and attendance. Joel always beamed as Monsignor complimented him and patted him on the back . . . at last, a man who recognized his worth. The other children might idolize Superman or a sports figure; Joel had Msgr. Carroll. While the others might don capes made from bathroom towels or table linens and career around their backyards chasing imaginary villains, Joel played the role of priest in endless pretend Masses and delivered fiery sermons to his less worthy siblings.

There is little doubt that the image of an ecclesiastical prelate took precedence over that of the priest-servant in Joel's mind when he applied for entrance into the seminary during his last year in high school. His dad threw one of his major tantrums, assuring Joel that he was throwing away his life, that he was too gifted intellectually for the priesthood, that he'd be stuck in some country parish tending to bumpkins and old ladies, and that he should devote his life to a more worthwhile profession like the law. He argued at length with Joel about a man's sexual needs, the abnormality of the celibate life, and the loss he would feel in not having a wife and children. He finished his argument with all the dramatic flair of concluding remarks to an awe struck jury, as he threatened to disown Joel if he continued in his desire to be a priest.

It is always a mistake to underestimate an opponent. The years of debating his father had not been wasted practice. Joel's face reddened as he prepared his rebuttal. Several minutes passed in absolute silence as his father glared at him. Joel's words were measured as he began quite softly.

"Dad, all my life I've watched you run the lives of everyone in this house as if someone had made you king instead of husband and father. I've seen you berate my mother and bring her to tears time and time again. My brothers and sister have long lost whatever love and respect they may have had for you. You have beaten them all down to submission. You've won every battle in this house and always gotten your way. How does it feel to be feared rather than loved in your own home?

"And then I watched you every Sunday take us all to Mass, put on your devout face, genuflect to this God you say you love, make the Act of Contrition, and receive

Jesus in Holy Communion. Where do you get the guts to do that? Don't you see the hypocrisy? Who do you think you're fooling? Not your family, and surely not God."

Joel heard his own voice becoming louder and more strident. "But you will not determine what I do with my life. You will not determine what God's will is for me. You will not stop me from being a priest. You will not blackmail me by threatening to disown me. Do you not know your own flesh and blood well enough to know that would cause me to be more sure about my decision, and to see clearly that I would have really nothing to lose by leaving a father who would reject his son because he was trying to follow God's will?"

And now it was time for Joel's closing argument. "Father, I have tried all my life to live up to your expectations. I've tried to make you proud. I've even tried to be like you in many ways. And, most of all, I've tried to love you. But I have another Father too, and He has first call on my life."

Something quite strange followed: Joel's father had nothing to say.

The bishop was delighted to receive Joel as a seminarian. His grades had always been superlative and he had received a glowing recommendation from the highly respected Msgr. Carroll. After four years of college in the diocesan seminary, he was sent to Rome to study at the North American College.

Joel loved Rome, the challenge of studying with others of exceptional intellect, and the opportunity to grow spiritually beyond his imagination. The very proximity of the college to Vatican City, the seat of Catholicism, was exciting. The place spoke to the pomp and power of the Church which had always intrigued him. He attended every ceremony at which the pope presided, and he relished the papal audiences as well as the pope's Sunday benediction.

The four years passed quickly, and his class was given the opportunity of being ordained by His Holiness John Paul II in St. Peter's Basilica. It was a dream come true for Joel. The eight years had given his father plenty of time to become accustomed to having a son in the priesthood, particularly since the other two sons had become law partners with him and had already given him grandchildren. Joel's sister had become a teacher and joined the faculty of the parish elementary school. All the family with their spouses, as well as several uncles and aunts, flew to Rome for his ordination. The Holy Father was at his best, deeply spiritual and yet jovial and warm—a perfect launching pad for any newly ordained priest.

However, the glow of ordination began to diminish within his first year as an assistant to Msgr. Dumbarski. Father Joel had arrived at the parish with the best of intentions, but he found the manner in which his pastor ran things both inefficient and archaic. He struggled within himself to accept the status quo but had to bite his lip often not to point out to Monsignor how he might improve the parish. Joel knew that the old monsignor was kind to his flock, never missing an opportunity to reach out to anyone who was hurting, and deeply loved by the children and most of the adults. BUT . . . .in Joel's mind, he was simply stupid; Joel began to think of him as Msgr. Dumb-ass-ski.

Seven months after he arrived, Joel felt he could no longer overlook the inadequacies of the pastor and his parish. After the final Sunday Mass, Joel came to the luncheon table in a furious mood. He slammed his chair back from the table, sat down heavily, glowered at his soup and then at his pastor.

"Would there be something bothering you, Father Joel?"

"Everything about this parish bothers me. That caterwauling from the balcony which passes for music bothers me. The poorly trained altar boys with dirty hands bother me. The inattentive come-late, leave-early, bored congregation bothers me. The ushers who joke noisily with one another in the vestibule during Mass bother me. The lack of parish organizations bothers me. Your ditzy parish secretary who can't get a telephone number correctly bothers me. The lousy religion teaching in the school bothers me. And that you who as pastor has seen it all go on for over twenty years would condone it with your silence really bothers me."

Msgr. Dumbarski blew over the soup in his spoon to cool it. "Well, it ain't exactly St. Peter's, I'll have to admit. But, then, you're not exactly the Cure´ of Ars either." He seemed to really enjoy the soup, and a satisfied smile crept over his face. He'd dealt with associates who were full of themselves before.

Joel tried unsuccessfully to muffle an exasperated scream. He stood up abruptly, toppling his chair, and stamped loudly from the dining room, slamming the door behind him. The noise alarmed the housekeeper, who emerged from the kitchen to find her pastor seated quietly, enjoying his soup. She sized up the situation, removed Joel's untasted soup, and gave Monsignor a knowing wink.

It took Joel the better part of a week to cool down. He kept reliving the dining room scene, thinking of things he could have said, burning righteously over the pastor's words, seething at the injustice of it all, and wondering if his father could have been right after all. He tried everything he could think of: exercising, visiting the Blessed Sacrament, sharing his feelings about Msgr. Dumb-ass-ski with his priest friends from

Rome, and barricading himself in his room while neglecting all his parish duties save daily Mass, even absenting himself from meals (surreptitiously sneaking out to Burger King). He was sure that his actions would eventually provoke some kind of response from the pastor; he was wrong. When he returned to meals the next Sunday, he suffered the further indignity of Monsignor's acting as if nothing had happened at all and seemingly enjoying his soup even more than the week before.

Joel returned to his ministry and attempted to overlook all the deficiencies of pastor and parish, but they grated too deeply upon what he deemed proper. Several months later, he wrote to the vicar general, Msgr. Clement Donnelly, and asked to be reassigned. The letter was four pages long, single spaced, enumerating all the liturgical and pastoral transgressions of Msgr. Dumbarski and suggesting that the pastor be retired immediately. Clem deemed it an unusually angry and self-righteous letter to be sent by a priest so young.

The letter of reassignment from the diocese arrived several weeks later with no mention of Joel's tirade. Joel was to report to a parish with a pastor who had a reputation for excellent relationships with his associates. Somehow Msgr. Dumbarski got over the loss and continued as pastor for thirteen more years before dying of a heart attack while visiting the sick. The church was overflowing with grieving parishioners at his funeral; the caterwauling from the balcony was even worse than usual. Joel had a previous engagement that day.

Joel's second assignment went well for almost two years. Father Jack Lawrence made a determined effort to meet with him once a week to discuss liturgy, parish activities, shared responsibility, their spiritual lives, and their relationship with one another. He sought Joel's opinions and ideas and really listened. He shared the pastoral duties equitably and tried to make certain that Joel felt fulfilled in his priesthood. Msgr. Donnelly had shared with him the difficulties that Joel had experienced with Msgr. Dumbarski, and they both wanted to help the young priest get a new start.

Father Jack worked hard personally, had an active parish council and finance committee, and a large parish school. He invited Joel to become a part of everything that was happening in the parish and asked that he teach religion in the school, show special interest in the senior citizens ministry, and visit the sick in the hospitals and their homes.

Joel enjoyed teaching religion to the kids in the seventh and eighth grades, but quickly tired of the lower grades as he felt that his talents, intelligence, and education were not well used with those so young. When the response of the elderly to his ministry was less than enthusiastic or stimulating, he also felt that he was casting his pearls of wisdom before those incapable of recognizing their value. Having a high opinion of his own intellectual superiority, he lacked patience with those of any age who seemed marginal.

During his second year with Father Jack, his sense of frustration with his duties to the young and old had grown. He now felt it almost impossible to walk into the classrooms of the early elementary school grades and was depressed whenever he had to visit the sick or the dying. He would have to force himself to enter the hospital room of the terminally ill.

Joel knew he was slipping away from the image of the priesthood of Jesus Christ. He felt his focus lessen bit by bit each day. The recognition his priesthood was faltering frightened him, and he did not understand it. All the examinations of conscience he had done throughout his life had not enabled him to see himself as he really was. Perhaps it was the early training in debating his father that allowed him to exonerate himself from any personal guilt and to defend his inflated self-image against the promptings of the Holy Spirit. The very essence of his tragic flaw also prohibited him from talking to a spiritual director.

Joel was surprised at the end of his second year with Father Jack when he received a letter from Msgr. Donnelly assigning him as pastor of a small parish. He was excited by the possibilities the assignment opened for him. He loved the thought of being able to run a parish the "right" way, celebrating the liturgies properly. Perhaps this assignment would refresh his enthusiasm for the priesthood as he would be free of the limitations placed upon him by pastors who were neither as intellectually gifted nor as well educated. While he respected Father Jack and appreciated what he had tried to do, he had also noticed deficiencies. Now a new day had come; now he could become the kind of priest God intended him to be. He remembered a line from a short story he had read in high school: "You can't keep a fast horse in a poor man's stable." Giddy-yap, ol' Joel!

As might have been predicted, the die had been cast. Almost five years passed before Joel's frustration reached the boiling point. The parishioners at his new assignment seemed slow to be awed by the gift of Father Joel's intelligence. The parish council was reluctant to accept the changes he wished to make, even offering resistance at times. The finance council refused to endorse his plans to renovate the sanctuary. The music director was frozen somewhere in Kumbaya-land. The parish secretary was a morose old bag who thought she ran the show instead of supporting his every whim. The rectory looked like something from Edgar Allan Poe; Joel kept listening for "Nevermore." At least, that's the way Joel saw it all. He was sure that the bishop was out to get him and that a grave injustice was once more being leveled upon him. Off went another tersely-worded four page epistle to Msgr. Clement, enumerating the slings and arrows of his outrageous fortune.

Upon receiving the letter, Clem read the indictment against Fr. Joel's parish, against the first two pastors under whom he had served, against the bishop who had the audacity to make the appointments, and against Clem, who along with the rest of the diocesan hierarchy, obviously had something against him. Clem placed the letter on his desk, sighed, and placed his head in his hands. It had been a long day. He had tried so hard to help Joel. He had no answer. He said a prayer to Jesus for Joel . . . and one for Joel's parish.

Prayers are often answered in unexpected ways. The members of the parish council in Joel's parish would long remember their meeting to discuss Father Joel's proposal concerning the urgent need of renovating the sanctuary. Joel had prepared a carefully crafted presentation that laid out the needs, execution, expenses, time lines, and benefits of the renovation. He had even hired an architect and presented his renderings of the proposed sanctuary. He concluded his argument by quoting the documents of Vatican II and the findings of the United States Conference of Catholic Bishops on the proper usage of liturgical space.

Joel sensed hostility in the room. He had noticed the absence of agreement in the faces and body posture of the members of the council during his presentation. Most looked at the floor, some showed discomfort, one yawned, another doodled. At first there was silence. Then one after another of the council began to voice their objections:

"The altar was given memory of my mother."

"Everyone in the parish likes the way things are now."

"Four generations of our loved loves have sacrificed to give us our beautiful sanctuary, and it would be an insult to their memory to change it."

"When the bishop was here for Confirmation, he said it was one of the most beautiful churches in the diocese."

"It simply isn't necessary, and the money could go to the school."

"How much money did you spend on the plans and did you seek our advice for that?"

Suddenly it was just too much for Joel. Again he was faced with absurdity and frustration from people who had no vision and less intelligence. With an ever reddening face, he rose, took the architect's rendering of the sanctuary and ripped it apart. "This is what you have done to my heart and priesthood. You are so uninformed, so dense, that you are unable to see what is obviously needed. I give up! Keep your antiquated sanctuary and your dismal little parish. Find another priest to dance to your Loony Tunes and Merrie Melodies." And with that he stormed from the room.

Within the week Clem had arranged for Joel to enter a counseling center to receive treatment for anger management issues. While the process was slow, it worked. For the first time in his life, Joel was able to see himself as he was. He saw the egotism that had plagued him and made every assignment he had received destined for failure. He understood the effect that his family life had upon his priesthood. A spiritual director was assigned to Joel, and he began to love Jesus for the first time in his priesthood. The Holy Spirit was active and doing his work. Joel even began to understand humility and to love the priesthood for the right reasons. As the year passed, he yearned for the day he would be able to serve the people with the heart of Christ. The most important and grace filled year of Joel's life had just concluded when he received the call from Clem to take Adam's place.

CHAPTER FOUR

FATHER JAMES CHUDY

Stephen Chudy was born to a farm family in 1950 and had seven siblings. His parents were deeply religious and reared their children according to strict Catholic tradition. No meal ever began without grace; no child ever went to bed without saying his prayers; crucifixes and religious pictures hung in every room; Sunday began with early Mass; and the family rosary was recited every evening after dinner.

Every child was expected to help on the farm. The effort extended beyond chores to an understanding that the farm would succeed only if all accepted responsibility according to their abilities and age. As Stephen was the oldest boy, he was expected to set an example for his siblings. By the time he was twelve, he was doing the work of a man. Farm accidents are not rare, particularly among the inexperienced. One day Stephen was driving the tractor, hit a deep rut, and was thrown to the ground, hitting his head on a stone.

When Stephen awoke, he could not see. The doctors explained to his parents that the condition would be permanent and left it to them to break the news to Stephen. Farmers are accustomed to trusting the will of God. They know that there will be good years with bumper crops and bad weather years with little yield. Their children are reared to understand that trusting in God is not reserved for the good times but is particularly important in the rough times. Such faith doesn't take away the pain of tragedy but does promote a philosophy that deters self-pity and prolonged depression.

Stephen seemed angrier with himself for not managing the tractor properly than he was frightened by the lack of sight. Once past their initial grief, his parents rapidly made plans for Stephen's future. He was to be sent to the School for the Blind in the nearby capital city, where he would learn to function with his blindness and receive training which would enable him to earn a living. Stephen accepted his future and steeled himself to be manly in leaving his family and depending entirely upon others.

Stephen was immersed in a deep sense of loneliness when his parents left him at the school. In unfamiliar surroundings with no sight, he felt abandoned. He had always been surrounded by his large family in a home he had known all his life. He was assigned a roommate from a family quite different from his own, urban and blessed both socially and financially. Age and lack of vision were all that they had in common.

Stephen's life began to brighten when he met Joanne, who had been sightless from the age of six. They were in the same class, connected immediately upon meeting, and were instinctively solicitous for one another's well-being. Here was an instance in which "the blind leading the blind" actually worked. Their Catholic faith was important to both, and their blindness had not dampened their belief that God was guiding them through life. They trusted that God had brought them together.

As soon as they had graduated from high school, Stephen and Joanne married. They had both been successful in obtaining jobs, Joanne as a receptionist and Stephen as a telemarketer. They attended Mass daily and prayed that God would give them a child. The prayer was answered eighteen months after their marriage.

James was a great joy to his parents and became their eyes to the outside world. He loved to describe his daily adventures to his parents to the least detail, always in glorious colors. He would describe each priest who was assigned to the parish so that his parents might better envision the celebration of the Mass. The joy of enriching his parents through his descriptions heightened his attention to detail. He didn't want to miss anything and rarely did.

Needless to say, Stephen and Joanne doted upon their only child. It was understandable that they had mixed feelings when James announced to them that he wished to enter the seminary and become a priest. They hated to admit to themselves a certain selfish reaction at the prospect of losing the sight James had provided for them, but they were also grateful and filled with pride that he would become a priest of the Church they both loved so deeply.

James was one of those all too rare people blessed with having a deep inner joy which spills over into the lives of those around him. His eyes and smile were captivating. When he looked at people, they felt that they were looking into the eyes of Jesus.

The seminary delighted James. He loved the structure; the emphasis upon the spiritual life; the camaraderie of exceptional, highly-motivated young men; and the simple pleasure of profoundly knowing that he was doing exactly what he was meant to do. His classmates saw something extraordinary in James, and even the class cynic could find no fault with him.

Eight years is sufficiently long for even holiest of candidates for the priesthood to have doubts concerning a vocation. The temptations that are common to all men were a part of Jesus' life, and they came and went with greater or lesser intensity in James's life. He was a virgin and when temptations of the flesh came to mind, he felt unworthy. Often he found himself on his knees before the Eucharist, asking God to forgive him and let him know if anyone so tempted should actually become a priest. When Monsignor

Clement Donnelly was appointed to hear the confessions of the seminarians once a week, James knew he had been blessed.

The first time that James entered the confessional and sat before Clem, he was confused and depressed. Clem had been a priest for twenty-five years and had heard tens of thousands of confessions; he was able to defuse all the anxiety that James had bottled up inside in short order. He assured James that his temptations and feelings were similar to those of all seminarians and that he had experienced them personally. He then spoke of a merciful Jesus who loved James more than he had been willing to admit. As he spoke, he could see the relief in James's eyes and Monsignor finally even coaxed a smile from him. That confession was the beginning of a friendship based upon the love of God that would last for the next for the next twelve years, until Clem's death.

In 1993, two years before James's ordination, he received a call to come to the rector's office. He instinctively knew that something was wrong. The rector was a sensitive and kind man, and he recognized what an extraordinary young man James was and what promise he would have as a priest. He had met James's parents on several occasions over the past six years and knew the closeness of the family. When James entered the room, the rector rose from his desk, walked to James, and gave him a long hug. The rector had always kept a certain distance from the seminarians to retain their respect. When the rector stepped back, James noticed tears in his eyes.

"James, draw up a chair. We need to talk. This will be one of the hardest things you will ever have to hear. This afternoon, while your dad was at work, he suffered an aneurysm of the brain. I have to tell you that your father died immediately."

"How? Why? He was fine. He's only forty-seven years old. What happened?"

"Aneurysms are unexpected and often fatal. His doctor said that it is possible that the tractor accident that caused his blindness may have triggered something in the brain that precipitated the aneurysm."

"But . . . Mom, where's Mom? She'll be lost without Dad." James broke down in deep sobs when he thought of his mother, so dependent on and so in love with his father.

"She's with your grandparents. I've asked the vice-rector to pack your bags, and I'll drive you home right away. You will stay as long as you need; we'll work things out for you here. You will get through this, Son. Your dad was as holy a man as I've ever met. He now has sight again, and he looks into the face of Our Lord. You will now give the comfort to your mother that no one else is capable of giving. As you have been her eyes from your childhood, now you must help her see God's love in all this."

The Chudy family never asked God, "Why?" They had always lived with difficulties. They simply never questioned their faith or God's love. And so the only son went to his blind mother, and they wept together, each seeking to comfort the other as they always had done. James made the funeral arrangements with the priest who had given him his First Communion and recommended him as a seminarian. He then took his mother to the funeral home and described to her each detail of the coffin they selected for Stephen. He guided his mother's hand over the smooth, varnished oak exterior and then over the satin lining. He took the one suit his father owned from the closet and selected the red tie that he had given him on the last Father's Day.

On the day of the funeral, Joanne and James went to the funeral home early to spend a few minutes with Stephen before his body was taken to the church. It was so very hard for both of them because such extraordinary love existed within their small family. Love can be very painful.

"Mom, he is with God, and that leaves just the two of us here. I'm going to leave the seminary and live with you. I can get a job, and we'll be fine. Dad would want me to help you now."

Joanne reached out and held her son's head between her two hands. "If you think that, you did not know your father as well as I thought you did. You were his joy and his pride. Every night we got on our knees and thanked God for giving you a vocation to the priesthood. Every night we prayed that you would always be good priest. We knew that you would help others see God, as you have always helped us see all that God had given us. God worked through our blindness to create the most loving and giving person I know, you. Now you must give that gift to God in the priesthood."

Then she smiled at James: "Besides, don't sell your mother short; God and I will work things out fine."

Three days later James returned to the seminary.

Two years elapsed, and the day of James' ordination arrived, May 26, 1995. The joy and exuberance that were so much a part of James had returned within a few months after Stephen's death. His mother had continued in her work and lived with her parents. She was buoyant as she entered the cathedral on the arm of her father and was seated in the front pew for the ordination of her son. It was the happiest and proudest day of her life; she knew that Stephen was there with her sharing in her joy. It had all been part of God's plan for her family and for her Church.

All who knew their story teared as Father James gave his first blessing to Joanne.

James radiated joy. The Holy Spirit was pulling out all the stops. Truly, this was the day the Lord had made.

From the first day of his ordination, James was everything that God intended him to be as a priest. Why not? He was hand-crafted by the Holy Spirit. He was so alive with God's presence that he was loved by the parishioners in every parish he served. They would see him daily kneeling before the Blessed Sacrament for an hour prior to each Mass he celebrated. The Masses were always said with such devotion and attention that even the most obdurate of heart were moved. He brought new meaning to the words of the Mass because he prayed them, not "said" them.

His homilies were obviously the product of a life of love and prayer and study. Here was a priest who cared. His eyes glistened as he described God's love and mercy, as he spoke of grace and the saints. When he encouraged people on how to live their lives in a moral fashion, he never did so with condescension or rebuke, but rather with a heart that understood and urgently wanted to help them come closer to God.

Within five years of his ordination, he was being asked to give retreats and speak at conferences. His speaking ability, sincerity, holiness had won respect and notice throughout the diocese. He was often referred to as the new Chrysostom (the "golden tongue"), a saint so named because of his superlative speaking ability.

James was always looking for something more to do for the Church. At this time the diocese experienced a large growth in its Latino population. Tens of thousands of Mexicans flooded the diocese to find work that would enable them to care for their families. But the diocese had only a few priests able to speak Spanish and thereby minister to its new Catholics. James saw the need and with a compassionate heart asked the bishop to send him away to study Spanish. Within a few years he had become proficient in Spanish and the diocesan Latinos looked upon him as their shepherd, which indeed he was. He was quick to see Jesus in the poor and the needy, and noticing the special gifts they possessed in their spirituality and humility and knowing that they could be a great asset to the Church.

James worked tirelessly for all the Church, and everybody wanted him. He knew that his ministry depended upon his prayer life, and he never let it take a back seat. He always found time for prayer, but not often for enough sleep or rest. He always found time to call Joanne daily, and he visited her every two or three weeks. He still wanted to describe to her in detail all that he had experienced.

July 28, 2003, was particularly hot. James had celebrated the early Mass at his parish, returned some phone calls, visited three sick parishioners at the hospital, and was hurrying to a neighboring parish to celebrate a funeral Mass for a Latino teenager who had been killed in an automobile accident. He had skipped lunch and felt really weak and nauseous. He made it through the funeral and the burial, excused himself, and made it to the rectory. He rushed to the bathroom, where he noticed considerable blood in his stool.

Parish priests can normally find a good Catholic doctor when they need one. James was in the doctor's office the next morning right after his early Mass. The doctor insisted over James's objections that he be admitted to hospital for tests immediately. After several days, the doctor informed the young priest that he had colon cancer, which they would attempt to treat through chemoradiotherapy, a combination of both chemotherapy and radiation therapy. It was difficult for the doctor to tell his own pastor whom he had grown to love that the therapy would probably be difficult, the outcome uncertain, and death probable. He watched James carefully as he detailed the clinical procedure and described what James could expect.

James had ministered to parishioners with various cancers throughout the eight years of his priesthood. He had thoughts of what his future might be from the moment he first saw his blood in the toilet bowl. He had prayed throughout the night before he met with the doctor and endured the three days of testing in the hospital, full well expecting exactly the diagnosis that his doctor had just delivered with such tact and kindness.

"Doctor, I'm thirty-three years old. I've been blessed all my life. I had the best parents anyone could possibly hope for, been surrounded all my life with God's love, and have had the joy in sharing in the priesthood of Jesus Christ for eight years. If the Father wants to call me to himself at the same age as he called His only son, how could I possibly be anything but grateful? If He wants me to suffer the way He asked His son to suffer, maybe my Calvary will also win a few souls. At any rate, you and I both know it's in God's hands, and He has never let me down before and won't now."

Even though he had heard James speak from the pulpit every Sunday, the doctor was not ready for his absolute graceful surrender to God's will. He had to turn away for a moment to hide the pain he felt for his pastor.

"And, so, Doc, I'll take chemo and the radiation and whatever else you suggest. But I ask one thing from you: respect the doctor-patient confidentiality pact and tell no one. I will tell both my mother and the bishop in confidence, as they both deserve that knowledge. But I will live out my priesthood with every ounce of strength that God gives me until the day I die, be it sooner or later. I was ordained to bring people to God and cancer will not rob me of that gift."

James left the hospital, made a visit to his mother and then to the bishop. Both received what James had to tell them as would be expected of people with love and faith. Both admonished him to save his strength, take things easier, and cut back on his duties. James thanked the bishop for his fatherly concern and told him he would let him know if he needed any help. When he was leaving the bishop's office, he turned, smiled broadly, and winked. The bishop accurately interpreted the wink and knew that this priest he had ordained only eight years before had absolutely no intention of following the advice he had given; he was never so impressed or moved by a priest's disobedience.

The visit with Joanne was harder; there was too much history there, too much love, too much shared joy and pain. But as always, James could rely upon the strength and support of his mother. After he had left, she thought of another mother who had given her son support as he made his way up Calvary; she resolved to do the same for her priest-son.

When James returned to his parish, he was met with the phone calls and problems that accumulate in a busy parish when the pastor is away for several days. He told his staff that he'd had a check up at the hospital but that they didn't need to be concerned.

His statement wasn't a lie: their concern would not change anything and they truly did not need to worry. That evening he met with a couple preparing for marriage and taught the RCIA class. All the catechumens thought that his presentation on penance was the best lecture he had ever given.

His chemotherapy and radiation treatments were scheduled on his "day off." The parishioners were happy to see he was finally taking a little time for himself. They noticed that James was looking tired and drawn, even a little shaky and distracted. They assumed he was working too hard, constantly giving himself to anyone in need; they were right. Outside of his therapy, James found himself working harder than ever. He forced himself out of bed every morning, disregarding his almost constant nausea, frequent diarrhea, and flu-like symptoms. Sensing that the end was coming sooner than either he or his doctors had envisioned, he prayed and worked with the urgency of someone who had to finish his assignment before the end of the work day.

This behavior continued until the day seven months after his diagnosis, when he collapsed at the altar during Mass. He had just elevated the chalice after the consecration, felt dizzy for a moment, tried vainly to steady himself, and then hit the marble floor heavily. When he came to, he saw the face of his doctor, who had been attending Mass, above him. An ambulance was called; he tried unsuccessfully to object over the doctor's insistence.

Msgr. Donnelly was summoned to the hospital to anoint James. The tumor had metastasized and the organs were shutting down. Word spread rapidly and a crowd gathered in the parking lot—primarily Latinos praying the rosary for their shepherd. They remained there into the night, sharing memories of this brave and holy priest who had given every ounce of his strength for them; no one had ever shown them such love or treated them with such respect and understanding.

James' strength was decreasing rapidly, and breathing was difficult. Joanne sat at the left of his bed, cradling the hand of her son. He summoned enough energy to squeeze his mother's hand gently, seeking to communicate the love he had for her that she could not see. His thumb traveled smoothly over the back of her hand.

Clem, on the right side of the bed, put his ear next to James's mouth and asked if he had anything to confess. It had been only three days before that James visited Clem to make his weekly confession that had begun ten years before in the seminary chapel. He could muster only enough strength to mouth, "I'm . . . sorry, and I love you." Absolution was given, and the anointing began. Clem made the sign of the cross with the oil on James's forehead and then the back of his hands. He placed a tiny fragment of the Precious Body that James had consecrated early that morning at his unfinished Mass on James' tongue, giving the remainder of the host to Joanne. After administering the Apostolic Blessing to James, Clem knelt by the bed, raised James's right hand and placed it upon his head, "Now, Father James, may I have your last blessing?" The slightest trace of the old smile returned to James's lips as his mouth formed the words, "Father, Son . . ."

Joanne felt life leave the hand of her son. She rose, sat on the bed, and hugged her son. Clem remained on his knees, knowing that he was watching a living Pieta.

So many attended the funeral that it had to be held in the parish gym rather than in the church. Still the crowds poured out into the parking lot. Clem preached a homily that left everyone in tears, including himself. He spoke of the priesthood of Jesus Christ and how James had lived it so fully. Joanne's composure and grace portrayed a mother who understood the meaning of life, death, and resurrection. She obviously could see more than many others whose eyes were clouded by tears. The steady stream of Latino mourners who passed by the coffin at the grave yard, each throwing a little dirt on the coffin, took nearly a half hour. They gathered around Padre Juan Romero-Martinez, a young priest from Chihuahua, Mexico, whom James had helped to secure for the diocese and who had become his closest friend.

One of the first cars to leave the cemetery grounds was a new Jaguar driven by another of James's close friends, Father Joseph Mulalley.

CHAPTER FIVE

FATHER ALAIN MOREAU

Alain Moreau was born in Megier, a small village eighteen kilometers west of Avignon, on July 4, 1978. His father worked in the famous vineyards of Chateauneuf du Papes. His mother was from the neighboring city of Uzes and daily filled their country kitchen with the rich aroma of sautéing onions and garlic, and soups made from hearty stock.

Some of Alain's earliest memories were centered on the small rock church in his village perched upon a hill overlooking the vineyards. Everyone in the tiny village attended the church and formed a community in every sense of the word. Built in the fifteenth century, it had remarkably survived the French Revolution and that seemed to add credence to the enduring quality of the faith. Alain would always remember the hardness of the antiquated pews and kneelers, the dim atmosphere which strangely added an aura of holiness, the slender stained glass windows of Joan of Arc, St. Louis, St. John Vianney, and his favorite saint, Jean de Brebeuf, whom he could envision standing among the Iroquois brashly professing his faith, suffering torture and death. He loved the simple, small-boned, stooped older priest sent from the larger church in Uzes to celebrate Mass at the mission church. Close to Megier was the old monastery of St. Castor which had been converted into an inn by an affable British-American couple. Alain often wandered through the grounds imagining himself a twelfth century monk.

As a child, Alain loved to run through the vineyards and watch the growth of the grapes as they matured in the sun. But, most of all, he loved to sit in the kitchen and watch as his mother created one culinary miracle after another. So entranced was he with the beauty and richness of food that he knew from the age of eight that he must become a chef. At the age of twelve, he found a job in Avignon washing dishes in the Michelin two star restaurant of the renowned chef Michel Gerard, L,Oignon; by thirteen he was bussing tables, by sixteen he was preparing the salads, and by seventeen he had become a sous-chef. He loved watching Chef Michel create dishes of remarkable complexity or a simple cassoulet with such subtle flavors that it achieved nobility.

When he was eighteen, Alain received an exciting invitation from Chef Michel to accompany him as his sous-chef to America, where he intended to open a gourmet restaurant. Alain rushed home to Megier, made a quick visit to his church where he prayed to St. Jean de Brebeuf to intercede for him with his parents to be allowed to go to that wonderful land where the saint had shed his blood. His parents saw this as an opportunity for their son to utilize the love that he had for food as well as what his father had taught him about wine and make a good life for himself. They prayed with their son and the next morning gave him their blessing.

In six months Alain found himself in a small apartment in the United States, working harder than ever, constantly learning from Chef Michel, and loving the American way of life, so very different from the countryside of Provence. His parents had impressed upon him that he would need to make extra effort to practice his faith with the chaotic hours of restaurant work and the dangers in living in a country without a strong Catholic heritage. It was excellent advice but probably unnecessary as Alain always connected his love of food and wine with the abundance of a generous God, who was the source of everything he loved and which had the effect of making God omnipresent in his life.

Fortunately Chef Michel's new bistro, also named L'Oignon, was closed on Sunday, allowing Alain the opportunity to attend Mass. He found a Catholic church only two miles from his apartment and walked there each Sunday for noon Mass. Although he had worked in Avignon within the shadow of the Palais de Papes, he found American churches surprisingly large and he missed the unity he had experienced in Megier. The same priest always celebrated the noon Mass and gave a marvelous homily. Alain began to feel welcome when the priest began to recognize him after Mass and exchange a few pleasantries. As the weeks elapsed, a few of the congregation began to recognize a new face, warming up to Alain and inviting him out to lunch or giving him a lift back to his apartment.

On the evening of October 19, 1997, business was a little slow at Bistro l'Oignon, and Alain had an opportunity to leave the kitchen and take a run through the dining room. He noticed a lone diner, a man in a dark sports coat and red shirt, whom he couldn't place at first glance. Their eyes met and in a moment of mutual recognition Alain saw his pastor, Msgr. Clement Donnelly. Clem greeted Alain warmly, and Alain was excited to be able to share his story and talk with this priest he had admired for the genuine quality of his homilies and the reverence with which he celebrated Mass. Recognizing that Alain was without family and friends in a new country, Clem invited him to have lunch with him at the rectory after Mass the next Sunday.

Lunch the following Sunday was definitely less tasty than dinner had been at l'Oignon but the quality of the conversation distracted both Clem and Alain from the deficiencies of the table. Clem had rarely met a young man so vibrant, so aware of all that surrounded him, and so filled with a deep sense of joy. Alain told him of his parents,

Megier, the love that he had for his little village church, his walks through the grounds of St. Castor, his love of the vineyards, and his wonder at the beauty of food and its potential not only to nourish but also to delight. Clem recognized that Alain had been endowed with a sense of the omnipresence of God that is generally found only in saints and poets. He felt his own heart elevated by the wonder that existed within Alain's soul and mind. Clem was reminded of Gerard Manley Hopkins' appreciation of God's Grandeur, "like shining from shook foil."

For the first time since Alain had arrived in the United States, he felt totally at ease. He heard himself speaking with the joy he felt in his heart. Somehow being with Clem relaxed him. It was like being with his parents; he knew he was accepted and loved without condition. His hearty provincial laughter flowed as Clem chided him for his exuberance. He listened as Clem told him of his journey to the priesthood and the fulfillment he had experienced throughout his ministry.

This was the first of weekly lunches that would last for almost nine months. A spiritual bond had been formed between Alain and Clem that was sufficient to bridge the almost thirty-five years that separated them. Alain was surprised and grateful to have found a wise and accepting father figure in his new life, and Clem was invigorated by the company of a young man so filled with life and faith.

On the following Monday, Chef Michel hired a new hostess. Michelle's parents were French Canadian from Quebec. She was twenty-two, poised, attractive, and intelligent. Alain was immediately attracted to her, and Monday evenings would normally find them together, enjoying pizza and a movie. They had a strong sexual attraction to one another, but they both were serious about their faith and fought temptations that became increasingly more urgent.

Alain found himself in a dilemma. His weekly talks with Clem had evoked thoughts of a possible vocation to the priesthood, but his almost daily contact with Michelle evoked thoughts of marriage and children. A nineteen year old Frenchman with his Gallic blood on low boil but his heart filled with a desire to know God more deeply and to serve him made an interesting tug-of-war. Regardless of how late he had worked at Bistro l'Oignon, Alain always knelt beside his bed to say his night prayers. Each night he would pray through the intercession of St. Jean de Brebeuf that God would give him the wisdom to choose the right path and the courage to follow it.

His prayers were answered in a strange manner. Every table at the bistro was double booked on the evening of February 14, 1998, with couples young and old who had come to celebrate St. Valentine's Day. An attractive blind lady entered on the arm of a young priest who had reserved a table under the name of James Chudy. Michelle ushered them to a table near the kitchen, reserving the better tables for hopefully more lucrative guests. Alain watched from the open kitchen and was moved by the loving concern of the priest for the lady he presumed to be his mother, their joy and humility, the pleasure they took in being with one another, their lack of familiarity with dining in a fine restaurant, and the manner in which they devoutly shared grace before their meal. He was equally put off by the manner in which Michelle ignored their table, but found plenty of time to visit and joke with the regular guests.

The Latino washing dishes caught sight of the couple and was immediately excited, telling Alain that this was his wonderful pastor. He spoke of how Padre James had come to his home with food for his family and clothes for his children when they first came to the United States.

Alain motioned for Michelle to come to the kitchen and told her that he would be picking up the bill for the Chudys' table and asked that she tell them that one of the guests had done so. Alain had little money, spent almost nothing personally, but wanted to be a part of the joy he saw shared at that table; he was reminded of his own family.

As Alain prayed that night before retiring, he knew what he wanted more than anything in his life; it was not Michelle. On Sunday he asked Clem if it would be possible for him to study for the priesthood. Clem knew with all his heart that this young man should be a priest and that he would make a great one. On May 30, the feast of St. Joan of Arc, Alain received his letter of acceptance as a diocesan seminarian, and on August 4th, the feast of St. John Vianney, he left for the seminary. The French always stick together, even in heaven. Eight years later he was ordained a priest in the Cathedral of St. Louis, with his parents beaming in the front pew.

Father Alain flew back with his parents and celebrated his First Mass in the little church he loved so deeply in Megier. As he said the words of consecration over the wine from the vineyards his earthly father had tended, he reflected on how his father's sweat had helped to form the grapes made wine that would now become Jesus Christ whom he would offer to his Heavenly Father. God's providence seemed amazingly clear to him. Msgr. Clement Donnelly spoke in very broken French as the homilist. The small community gathered outside for his reception following the Mass. Chef Michel Gerard accompanied the family to Megier and prepared the most exquisite food the villagers had ever tasted, and the management of the neighboring Chateauneuf du Pape vineyards donated several cases of their very best wine. As they stood in the warm autumn sunlight, looking down upon the russet leaves of the vineyard, Father Alain toasted a priest who had died two years before and his gallant mother Joanne who had accompanied Msgr. Clement to Megier. This was a day that the Lord had made and they all rejoiced in it.

Msgr. Clement had a letter of appointment from the bishop to Father Alain. Alain's eyes teared with joy as he read that he was now the associate of the priest standing by his side whom he had grown to love so deeply. Neither had any way of knowing the relationship that had added so much to both of their lives was to end just five months later when Alain would find Clem dead in his chair.

Alain's charm was enormously helpful in soothing the hearts of Clem's parishioners at Clem's death. They knew that Alain had loved Clem as deeply as they had and shared in their grief. He cared for the parish himself for two months before a new pastor was appointed, Father Jason Arnold.

Alain had met few people like Father Jason; his style and approach to ministry and liturgy could not have been more divergent from that of Clem. The parishioners attempted to be welcoming and indulgent but all too often Alain had to soothe bruised egos, allay suspicions, and preach the gospel of love and understanding. Alain doubtlessly saved Jason's ministry and cleared his way through a sea of parochial discontent. The bishop recognized Alain's accomplishments and six months later gave him his own small parish, the first of several which were experiencing unrest and which he was to placate and infuse the life of the Spirit. Without his recognizing it, he had become the bishop's peacemaker, and the Holy Spirit found innumerable ways to manipulate his Gallic charm for the good of the Church.

It was, however, that same charm that would lead to the most traumatic experience of his priesthood.

CHAPTER SIX

FATHER JOSEPH MULALLEY

Silver spoons in the mouths of babes rarely foreshadow vocations to the priesthood. Michael Joseph Mulalley had frankly cleaned up in the stock market and made a bundle. He proceeded to marry Eugenia the daughter of a wealthy Presbyterian businessman who had little use for Catholics and their popish ways. Nor did it help that Michael had come from a family that owned a liquor store. Eugenia's father suspected that the Mulalleys were their own best customers. But Eugenia was adamant and so she and Michael married in a private ceremony in the rectory of the Catholic church; her father did not attend. The reception was at the Country Club and was probably the most lavish ever experienced by most of the guests.

Michael never particularly liked his father-in-law and was determined not only to distance Eugenia from her parents but to embarrass them by building a home so extravagant and so huge that even their opulent home would appear insignificant by comparison. It might have been gilding the lily just a bit when he built a similar mansion for his parents on the empty lot immediately adjoining Eugenia's parents.

The birth of Michael and Eugenia's first child, Joseph Seagrams Mulalley, offered Michael another opportunity to rub salt in Eugenia's father's damaged ego. Michael viewed the baptismal ceremony for Joseph as manna from heaven. While donating $100,000 to the bishop's favorite charity, he asked the bishop if he might find time to baptize his son. The bishop was delighted. Invitations were sent out for the baptismal reception to follow. Every prestigious person in town was invited to a garden party at his estate. Chef Michel Gerard, whom Michael had met on his honeymoon with Eugenia to

Provence, was employed to cater the formal dinner and an orchestra was to be flown in from New York. It would not be an overstatement to say that the festivities overshadowed the reason for the celebration. As Eugenia's father had made it known he would attend no baptism of his grandson performed in a Catholic church, bishop or no, it was assumed that he would not wish to receive an invitation to the reception. It did not concern Michael that Joseph would be burdened by bearing the name of a liquor distiller for his middle name because he knew how much it would irritate the old codger. Never cross an Irishman.

Eugenia never converted to Catholicism as she did not wish to anger her father, thereby endangering the possibility of a large inheritance, and she had little interest in any religion. Michael made it a point to attend Sunday Mass whenever nothing else of interest captured his attention or the golf course was closed due to snow. Whether it was to irritate Eugenia's family or because he thought religion could be of some use, he made certain that Joseph was always at Mass on Sunday and attended Catholic school from elementary school through college. He would instruct Eugenia to drive the boy to Mass on Sunday and pick him up when it was over.

So from the time he was five, Joseph would be dressed in a suit and tie, dropped off at the church entrance to sit by himself as instructed in the front pew and absorb as much of the liturgy as a five-year-old was capable. Strangely enough, he was capable of appreciating a great deal. He loved the colorful vestments, the altar servers in their cassocks and surplices, the singing, the ringing of bells, the smell of incense and beeswax candles, and the reverence of the congregation. When his mind would wander, he'd gaze at the stained glass windows, the huge crucifix behind the altar, or the beautiful statues of

Mary and Joseph. He was sure that Mary's eyes were always looking at him; they seemed to follow him when he moved, and he'd wiggle about in his pew to check whether she was still looking at him. He didn't tell his parents how much he liked going to Mass for fear that they would laugh at him. The pastor would notice the lone little boy in the front pew all dressed up in suit and tie. He felt sorry for Joseph and would take special care to shake his hand after Mass and tell him how happy he was to see him; it made Joseph feel like a grown up.

For his sixteenth birthday Joseph received a red Corvette convertible from Michael, arrangements for him and a friend to travel through Europe the following summer from Eugenia, a check for $5,000 from his maternal grandfather, and a six pack of Bud from his paternal grandfather. Joseph took his affluence pretty much for granted and was beginning to enjoy "the good life" a bit too much. He was a nice looking guy and could have anything or anyone he wished. His parents placed no restrictions upon him, but he didn't really seem to need any. Even though he was surrounded by wealth and all it can buy, he continued to attend Mass regularly and live a moral life.

It was Eugenia's gift that changed his life. He invited Desmond Dunleavy to be his guest for the trip to Europe. Desmond's family had little money and many kids; Eugenia assured his parents that no cost would be involved and that it was Desmond's golden opportunity. She slipped Desmond a thousand dollars in spending money and asked him to make sure that Joseph had a great summer.

Joe and Des thought alike, acted alike, dressed alike (Des in Joe's cast-offs), and had similar desires. Now not every sixteen year old boy without supervision would make the right choices visiting Europe for the first time; Joe and Des were no exceptions.

Landing in London, they placed their bags in the hotel and made for the nearest pub. That night they both drank heavily and lost their dinners and their virginity. It's doubtful that was what Eugenia had in mind with his birthday gift.

They awoke early the next afternoon, felt miserable physically and remorseful spiritually. They were both Catholics, both sincere about their faith, and both realized that the evening filled with booze and broads that almost all high school boys dream of having was a serious mistake for them. They felt unfaithful to what was expected of them, ungrateful for screwing up the gift they were sharing, and shaken by the guilt that accompanies serious sin for those who truly try to love God. They located a Catholic church, went to Confession, and were determined to change their focus for the remainder of their trip.

Visitors to Europe often jest that if they see one more cathedral they will have to be committed. Joe suffered no such malady; he was absolutely enthralled both by their grandeur and the impact they had upon him spiritually. While Des would look around for fifteen minutes or so, Joe wanted to sit, gaze, pray, absorb, meditate. He had feelings he had never experienced; his heart would beat more rapidly but his breathing was almost imperceptible. He knew that the Holy Spirit was doing something in his life, and that recognition frightened him.

Lourdes was the point of no return for Joe. Des and he joked about the shoddy, cheap commercialism of the town as they approached the shrine, but they were unprepared for the beauty of the Basilica of the Blessed Virgin. As Joe knelt before the statue of the Blessed Virgin, he again felt her eyes upon him; this time it was not the eyes of a statue that followed him but the eyes of Mary herself looking at him and beckoning him to follow her son. Her words to the servants at the wedding feast at Cana came to him: "Do whatever He tells you." Joe began to shake physically and perspire; this wasn't in his plans for his future. Des saw that his friend was upset, touched his shoulder, and beckoned for him to come outside. "No, I won't follow You," Joe said. Des erroneously thought that Joe was speaking to him. Joe bolted from the pew and almost ran outside, where he grasped the iron railing and stared down at the Gave River.

Then, in the distance Joe heard the singing of the "Ave Maria." As he looked down from the basilica steps, he saw an almost endless procession of invalids in wheelchairs, crossing the bridge from the opposite side of the river in preparation for Mass. As he turned, he saw a young father carrying his little boy who was obviously seriously ill. Joe had a meltdown. He returned to the basilica and with great humility looked up at the statue of the Blessed Mother: "Okay, I get it . . . I'll follow your son."

That night over a beer he told Des he had decided to become a priest.

"Gosh, that's exciting, Joe; I'm really happy for you. But, what about all the stuff you've had all your life? Can really leave all that behind you?"

"Frankly, the 'stuff,' as you call it, doesn't mean much to me. I don't think I'll miss it that much. I always thought of it as my parents' 'stuff' anyway. At any rate, I'd become a diocesan priest and wouldn't take the vow of poverty. Maybe I can do some good with my 'stuff.'"

"And how about girls, women? We've talked about them, yearned for them since we were twelve or so. That night in London was pretty seedy, what I can remember of it, but it wasn't all bad."

"As far as I'm concerned, it was 'all bad.' For me it was an act, something expected of me in the rites of passage. It wasn't ME at all; it was what people expect me to do and be. I'll find a way to deal with my sexual temptations, but that won't be a part of it."

After several other stops, Rome was their final destination. Whatever lingering doubts Joe may have had about having a vocation were laid to rest in the Blessed Sacrament chapel of St. Peter's Basilica. With his spiritual motors running on overload after three hours of gazing with wonder at the interior of St. Peter's, he knelt before the Eucharist and asked God to help him become a priest.

That night Des and Joe shared carbonara at Ristorante Alla Rampa at the foot of the Spanish Steps. It was their final meal in Europe, and so much had happened to them both. They shared two large carafes of vino blanco and returned to their hotel room. Des went into the bathroom to shower as Joe lay on his bed. Des had left the door half open to diminish the steam. Joe found himself watching Des as he undressed and showered. He turned away, both confused and ashamed of the feelings he was experiencing. "Too much wine," he assured himself.

During his seminary years, Joe was largely successful in detaching himself from the material things of the world and concentrating on Jesus. In many ways he was a model seminarian: he had a good mind, got along well with his classmates, spent hours in prayer, and was liked by the faculty. While his parents continued to immerse him in gifts during periods of vacation, they could see that the gifts meant little to him. Joe was so accustomed to fine material things that he simply took them for granted. He was generous with his fellow seminarians and treated his friends to expensive dinners on their rare nights out. He never attempted to buy friendships, but it would be hard to deny that some were attracted to him because of his generous nature and easy spending habits. Joe saw no need to be thrifty as his parents had plenty of money, put no restrictions on the use of his credit cards, and saw that others could benefit from his generosity.

The preparations for Joe's First Mass were handled by an event planner hired by Mike and Eugenia. His chalice was made by Cartier and had a cross encrusted with diamonds on its base and emeralds around the node to emphasize his Irish heritage. His vestments were made by the tailor of papal garments in Rome, Gamarelli. The string quartet from the Boston Symphony Orchestra provided the music prior to the Mass and a tenor from the Metropolitan Opera sang during the Mass. The scent of lilies tastefully mixed with bells of Ireland filled the church.

None of these preparations seemed excessive to Joe who took it all pretty much for granted. And, in truth, none of it meant much to Joe for he was centered upon the spiritual aspects of becoming a priest and uniting himself with Jesus Christ in the Holy Sacrifice of Mass. His heart was truly with Jesus; his parents and their hired planner took care of all the rest. The Mass was exquisite by anyone's standards, spiritual or temporal, and would be the talk of the diocese for weeks to come.

Father Joe made a good associate priest for several pastors after his ordination in 1987. Simultaneously he was assigned to teach English at the Catholic High School for Boys. After that, he was assigned as pastor in a series of parishes with an average stay of about three years. A joke emerged among his fellow priests that they all wanted to follow Joe wherever he had been pastor as he totally refurbished the rectory at his own expense. And when Joe left each appointment, he left with only his clothes, leaving behind all the new electronic equipment and furniture he had purchased.

Even though Joe took very good care of himself, he was even more generous with anyone in the parish who needed help. He worked particularly well with the poor, who often found that some anonymous person had paid their overdue utility bills or rent. Joe never told anyone of his generosity; and many, seeing all his personal possessions, the expensive cars he drove, and the vacations he enjoyed, unjustly accused him of selfishness. He was simply living the life he had always lived and simultaneously caring for the needs of others.

In the summer of 2006 Father Joe received an invitation to the ordination of Alain Moreau. Joe had seen Alain in passing throughout his seminary years. Joe was impressed with Alain's élan and good looks. As Joe was known in every gourmet restaurant in the state, he was impressed to learn of Alain's history as a chef. He attended the ordination and sent Alain a congratulatory check for a thousand dollars. When Msgr. Clem died, he was pleased to learn how expertly Father Alain had handled his parish.

As the years elapsed Joe became increasingly interested in Alain. As they were stationed in the same city, Joe would often take him out for dinner. The almost twenty year difference in their ages did not deter a growing friendship. Alain became the recipient of Joe's generosity, receiving rich vestments from Europe and tailor-made clothes from Neiman Marcus. It gave Joe genuine pleasure to provide nice things for this young, charismatic French priest.

Joe's family had a rarely used elaborate lake home with a state of the art kitchen.

Alain had been ordained only five years when Joe suggested they spend a couple of nights there, do a little fishing and swimming, and give Alain an opportunity to utilize his culinary skills. Joe was getting ready to leave for a few days in New York City as he often did to attend the theatre and thought he would make a week of it by meeting Alain at the house on Sunday evening after their last Masses.

The September weather was still warm enough for a swim before dinner. When Alain climbed up on the dock, Joe had already opened a bottle of Chateauneuf du Pape and handed him a glass. After finishing the bottle, they went inside to prepare dinner. About midway through the second bottle, Joe noticed how very handsome Alain looked in his swimsuit as he deftly floured the veal for scaloppini. The meal was extraordinary, from the endive salad to the bananas Foster; at least the third bottle of wine made it seem so.

With the last bite of dessert, Alain announced that he was tired, had consumed too much of his favorite wine, and needed to retire. He went to his room, flopped on his bed, and was immediately asleep. While Joe cleaned up the kitchen, he had trouble getting Alain out of his mind. He recognized the same feelings that had shamed him almost thirty years before in Rome as he watched his friend Des shower. This time he did not dismiss those thoughts.

When he went to his room, Joe found himself unable to sleep with constant thoughts of Alain. He longed to know the embrace of another person. With the exception of the far-from-satisfying experience in London when he lost his virginity, he had remained celibate. Alain seemed so appealing, so open, so warm. Joe finally stopped fighting. He rose from his bed and walked quietly into Alain's room. He listened to Alain's breathing as he slept soundly. Joe carefully lowered himself onto the bed and lay silently next to Alain for several minutes. He gently placed his arm across Alain's chest. With that, Alain awoke. It took a moment for him to recognize what was happening. Alain leapt from the bed, "Merde! What the hell are you doing? For God's sake, we're priests! Get the hell out of my room!"

"I'm sorry . . . I didn't mean . . . I just . . ." Joe left, returned to his own room. Shame held off sleep for several hours, and then it came fitfully and briefly. When he knocked on Alain's door the next morning, there was no answer. He looked outside to find Alain's car gone. As he drank his coffee, he looked at the lake and pondered what had happened. Had it been too much Chateauneuf du Pape? Was he indeed homosexual, as he had feared since that night in Rome with Des? Was this the end of his priesthood? Would Alain go to the bishop? Had he become so distant in his relationship with Christ that he would attempt such an action with Alain and endanger both their vocations? Should he cancel his trip to New York and go to the bishop himself?

He left that afternoon for New York as planned. He went to a musical comedy that night, unable to concentrate on it, worried about his future and his relationship with God. The next morning he rose at five. He remembered having heard of a Franciscan church near Grand Central where the priests heard confessions early each morning prior to Mass. He was there before seven. On a side altar of the old church there was a statue of the Blessed Mother that reminded him of the one at Lourdes, where he had reluctantly accepted her call to follow Jesus. As he knelt there he grieved that his bodily temptations had led him away from the love of his savior and the vows he had made. There was a crushing emptiness in his heart. He hated what he saw in himself. He hated having betrayed Jesus. He hated the distance that he perceived within himself to the very source of all that was true and good and loving.

An elderly priest entered the confessional in the darkened church. Joe followed. For the next fifteen minutes, he opened his soul to the confessor. He spoke of his privileged upbringing, his love of the Church, his attraction to material goods, his sexual longings, his drift from the first fervor of the priesthood, his attraction to Alain and his advances toward him. And he cried in shame, confusion, and recognition of his poverty in not being close to Jesus. The confessor responded with the wisdom earned through having heard confessions for over fifty years, the wisdom of a prayerful life, the wisdom of knowing a merciful Lord who died to take away sin. He imparted a sense of peace, hope, and most of all forgiveness.

Joe had not known such peace and hope for several years. He was elated as he left the church after Mass and headed down towards Wall Street to enjoy a good breakfast. The sky was clear and he was on top of the world. His sense of euphoria was broken by a young woman sitting on the sidewalk cradling what appeared to be a baby in her arms. She looked quite desperate and was begging passersby for money to feed her child. Joe was moved and with characteristic generosity took out his wallet with the intention of giving her a hundred dollar bill. As he bent down to give her the money, she drew a gun from beneath a doll she had been using as a prop, shot Joe three times rapidly in the chest, took his wallet and ran. Joe died there on the sidewalk, surrounded by strangers, killed by a young woman needing money to buy drugs.

Joe's funeral was held two weeks later. The bishop presided. His parents, Michael and Eugenia, arrived in their chauffeured limousine, looking dazed that their only son could really be gone. Almost every priest in the diocese attended, many having benefited from Joe's generosity. But most of the church was filled with blue collar workers and the poor, each with a story of Joe's having paid their hospital bills or rent or education. Some remembered the times he had shown up at their doors with huge baskets of food; others remembered the jobs he had obtained for them, even used cars purchased enabling them to get to work. Many cried as they looked at their children, thinking of the hardships that would have been theirs had it not been for Joe's generosity.

No one in the church seemed more ill at ease than Father Alain Moreau. Of all those present, he was the last to have seen Joe alive. Alain had phoned the day following that strange night at the lake and asked to see the bishop for personal reasons. The appointment was made for the Monday following Joe's funeral. As Alain heard one story after another of Joe's care for the poor, he knew what he must do. At the cemetery, Alain saw the bishop's secretary and canceled his meeting. Alain never spoke of the night at the lake to anyone.

CHAPTER SEVEN

FATHER GREGORY OWENS

"Just remember who you are. Your daddy was president of the Metropolitan Bank and Trust; he wasn't always a salesman at Western Auto. When the crash came, he took the only job he could get. And I didn't always work at S. H. Kress & Company; we even had a maid back then. Your daddy and I were 'victims of circumstance'; that's what we were, 'victims of circumstance.'"

Marlene often reminded her son Gregory about who he was, what his father had been, and the social standing she once had in the community. She didn't want him to kowtow to anyone. She had looked down her nose at the community when she was the wife of a bank president, and she continued that practice as she condescendingly chose to wait on customers at the five-and-dime store. She desired to instill that same sense of haughtiness in her son as protection against people who might judge him on the basis of their present economic status.

Gregory's father, Winston, was a beaten man who had never recovered emotionally or financially from having lost everything when the bank closed. He had the look of hopelessness written upon his face, and the shame he had endured in the crash was so deeply ingrained that he never directly looked at anyone. Marlene's overpowering demeanor did nothing to bolster her husband's ego but rather was another reminder that he was a failure.

Gregory was born in 1934 three weeks prior to Clement Donnelly in the same hospital. Marlene and Winston had given up on ever being able to conceive a child, and then when they were least able to afford one, Gregory came along. There was little joy over his birth; rather his parents again felt themselves "victims of circumstance." It took Winston almost five months to pay off the hospital and delivery bill, which amounted to almost $27.

While Clem grew up surrounded by love of parents and brother, Gregory grew up as an only child in a quiet house filled with depression, remorse, and pessimism. The two became friends in the first grade, and Clem was a ray of sunshine in Greg's life. They did everything together. Since the boys lived just a few blocks away from one another, the neighbors began to call them Tweedledee and Tweedledum. Clem was blond and Greg had dark, curly hair which led to the additional appellation of Vanilla and Chocolate.

Greg was so much happier in Clem's house than his own that the boys often contrived reasons to have Greg sleep over. Initially, Marlene was reluctant to grant permission, but as time went by she began to view it as a convenience, one less person to cook for and clean up after, following her humiliating day at Kress's. But Marlene was defensive about the Donnellys. Before Greg would leave the house, Marlene would always warn: "Now remember, Greg, the Donnellys may have some things that we don't, but they are no better than us. Remember, your daddy was president of the bank . . . " Before she could finish the litany of the "victims of circumstance," Greg had bolted out the front door on his way to Clem's. Al, Clem's dad, always took a special interest in Greg, knowing that his life with his parents had to be difficult. Greg returned that love but was uneasy with the knowledge that Al really belonged to Tim and Clem and that he was really not a part of the family regardless of how much he wished he could be.

Clem and Greg's closeness continued in high school. They shared their first furtive cigarette and beer, both of which made them feel ill, although neither would admit to that lack of "manliness." They debated the beauty of girls incessantly and their first date, driven by Al, was a double date. The studied together, sang in the school choir together, and served Mass together. Both sensed that their friendship would be lifelong.

But the seeds that Marlene had planted bore fruit. Greg viewed each of Clem's successes in high school as either a challenge or an insult to his own abilities. If, as Marlene had constantly reminded him, it was true that he was better than Clem, why did Clem always end up with better grades, more friends, prettier girls, and considerably less acne that he had. Was he also a "victim of circumstances" with Clem always getting the breaks while he came up short?

The crowning blow for Greg came with the casting of the senior play *Our Town*. He read for the part of the stage manager and wanted it more than anything he could imagine. If he could just get this part, it would show that he was better than Clem, who had also read for the part, and would win the admiration of others. He was livid when the drama teacher announced the cast, with Clem as the stage manager and Greg as one of the minor voices from the grave. Clem could not help noticing Greg's angry exit from the room, and he was nowhere to be found after school.

Greg's anger was no match for that of Marlene's, who called the drama coach at her home that night, cursed her, and threatened to have her fired. "My son is better than ten Clem Donnellys. You've never liked Greg, so you gave the part to your precious little Clem. Do you have any idea who I am? Do you know my husband was the president of a bank? We have connections, and I'm going to use them." In her fury Marlene failed to recognize that the line had gone dead and continued her tirade for several minutes.

Teenage boys rarely hold grudges, and Clem and Greg patched things up before the week was out. Greg couldn't bear to think of missing out of being in the play with his best friend in their last year of school together. Marlene put her wrath on simmer but did not attend the play, nor was she missed, even by Greg. Winston told Marlene he had to take inventory at Western Auto that evening and in a rare show of independence watched Greg deliver his three lines in the play.

Two months prior to graduation, Clem received news of his scholarship to Regis University. He knew that Greg would not be joining him and that the friendship that had meant so much to them both would have to be interrupted. He had also begun to understand Greg's jealousy. He did not love him less for it, but understood it as a natural response to his mother's fixation on the glories of her past. Greg really tried to be happy for Clem's scholarship; but when he thought of being stuck in town, going to the community college, and living with his parents, he felt that he had suffered still another injustice. Marlene developed a migraine when she heard of Clem's scholarship, accused Greg of never trying his best for her, told Winston that it was the lack of his involvement in Greg's life that caused his son to be a failure, and took to her bed to sulk.

The summer was a tense one between the two. Both boys knew what was happening between them, and neither could find the courage to bring it out in the open. They were like twins and could read one another clearly. The day finally came for Clem to leave for Regis. Greg went to the train station to see Clem off. They looked at one another, and both felt the bond of friendship born from eighteen years of sharing in one another's lives. Clem threw his arms around Greg: "I'll miss you so much, Greg. Thank you for always being there, for all the times we shared. I'm sorry this summer has put distance between us. You are a brother to me, and I will always love you." Greg couldn't stand it; Clem had again shown himself to be the better man. Greg said not a word in reply, drew back from Clem's embrace, and ran behind the station and wept. He hated himself for not responding to Clem's love; he was sorry for himself for losing his best friend and having to stay in a town which would be empty without him. And he became almost despondent when he thought of living the next four years with a mother he no longer loved and a father he no longer respected. "Shit! Shit! Shit!"

It took two weeks for Greg to write Clem, apologizing for his coldness at the train station. He tried as best he could to explain his actions without admitting jealousy, even to himself. He wrote that he was overwhelmed at losing his best buddy and would look forward to seeing him at Christmas break. Clem was quick to respond to Greg's letter, and they began writing one another weekly. As the year progressed, Greg noticed a change in the mood of Clem's letters. They became more serious, and it appeared that almost all of his life at Regis was centered on the Newman Center.

Greg, on the other hand, had attempted to fill his life with the diversions that college freshmen often adopt. Each weekend was a celebration of binge drinking, and his choice of female companionship could best be described as "easy." This led to heated rows between Greg and his mother, who had lost none of her thirst for a no-holds-barred battle. On a frosty February morning, both outside and attitudinally inside, Greg came to the breakfast table with a terrible hangover and Marlene decided that this was the perfect time to tear into him.

"Welcome to the table, my son. Or, should I say 'my drunken sot.' I heard when you came in this morning at three. I don't even care to imagine what you must have up to this time. You still reek of beer and cigarettes, mixed with the odor of the cheap perfume obviously worn by your equally cheap lady of the evening. You must be very proud of yourself, and certainly in a good state to receive communion this morning. You insult me with your conduct, and now you will go to the church and insult God by receiving the Eucharist in mortal sin."

Greg glared. "I wonder, Sweet Mother, or should I say 'my old dragon,' if you ever considered that the reason I have to drink and get out of this house is that I hate being around you so much?"

Marlene slapped Greg so hard that it knocked him off his chair and onto the linoleum floor. He lay there for a minute or two, got up, looked with disbelief at his mother and then at his father. "Goodbye, Dad. That's all I can take. I don't know how you've done it all these years." He threw some of his clothes in a suitcase and left, with Marlene screaming after him: "You're no good; you'll never be any good."

Greg paused, turned, and looked straight at her. "Thanks for the vote of confidence, Mom. I'll always have that to remember you by."

After arranging to stay with a fraternity brother, later that afternoon Greg called Clem and told him about the morning bout and the near kayo from the dragon lady. Clem calmed him down and tried to convince Greg that part of the problem was the manner in which he was choosing to live, and reminding him of the love of Jesus Christ that they had shared throughout the years. Later that afternoon Greg rang the doorbell of his pastor and asked him to hear his confession. Once more assured of the love of God and the love of Clem, he began to live a better life. He got a part time job, studied harder, and quit drinking. He did not, however, return home. He stopped by the Western Auto store from time to time to visit with his dad, but had no contact with is mother for the next three months.

Mid-March he received a letter from Clem that made him gasp and his stomach turn cold. Clem had decided to enter the seminary in the fall and study for the priesthood. Greg didn't know what to do or say. He found himself in his parish church on his knees. He begged God to help Clem, and for the next hour sat staring at the crucifix above the altar. "God, you've got to tell me what to do. I seem to lose everything that I held dear when Clem left. I hurt you and myself the way I acted last fall. None of the stuff that I thought might bring me happiness worked out well. I can't stand the mother you gave me, and I can't stand myself for not being able to stand her. Now you've called my only real friend to follow you, which I know will take him farther from me. Are you punishing me for my jealousy toward him? But why, why, why did you call Clem . . . and why did you not call me?"

That same prayer took many forms during the next two months, but the essence was always the same: Clem was anchored in the safe harbor of God's love while Greg was adrift in the perilous waters that took him farther and farther away from God and Clem. And then one Sunday in May, he heard his pastor give a homily on the Prodigal Son. At first he saw himself as the prodigal son but as the Gospel unfolded he knew that he was really like the son who remained home and resented and envied his brother who had left. He had always resented everything that Clem had achieved, resented his leaving, resented his scholarship, and now resented his being called to the priesthood. But then came the words of the father to his son in the Gospel: "You are with me always. Everything I have is yours . . ." Then Greg knew what he must do.

Greg's pastor was surprised when Greg told him later in the afternoon that he felt called to the priesthood and wanted to enter the seminary along with Clem. He knew of the family problems that Greg had experienced and that he was living away from home.

"What do your parents think of this decision of yours?"

"They don't know yet, Father; I wanted to talk with you first."

"Do you think they'll be supportive?" Father had dealt with Marlene before and knew that she could be difficult.

"Does it matter if that is what God wants of me? Didn't Jesus say something about even the closest of relatives turning against one another because of His word?"

"Well, yes, I guess He did at that. I'm impressed that you know so much Scripture."

"Why not? I've listened to you preach every Sunday all my life."

"I'll tell you what I'll do, Greg. If you talk with your parents and work things out there, I'll talk with the bishop about your attending the seminary."

Greg did not welcome the idea of having to eat humble pie and then spring his desire to become a priest on his mother all in one sitting, but he was willing to do whatever it took to enter the seminary. So, three months after leaving his parents' home, he rang the doorbell and waited patiently for someone to answer. Marlene hurriedly opened the door and was shocked to see Greg standing there. For a moment no words were spoken by either; they just looked at one another, like chess players trying to anticipate their opponent's next move.

"Well, don't just stand there. Come in."

"Mother, I'm sorry . . . about everything."

"While that doesn't change the words that were said or the pain that I have endured, I know that I must forgive you, and perhaps the pain will subside in time. How have you been?"

"I've been really well, Mom. My grades have improved and I don't drink or smoke anymore. I'm living with Tom Wilbanks, who is a Baptist, and he'd throw me out if I did."

"It's a blessing that the Baptists finally got something right," Marlene chuckled.

"I need to talk with you and Dad about something important."

"You haven't gotten some tramp pregnant, have you?"

Now it was Greg's chance to chuckle. "Oh, for heaven's sakes, Mom, NO! I've also given up those 'cheap ladies of the evening' as you often called them."

Winston returned home from work, and the family sat around the kitchen table that had served as the field of battle three months before. The mood was quite different now: Greg was sober and self-assured, and Marlene was distant but not aggressive. And then with as much tact and finesse as he could possibly muster, he told his parents of his desire to become a priest and his plans to enter the seminary in the fall.

Winston's face flushed with pride and excitement for his son. Marlene was trying to process whether this was still another injustice that she was about to suffer or whether she should play the part of the Blessed Mother and heroically offer her son to God. She decided on the latter.

"Well, now people will see what a holy person you are. Everyone in the parish will know that the Owens knew how to rear a son. Wait until Clem's parents hear of this. How they will wish that Clem was studying to be a priest of the Church!"

"Ah, Mom, there's one other thing I forgot to mention . . ."

The bishop sent them to the same seminary and during the seven years of preparation their devotion to Jesus Christ and his Church grew. The shared goal of the priesthood brought them even closer together. They spent hours discussing how they would live out their vocations.

When the date of the ordination finally arrived, they walked down the cathedral aisle side by side. Tweedledee and Tweedledum, Vanilla and Chocolate, were about to become Father Donnelly and Father Owens. They prostrated themselves before the bishop, and each prayed for the other as well as himself. The bishop imposed hands upon their heads and anointed their hands with oil. Standing on either side of the bishop, they celebrated their First Mass.

Marlene and Winston sat in the front pew on the left and Ann Margaret, Al, and Clem's brother Tim and his wife sat in the front pew on the right. Marlene was on her good behavior and even worked up a polite smile for Ann Margaret and Al. While it irritated her that Clem was ordained before Greg, she recognized that alphabetical order often created "victims of circumstance." Ann Margaret wore a simple brown suit and small pillbox hat to match; Marlene's red hat was of sufficient size to block the view of the altar for two rows behind her and matched the red polka dot suit she had proudly ordered from Maison Blanche. She planned to outshine Clem's mother and indeed she did, as well as the bishop. Ann Margaret and Al were almost as happy and proud of Greg as they were of Clem, as he had spent so much time at their home with Clem that they looked upon him as another son.

The reception that followed the ordination was held in the cathedral hall and both priests stood in the same receiving line along with their parents. Marlene couldn't have been more effusive if someone had lit her polka dot suit on fire. She hugged, kissed, chortled, and flailed her arms about in such an uncharacteristic fashion that those who knew her wondered what "medication" she might have taken. Greg and Clem shared an understanding look, and Winston and Al looked decidedly uncomfortable. Ann Margaret, possessing both charm and grace, appeared not to notice Marlene's antics at all.

It's strange how rapidly a person's attitude can change. The bishop went to the microphone and announced the first assignments for Fathers Donnelly and Owens. As was expected by most, they were assigned to small agrarian parishes with solid pastors to guide them. But Marlene's expectations were rarely in sync with the majority. Those close to her noticed the rose wilt. As soon as the bishop had finished his congratulatory remarks, she was off to corner him. Greg caught sight of what was about to occur and if he could have intervened by tackling Marlene, he would have done so, but it was too late.

"Bishop, what a nice little talk. I was wondering, however, if you really think that is a good assignment for my son Gregory. You know, he is so talented and it's so important that he get a really good start in the priesthood. Don't you think something in a larger city, perhaps even here, might serve both him and the Church better?"

In 1960 it was rare that anyone questioned the decisions of a bishop, and never had a mother of a newly ordained priest taken that position. He was really quite stunned, but had heard about Mrs. Owens before.

"First let me congratulate you on having such a fine son called to the priesthood by Our Lord. You must be justifiably very proud of him, as well as extremely grateful to God for that honor. You are correct in discerning that the first assignment of a priest is crucial in the further development of his ministry. And that, my dear, is precisely why I have given him the assignment I announced. I know that you will support him with your love and your prayers, and that the good pastor of that parish will train him to become the extraordinary priest we both wish. Thank you for your suggestion." Checkmate.

Their first two years as associate pastors were quite similar. Both had been assigned to understanding pastors who did their best to impart whatever practical pastoral experience they had. But when Clem was reassigned to a parish after that and Greg was not, Greg felt unfairly treated. He was tired of his assignment, and the pastor's personality traits had begun to wear on him. Even though Clem's new pastor had a well-known alcoholic problem, at least the parish was a bit larger and there were more opportunities. The jealousy that had been suppressed for the past nine years began to reappear in Greg's heart and mind. Marlene's subtle comments to him about how nice Clem's new parish was did not help matters. She looked upon Greg's continued presence in the same parish after two years in the same manner she would view a student being held back in grade school. "Goodness gracious, you're smarter than that old poop you were assigned to anyway."

By the end of his third year, Greg had requested an immediate reassignment and was given one. He looked upon his new pastor as domineering and dictatorial. Good grief, he was now 28 years old and the pastor dared to set a curfew for him, assign him duties he disdained, and reprimand him when he deemed it necessary. He knew that Clem was covering for his own pastor's alcoholic failings, but at least he was able to do what he thought was right. Many of the priests were talking about what a great job Clem was doing and wondered how long it would be before his pastor was sent away for treatment. Greg again went to the bishop and asked to be reassigned. The bishop began to recognize that Greg would probably not be happy under any pastor and that perhaps he could handle a small parish on his own. So, after only three years as an associate, he was given a small parish with two missions.

Marlene was delighted that Greg was now a pastor, while Clem continued to serve as an associate. Perhaps the scales of justice were beginning to tilt in her favor. She was not, however, pleased that her son was given two mission churches and suggested to him that perhaps some other neighboring parish could take over at least one of the missions and that he might mention that possibility to the bishop. She had seen at the reception that the bishop was not open to her ideas and presumed he simply didn't like women. The idea seemed attractive to Greg, but he thought he'd better not push his luck with the bishop quite so soon after having been named a pastor.

The first year as a pastor was a better one for Greg. He worked hard to serve his parish and its mission churches, and the people were eager to give the young priest a good chance. He would generally spend his day off with Clem, who had a unique ability to help him keep his eyes trained on what the priesthood was really about. Clem also tried to calm him down concerning the little problems of ministry that he had a tendency to exaggerate. Clem rarely mentioned his own problems in dealing with his pastor's ever increasing problematic behavior and was even able to find humor in it. They'd have dinner, maybe take in a movie, and Greg always felt better after having visited Clem.

Clem's pastor was finally sent away for counseling, and Clem ran the parish just as he had been doing practically speaking since he arrived two years earlier. Recognizing his exceptional service to the parish, the bishop reassigned Clem to become the pastor of a parish normally reserved for priests who had served the diocese for fifteen or twenty years—and it was a parish without missions. When Greg received the letter detailing all the assignments for the diocese and saw Clem's plum, he was deflated emotionally. His first thoughts were what Marlene would think, and he knew that he would be receiving a call from her as soon as the assignments were made known to the laity.

Over the years, the pattern repeated itself time and again. Regardless of how hard Greg saw himself working, Clem was always more highly esteemed, better liked by his parishioners and brother priests, and always received the better assignments. Greg became embittered and his resentment was obvious in the manner in which he treated his parishioners. Clem was smart enough to comprehend the reason for the obvious distance growing between them and attempted to talk it over with Greg, who viewed those attempts as condescending and demeaning. When Clem was appointed as the vicar general for the diocese, a rift resulted between them that lasted many years. Greg lacked the emotional tools to deal with his friend being his ecclesiastical superior.

When Marlene heard the news of Clem's appointment as vicar general, she wrote a letter to him with a copy to the bishop, letting them both know of the injustices she felt had been heaped upon Greg from his first appointment on—he had been set up for failure repeatedly. She stated that having known Clem all his life, she knew he was intellectually incapable of fulfilling his assignment, and she would no longer be donating to the Church which had treated her son so shamefully. Clem tried unsuccessfully to make peace with Marlene, writing her the kindest letter he could compose, and the bishop acknowledged her letter and assured her of his love and respect for Greg. She threw both letters into the trash can.

Greg's father died in 1985. The bishop spoke at his funeral and did his best to comfort Marlene, who responded with coldness. Clem went to see Greg as soon as he heard of Winston's death, and they spoke of the disappointments and trials of his father's life, neither mentioning Marlene.

Marlene died seven years later. Greg had the funeral Mass for his mother and delivered the homily. He spoke of how she had attempted to guide him throughout his life and was successful in imbuing him with her own philosophy. He was still sorting out in his mind the positive and negative effects she had upon him. Greg told the congregation that she was a woman of strongly held principles and sometimes acted upon them in a manner hurtful to others, but she had been indeed a "victim of circumstances." He began to break down as he concluded his homily, recognizing the love/hate relationship they had, one that had tarnished his life and his priesthood.

No one knew more than Clem how deeply Marlene had hurt Greg and damaged the caliber of priest he could have been. Clem knew what Greg must have suffered as he had also been the target of her jealousy on numerous occasions. After Marlene's body was lowered into the ground, Clem hugged Greg hard as they had not done in many years.   He kissed him on the cheek, drew back, looked him straight in the eye: "I'll tell you what I told you at the train station forty years ago—'You're my brother, and I'll always love you.' I'm your family now."   From that moment on they were the best of friends and jealousy never raised it head again.   The seeds that Marlene had planted in her son's heart died with her.

When Clem died in 2006, he and Greg had shared dinner the night before at a local steak house. They reminisced over the seventy-two years of their lives, laughing a great deal, but also sharing a few tears. They told each other how much they treasured their lifelong friendship and saw it as one of God's great gifts to them.

"You know, Greg, for those of us who have been called to a celibate life, serving Christ, having a friend like you meant everything to me. Even during times when we were not close to one another, I always knew that you were my brother and that I could count on you. I can't tell you how much I treasure the friendship that Jesus gave us."

Greg said nothing for a few moments and then looked thoughtfully at his old friend. "When I got that letter from you telling me you were going to become a priest, it didn't take me long to know that I had to also follow that path. But it has taken me the better part of my priesthood to figure out whether I really wanted to follow Jesus . . . or you. And maybe the best compliment I can pay you is that I can't see much difference."

It was a little after ten, when Greg's phone rang the next evening and Father Moreau told him that his good friend, his brother, had just died. Greg lived and served the Church for almost another ten years. At each one of his daily Masses, he stopped to remember Clem.

CHAPTER EIGHT

FATHER MARK SANDERS

Orville Sanders returned from World War II determined to build a new life and reap the benefits of the country he had fought to defend. By the spring of 1946, he had secured a good-paying job at a local dairy, married his high school sweetheart, and put a down payment on a comfortable home. By the following January, his wife Gertrude had given birth to their first child, Irene; a year later came Mark, followed a year later by Bette.

The Sanders attended the First Missionary Baptist Church at a time in the history of our country when churches were being built at a rate never seen before or since. Orville often gave his testimony in church meetings and taught Sunday school each week. He led his little family in prayer before each meal and each evening knelt with the children by the side of their beds to lead them in prayer. He had seen much in World War II, and he knew how deeply he depended upon God for all things.

Mark idolized his father and imitated whatever he did. As soon as he could read, he would pour over the family Bible and act out scenes from the Old and New Testaments with his sisters. At one time he was Moses crossing the Red Sea; at another, Samson slaying the Philistines; at another, Daniel in the lions' den. But his favorite role was that of Jesus—with Irene and Bette in supporting roles of Martha and Mary. In his eleventh summer, his church held a revival and during a particularly emotional altar call, he received Jesus into his heart and was baptized later that summer.

School was of little interest to Mark, but his grades were average or a little better at times. Mark was BIG, much bigger than the other boys in his class. His athletic ability was natural, and Orville spent hours with him in their backyard playing football. As he grew in age the backyard became more crowded with every boy in the neighborhood meeting right after school to play football. By junior high school, Mark was already six feet tall and weighed 165 well-distributed pounds. When he walked through the gym door for football tryouts, the coach almost salivated. "Holy Moses! Thank you, Jesus!"

From that moment on, the position of tackle went undisputed throughout junior and senior high school. Mark loved the game, his teammates, the coach, and particularly the tackling. His only problem came with the locker room conversations and jesting. Mark allowed no one to take God's name in vain. He would confront any teammate immediately, and his size always won the argument. At halftime one Friday evening in a game against his school's arch rival, the coach got carried away in his exhortations to the boys and laced his remarks with both profanities and blasphemies.

"Coach, I don't mean any disrespect, but I don't appreciate your using our Lord's name that way, and I'm really embarrassed by the other things you said to us. I can't go back on that field knowing that I'm playing for a man who doesn't respect God or us." Mark delivered his words softly and without malice while looking directly into the coach's eyes.

There was no sound in the locker room. His teammates were frozen, sitting on their benches, looking intently at the coach for his reaction. The coach looked hard at Mark, examining the purity of his motivations and pondering the proper response. He took a deep breath: "Team, Mark is right. I got carried away and he brought me back to where we all need to be. You've never heard me speak that way before, and you won't again. I'm sorry."

Mark led the team in three cheers for the coach . . . and they won the game.

It was no surprise to anyone that Mark received an athletic scholarship to college. He was now an impressive six feet four inches, 245 pound man with an easy and gentle demeanor. He loved his freshman year, handled his studies satisfactorily, played great football, and met a girl. She was the smartest girl in his English literature class, and he only had to maneuver a couple of guys out of the way to secure the desk next to hers. By the third class, he invited Dorothy out to dinner. He picked her up at her sorority house, and they walked to a restaurant close to the campus. He took her left hand in his and invited her to pray with him prior to dinner. She smiled, nodded, and crossed herself with her right hand.

As the meal progressed, he seemed to have some difficulty in asking her a question. "So, you're a Catholic?"

"Yes, always have been . . . and always will be."

"Well, have you been saved?"

"Yeah, Mark. We believe that Jesus did that 2,000 years ago."

"Well, I don't mean any disrespect, you understand, but you might be going to hell."

At that, Dorothy's head went back, and she laughed so hard that everyone in the restaurant turned to look. As she dried the tears of laughter from her face and looked at the red-faced young man across the table, she spoke very kindly. "You're a really nice guy, and I enjoy being with you. Who knows, maybe something else could develop between us in the future, but you need to understand I'm as devoted to Jesus as you are, that I believe He gave me my Church, and if your prejudice against Catholics is not something you can overcome, this will be our last date."

Little of consequence was said during the remainder of the dinner or on the walk back to her sorority house. As Mark left her at the door, he said: "I'm sorry about tonight. I need to time to think."

Without comment, she gave him a kiss on the cheek and went inside.

Mark prayed, phoned and talked about Dorothy with his dad, who recommended that he turn to his minister, whose counsel did not bring any peace. He and Dorothy had a few more dates, but each felt the barrier of faith that separated them. Mark knew that he was in love with Dorothy, but years of prejudice against Catholics would not let him pursue a deeper relationship.

Another cloud had found its way into Mark's life, the Vietnam War. Several of his friends from high school had already enlisted. Each day the news was filled with the bloodshed of American boys. Mark believed it was a just war, and his Christian ethic of helping those who were in need made him feel guilty about pursuing his own interests while other young men were enlisting. All those images of King David, Samson, Moses, and Daniel that he had imitated as a child filled his heart with a fervor that impelled him to enlist in the Marines after his first year of college, in the summer of 1967.

Vietnam was even worse than he had feared or imagined. Within a few weeks of arriving, he was in midst of the fighting. Mark was tough, but it drained even his strength, both physically and emotionally. He would never forget the look in the eyes of the first man he killed, the bodies of his Marine buddies blown apart by hidden bombs, endless hours of waiting between battles, the uncertainly as to whether he would ever make it home, the swamps, the snakes, the jungle, the heat. He prayed as he had never prayed before.

God had a surprise in store for Mark. He and two of his buddies had been sent to search an area for possible snipers. As they made their way through the rice paddy, a land mine exploded that sent the Marine to his right flying into the air. Mark was knocked to the ground as he felt the shrapnel enter his legs and his back. He quickly lost consciousness. The next thing he knew, someone was dragging him through the rice field. He had never known such pain. The voice told him: "Keep down and keep quiet. We've got to make it through this field, or we'll both be killed by the snipers." Tug by tug, his rescuer pulled him for perhaps a hundred or more yards. Reaching the cover of the trees, he pulled him up on his back, struggling to support Mark's weight, and carried him through the jungle to the safety of his company.

Before blacking out, Mark saw his rescuer make the sign of cross over him. He was evacuated, and the first of many operations took place. Mark was later told that both of his buddies had died, one from the bomb, the other from a sniper's bullet and that if the padre, his rescuer, had not put his own life on the line Mark would have been shot. The area had been crawling with the enemy. Surgeons informed Mark that one piece of shrapnel was lodged in his spinal column, and if they were to attempt to remove it he could become a quadriplegic. If they were to leave it, he would have considerable pain throughout his life, with the possibility of its eventually disabling him. Mark chose to leave it.

He had been in the hospital for seven weeks and had been through three operations when he was told he had a visitor. As soon as he saw the man's face, he recognized him as the one who had pulled him to safety and blessed him.

"How we doin', fella?" asked the same voice that had told him to keep quiet and keep his head down. The priest was of average size and was on crutches.

"I hear I owe you my life."

"You and I both know that's not true and who you really owe your life to."

At that, Mark cried for the first time since he had been injured. He could take the physical pain. But the knowledge of God's presence was too overpowering. "You're a Catholic priest?"

"Yeah, we have a way of showing up in people's lives from time to time."

"I'm a Baptist."

"I noticed that on your chart. You are also my brother in Christ. Let me help you. Let's pray together." And just as he had dragged Mark through the rice paddies, he now pulled him out of his prejudice and made him comfortable in praying with a Catholic priest. It was the beginning of Mark's journey to Catholicism.

Three months later Mark was given an honorable discharge from the Marines along with a Purple Heart, returned to his family, and then to the university. He began to visit the parish priest to take instructions in the faith. He had been able to spend a good deal of time during his convalescence with the military chaplain who had come to his rescue and now loved the Church he once misunderstood. Due to his time in Vietnam, Dorothy was now a senior in college while he was a sophomore. She had fallen in love with another Catholic, and they planned to be married in July. Even though

Mark had dreamed about a future with her, he felt strangely comfortable with her decision and even asked her and her fiancé to be his sponsors when he was confirmed as a Catholic.

Mark's parents were far more understanding about his becoming a Catholic than he had expected them to be. When he told them about how the priest had saved his life, they seemed to accept this as a sign from God. They still had reservations about Catholicism, but Mark was now an adult and this was a decision he would have to make.

During the next two years in college, Mark became increasingly active in the Church. Additionally, he read the early fathers of the Church and couldn't understand how anyone could be anything else but a Catholic. The truth was there. He was so filled with the Spirit of God that he wanted to help others see the wonderful truths he had found. He knew he must become a priest.

The seminary years were wonderful for Mark spiritually, but he had some difficulties in relating to his classmates who seemed at times shallow. He was older than most, and his war experiences had made him considerably more mature. Just as his father had learned in World War II, he knew how precious life can be and how dependent man is upon God. There was no doubt in his mind that God was controlling his life; he had seen it. He had to deal with the emotional pain of the war and the physical pain that would remain with him throughout life.

The day of his ordination was the happiest in Mark's life. His parents' negative feelings about Catholicism had dwindled over the years, and they both beamed with pride as they saw Mark enter the cathedral in his alb. Irene, now the mother of three children, was there with her husband. Bette had a married a Catholic and converted.

Mark had asked Father Joel Taylor, who had been ordained two years before, to vest him in his chasuble at the ordination.   Earlier that morning, Father Joel had been introduced to a priest from outside the diocese who asked him for an unusual favor. When the time for the vesting arrived, Mark stood expecting Father Joel to approach with his chasuble. He looked at Joel who was making no signs of moving from his place in the sanctuary. At that same moment the priest who had approached Joel earlier, stepped in front of Mark with his chasuble. Mark looked into the same eyes he had seen above him making the sign of the cross after he had been injured in Vietnam.

"What . . .?"

"I told you that we have a way of showing up from time to time." He placed the chasuble over Mark's head and upon his shoulders and hugged him. Still in awe, Mark watched the priest limp away. He had not seen or heard from him in seven years. At the end of the Ordination Mass, Mark blessed his parents, his sisters and their husbands, and then he returned the sign of the cross to the priest who had saved his life and introduced him to Catholicism.

Mark's priestly career was filled with enthusiasm and joy. He approached evangelism in the same manner he had approached football; he gave it every ounce of his strength. Perhaps it was his Baptist upbringing that helped bring such vigor to his own personal testimony and zeal for the Gospel. He was never reluctant to approach the lost sheep, both those who had never known God and those who had wandered away. He was still going for that tackle. He would never be known for his erudition, but it was so obvious that he was filled with the Spirit of God that he brought hundreds to the faith.

He became the best apologist in the diocese as he could read the minds of those who were distrustful and wary of the Church and what it had to teach.

As a young priest he was given small rural churches with missions. He bought the biggest Jeep he could find and rejoiced in tearing around from one place to another. The pain from his injury was heightened by the rough country roads, but that never seemed to diminish his joy in doing what he knew to be the most important thing in the world, spreading the Gospel of Jesus Christ, and bringing people to the knowledge of the fullness of the truth to be found only the Catholic Church.

The greatest joy of his priesthood was bringing his own parents into the Church on the twentieth anniversary of his ordination. Orville was seventy-eight years old and Gertrude seventy-six. They had introduced their son to Jesus, taught him his first prayers, and shared the stories of the Bible with him. Now he anointed them with Chrism, confirming them with the Spirit of the Lord, and fed them the Body and Blood of the Savior who had guided their family. As Mark looked at his mother and father, he realized how blessed he had been and became aware of the oneness that was theirs.

Mark had proven to be such an extraordinary evangelist with absolutely no boundaries to his enthusiasm that the bishop offered him a really nice city parish after he had been ordained seven years. That would be the first of three times he would make such an offer. Each time Mark would beg him to leave him on the mission circuit where he would be free to seek out those most unlikely to be exposed to the truth of the Catholic Church. He told the bishop that he knew the minds and hearts of these people, that they were often prejudiced against the Church, had little education and less money. He could connect with them because he had grown up thinking the way they did. He explained to the bishop that he saw these people as the sheep that had strayed far into the wilderness and needed a shepherd to bring them back. Each time the bishop would relent because he recognized that Mark really did have a special gift in seeking out souls that would otherwise be forgotten.

Sixteen years after his ordination Mark received a letter from the military chaplain who had saved his life, Father Israel Tatum, OSB. Even though he had prayed daily for this priest who had a way of "showing up from time to time," he had not kept in contact with him. Father Israel wrote that his injuries had forced him to retire from the military and return to his monastery. He was dying and didn't want to leave without telling Mark what a blessing he had been to his priesthood. Israel had always been able to see God's hand in Mark's life, and that insight had strengthened his own faith. He knew that it was the Holy Spirit who led him to Mark in the midst of the rice paddies and had given him the strength to drag his almost lifeless body back to camp. He never shared with Mark that the reason for his limp was he had been shot during that rescue.

Mark left the evening he received the letter to drive through two states to Father Israel's monastery. He was warmly greeted by the abbot in true Benedictine hospitality and shown to the infirmary. The abbot told Mark that Israel was rarely conscious and that one of the last things he was able to do was to dictate the letter he had received. Mark knelt by Israel's bed and quietly prayed the rosary as Israel's breath became increasingly shallow. Knowing that the dying are often more aware than they appear to be, Mark began to speak to him.

"Oh, Father Israel, my brother priest, just as you dragged me from the rice fields and then dragged me into the Church through your kindness and wisdom, your image has been a part of every conversion that the Holy Spirit guided me to make throughout the years of my priesthood. I often found myself using the same words, the same reasoning, you used with me to soften my heart and remedy my thinking. Just as you carried me on your back to safety, I have carried you in my heart as I tried to carry others to the heart of Jesus. Jesus used you to save my life and then to save my soul. God has taken me by the hand, your hand, and led me to a life filled with grace and joy. How can I ever thank God and you enough?"

A tear crept from Israel's closed eyes and made its way down his cheek and onto his pillow. His eyes opened a little, and he looked at Mark. With a soft voice he whispered, ". . . from time to time."

Mark felt that he had lost his father when Israel died. And, in a sense, he had. He stayed at the monastery and concelebrated Israel's funeral Mass. That afternoon he went to confession to the abbot and spoke to him for some time. After he had shared the evening meal with the monks, he set out to return to his missions, emotionally drained but joyous at having experienced such holiness in Israel and in the monastery itself. He intended to drive through the night as he needed to get back to the missions for his weekend Masses.

Mark probably never knew what hit him that night. A teenager who had been celebrating his football team's victory that Friday evening with a few too many beers, fell asleep at the wheel of his pickup truck and at the last moment veered across the center line, hitting Mark's Jeep head on. Mark was killed instantly; the teenager miraculously escaped major injury. Israel may have once more put Mark on his back and brought him to Jesus.

CHAPTER NINE

FATHER YANCY TROTTER

Dawn Jones came from a country family and had five older brothers and no sisters. They had nothing. Her father had lost his job at the mill when he was thirty-two and used that as an excuse never to seek employment again. Her brothers took after their dad, never finished high school, and worked as little as possible. They fought incessantly with one another and with anyone who dared to disagree with them. By the time Dawn arrived, her mother was worn down by the demands of a husband who abused her and sons who had learned from their father that she was unworthy of their respect or kindness.

Dawn was in the fifth grade, eleven years old, when she was first raped by her father. Within the next two years, all but one of her brothers had followed his example. Her teachers wondered why she always looked troubled and sad. Her father had warned her that if she told anyone of the rapes he would throw her out on the streets. And she had learned from her mother simply to take whatever the men had to offer; that was the way life was for women in their family.

At fifteen Dawn found that she was pregnant. She had no way of knowing who the father was, only that it was one of her own family. That year she met a junior in high school, eighteen years old, who was the first man who ever showed her any genuine kindness and wanted nothing in return. His family was poor but honorable. Dawn finally let her secret out to Leroy, who told her that he loved her and would rear the child as his own. They eloped and ran off to a neighboring city where Leroy got a job washing dishes. They rented a one-room apartment over a drugstore, and Dawn was happier than she had ever been. Seven months later on December 25, 1970, Yancy Trotter was born.

Yancy seemed to defy scientific knowledge concerning the physical and mental defects that are likely results of inbreeding. Although she was only a sixteen-year-old child herself, Dawn delighted in her beautiful, healthy baby. Leroy also loved the baby and got an additional job, fixing tires, at the local Goodyear store.

When Yancy was two, Leroy started smoking pot, lost both interest and motivation in providing for his family, and lost his second job. He had worked his way up to bartender in the restaurant, a situation which placed temptation only as far as the nearest bottle or lonely woman. He began staying out later and later and often did not return to the apartment at all. Finally he told Dawn that their marriage had been a mistake from the start, that he was just being a nice guy because she was pregnant by her father or one of her brothers, that he hated rearing a kid who wasn't even his, that he had met a wonderful girl at the bar, and that he was leaving Dawn to marry her. He packed and left.

Needless to say, Dawn's already low estimation of men in general took still another step south. She had $38, a two-year-old boy, and no one to turn to for help. She could not, would not, go back to that place she called home as a child. The next morning she took to the streets in search of a job with Yancy in tow. After repeated refusals, at three that afternoon she walked into one of the finer shoe stores in town and asked if they needed any help. The manager, a man of about thirty, sized up the situation. "Honey, we ought to be able to work something out." She wasn't sure what he meant, but it made her feel uncomfortable. "Get a new dress, fix yourself up, and come back tomorrow at 9:00 a.m. sharp."

From there, Dawn went to a lady who had advertised that she kept children during the day, gave her $10, and told her she would be back with Yancy at 8:30 in the morning. She knew she couldn't afford that new dress, so she put on a blouse and skirt, her only other outfit. She hoped that the scarf that Leroy had given her for their first anniversary would make it look more "citified."

Having dropped off Yancy, she showed up at 8:50 a.m., ready to start a new life and provide for her son. Clifford Hoover, the store manager, taught her how to treat customers and how to sell shoes. She caught on quickly; hunger is a great motivator. Within six weeks, she had become the top salesperson, and the customers often asked for her personally. For the first time in her life, Dawn was beginning to have some self-respect. She was supporting herself and her son.

Clifford Hoover had lost his wife of ten years to cancer. He was left with a son and two daughters. He had little idea how to rear a son and absolutely no understanding of the girls. And Clifford was lonely, very lonely. He saw Dawn as the answer to his problems. Within three months, they married. Dawn had visions of a secure home, stability for Yancy, and a husband who would take care of them both.

However, within two months, Clifford informed Dawn that he was uncomfortable with another man's son in his home, as well as with the financial drain it caused, and that she would have to make other arrangements for Yancy. She pleaded with Clifford, who told her to shut up and get rid of Yancy so she could be a proper mother to his children.

It was clear to Dawn that once more she was being used by a man for his own purposes, but like her mother she saw no alternative. As much as she loved Yancy, she had become dependent upon Clifford and knew that his children also needed her. She feared that what had happened to her as a girl could happen to his daughters. Dawn was aware of an orphanage in town run by an order of Catholic nuns whom everyone seemed to respect. Being totally ignorant of all religion, she was suspicious of them but had no particular prejudice against Catholics.

The orphanage was an imposing structure, rather dark and not quite as well kept as Dawn would have hoped. Her interview with Mother Superior was intimidating, but somehow she felt that she could trust these women in black habits with the person she loved most. She opened up to Sister Patricia and told her the whole story of her life, the sexual abuse, the unfaithful husband, and now the uncaring one who wanted only to use her. Sister Patricia could hear the despair in Dawn's voice and knew that she needed them. She agreed to accept little Yancy, who was now totally confused about whom to trust and whom, if anyone, to count on for love. Dawn left him with the nuns and promised to return once a month on visiting days. She returned to Clifford, who would use her to sell shoes during the day, care for his children in the evening, and share his bed at night. It worked out well . . . for Clifford.

Initially Yancy was terribly frightened to be without Dawn. He had never been without her at night. As Sister Patricia checked the beds in the dormitory, she heard his crying and stopped by his bed. She sat on the side of his bed, took him in her arms, patted his back, and sang one of the Austrian lullabies of her homeland. She did this almost every evening for six weeks. Finally Yancy began to trust her and look upon her as his new mother. He loved being with the other twenty-eight children in the orphanage. He had never had other children with whom to play and delighted in their company.

The nuns were strict, but they were also fair. They saw it as their vocation to lead the children to God and to care for their physical and emotional well-being. They taught Yancy about Jesus and led the children in religious songs. They instilled a strong sense of personal responsibility, and each was assigned chores that contributed to the good of the whole.

Dawn came to visit Yancy on the first Sunday of each month. Those visits lasted for about a year, when they became less and less frequent. Yancy really didn't mind as he felt increasingly uncomfortable with his mother and the time between them seemed forced and awkward. He would have much preferred to be playing with his friends than cooped up in the visiting parlor with his mother who always asked him the same questions and spoke increasingly about his stepbrother and sisters whom he could not even remember.

With Dawn's reluctant approval, Yancy was baptized into the Catholic faith, and when he was seven, he received his First Holy Communion. By the time of his confirmation, he and Sister Patricia had become as close as any mother and son. She made arrangements for him to enter the local Catholic high school for boys, where he excelled in his studies; Sister Patricia made sure of that. Recognizing the need for male figures in his life, Father Joel Taylor, who was teaching religion in the high school, took a special interest in Yancy. He arranged for him to serve his daily Mass, took him to ball games, and taught him to speak well and debate intelligently. As Sister Patricia had become his surrogate mother, now Father Joel became not only his respected mentor but also his loved surrogate father.

Father Joel was not surprised when Yancy came to him half way through his senior year in high school and told him he had decided to become a priest. Joel knew the struggles that Yancy had experienced in growing up without parents and questioned him thoroughly about the motives for his decision. Was Yancy really only looking for security, respect, and the family he would always have as priest? The young man assured him that the love of Christ he had always witnessed in and received from Sister Patricia and Father Joel had brought him to the realization that he wished to be able to give that same love to others. Father Joel set up appointments for Yancy with the diocesan vocations director. Knowing little of his background, the director arranged for multiple psychological interviews prior to his acceptance.

Yancy had never been told of his possible paternal parentage and believed that Leroy was his real father and that he had abandoned him when he was two. He had always been content with that explanation and had no desire to have any further relationship with the father who had turned his back on him. Dawn had evolved into more of a distant older sister role than a mother to him, and her visits were now only around his birthday at Christmas. The orphanage was his home, and the people there were his family. Sister Patricia and Father Joel were the guiding and loved adults in his life, and he was perfectly at peace with that situation; it was really all he had known since he was three years old.

The psychological testing unearthed no appreciable danger signals, and Yancy was admitted to the seminary the fall immediately following his high school graduation.

As he was accustomed to institutional living, the transition was probably easier for him than for the young men who came from traditional families. His easy, relaxed manner made him popular among his peers, and he became a natural leader. His intelligence and his comfortable attitude around priests that had resulted from his relationship with Father Joel made him popular among the priest faculty.

On holidays Yancy would often return to the orphanage, where the nuns were always excited to see him and were proud that one of their children was studying to be a priest. At other times, he would visit Father Joel at his rectory and help out in whatever manner he was asked. He became such a regular around Father Joel's parish that the parishioners helped support him and some of the ladies in the parish began to heap motherly affection upon him. He was readily and genuinely welcomed into many families who found his easy-going, warm, thoughtful, and prayerful persona a pleasant addition and a great example to their own children.

When Yancy was called to ordination to the priesthood on Pentecost Sunday of 1996, the cathedral was filled with the families that had followed his progress from his childhood in the orphanage, through his Catholic high school years and his formative years in the seminary. This handsome young man of twenty-six, stood before them ready to begin a life as a priest. While the others being ordained were supported by mothers, fathers, and siblings, he was filled with gratitude for the glorious family of the Church that had surrounded him with love and protection from the time that he was three. Self-pity had never been a temptation for Yancy; he loved the family God had given him.

Father Joel had a chalice made for Yancy, who would remember him in prayer each time he celebrated Mass. Father Joseph Mulalley heard Yancy's story and gave him a new Buick the week before his ordination. He celebrated his First Mass in the chapel at the orphanage, with the boys living there serving the Mass and the girls singing in the choir. The nuns outdid themselves preparing the most elaborate meal they had ever attempted for his guests. No family could have been more unified in their love than the nuns were for "their priest."

Dawn sent Yancy a nice card, stating that she was sorry she could not attend but that she hoped to see him soon. Clifford had forbidden her to go. He told her that she needed to put that part of her life behind her, that Yancy had been a mistake from the beginning, and that Catholic hocus pocus was just so much superstition. In reality, Clifford had planned a fishing trip with his son that weekend and needed someone to look after the shoe store.

Wherever the bishop assigned Yancy over the years, he immediately became a part of the lives of the people. His love and enthusiasm were never half-hearted. Because he saw the Church as his family, the elderly were his grandparents; the established, his parents; the young, his siblings; and the children, his children. Each day he thanked God for his priesthood and for the family He had given him. His homilies were like love letters to his parishioners, constantly encouraging them to form a deeper love for Christ. The parishioners knew that every word he spoke was from the heart, without pomp or frills or ambiguities—here was the love of the Gospels, pure and unvarnished.

But Yancy had a special love which made a minority of the faithful uneasy about him, and some of his more liberal brother priests contemptuous of him. He had a tremendous love for the unborn child. It wasn't difficult to understand how that love developed. His life in the orphanage taught him that every child had worth, even those discarded by their parents. It hurt him each time he saw parents leave their children at the orphanage as if they were just too inconvenient to deal with. He didn't understand why Dawn had forsaken him or why Leroy had left him, but he knew it wasn't right. And he knew it was horrible to kill a child.

Unlike many who would claim to be pro-life, he did something about it. In fact, he did a great deal about it. From his own savings and what he could beg, he bought a store opposite the local abortion clinic. There he organized volunteers to do sidewalk counseling for those approaching the abortion mill. He filled the store with items that mothers living in poverty could use for their children. He wrote articles for the local papers and gave talks throughout the state and ultimately around the country protesting abortion and proclaiming the right of a child to live. Throughout it all, he never lost sight of the dignity of the mother or the love and support she needed, even when she had an abortion. His love was like the seamless garment; it started with the child but encompassed the needs of the mother.

When he became a pastor, he lost a few parishioners who were offended by what they deemed an over emphasis on the protection of the life of the unborn. It was not unusual for one or more ladies to leave Mass during his homilies on the sanctity of life. Most of those were dealing with the guilt of having had an abortion. A few of his brother priests pointed out to him that there were other issues involving the sanctity of life that he should address. What they failed to recognize was that he was addressing those issues also, but did not use them as an excuse to avoid doing everything in his power to eliminate abortion.

Yancy had the full backing of his bishop on his love for the unborn. Letters sent to the bishop protesting Yancy's unwavering stance were responded to with firm, pastoral counsel that they should follow his example. Priests who might approach the bishop concerning the topic were told that they were on shaky ground and should return to the teachings of the Church. Yancy, for his part, never treated any of his detractors with anything but respect and patience. He knew that their thinking might be askew, but they were his sisters and brothers and should also be treated with love.

One day while counseling a young woman at his pro-life center who was contemplating an abortion, a grizzled man broke into his office. "What the hell do you think you're doing, you bastard? This is my girl friend and I brung her to the place across the street to get rid of the kid she's carrying. We don't want it, and it's none of your damned business." The woman was obviously afraid and shrank back against the wall.

Yancy finally calmed the man enough for him to sit down. "Now, please, tell me your fears about having this child, and let me see if we can help you and your girlfriend."

"It's the same thing that happened to my sister Dawn. She got knocked up as a kid and should have gotten rid of it, but didn't. She just took off and married some local dope called Leroy. It didn't last long and now she's trapped in marriage with a guy twice her age who makes her life miserable. If she had just gotten an abortion, everything would have been just fine."

Yancy paled. "What's wrong, Padre? No more big-shot answers?"

"It's possible that your sister Dawn and Leroy were excited about their child and thought that it was God's blessing upon their love."

"Oh, hell, it wasn't Leroy's kid. All of us men folk in the house had our way with her, except my little brother who turned out to be gay. We had no idea who Big Daddy was, still don't. She should never have had the little bastard."

Yancy had a great deal to process. He had just found out he was illegitimate, that his mother had lied to him all his life, and that either his grandfather or one of his uncles was his real father. He was stunned, angry, hurting, and he wanted to throw up. But he still knew that the girl sitting in front of him was carrying a child, some sort of a relative of his own, and that he had to figure out a way to save that child from becoming the victim of abortion.

"Don't you think it's possible that God had plans for Dawn's child and that He also has plans for the child your girlfriend is carrying?"

"You still don't get it, do you, Padre? We're back hills people. None of us ever amounted to shit and none of us ever will. But we're real men. We tell the womenfolk what to do and they do it. And I'm telling my woman right now to get up off her ass, go across the street, and get rid of the kid."

"And I'm telling you that she not going to do that. You'll have to kill me first. And while you may be willing to kill your child she's carrying, you're probably not ready to kill your own son standing in front of you. Your sister Dawn is my mother, and from what I can put together there is a least one in five chances that you are my father."

"Well, I'll be damned!"

"Yes, very probably. Now get out of here before I call the police to arrest you for trespassing." And he left, without "his woman."

Yancy attempted to appear calm as he told the receptionist to take care of the young lady and make sure that she had enough money to rent a motel room while they arranged a more permanent situation where she could be safe while she waited for the birth of her child. Once she was gone, he ran to the bathroom and vomited. He began to shake as he realized who he really was and where he had come from. His background was the antithesis of everything he held holy and good. The man who had just stood in front of him, who could be his real father, was the embodiment of all the sins that Sister Patricia had warned him against. All his life he had avoided self-pity but never had he been so tempted as he now was to despondency. He sat on the floor with his back resting against the toilet.

"Okay, God, where do we go from here?"

Over an hour passed before he was aware of moving a muscle. His receptionist was knocking on the bathroom door asking if he was all right. "I'm fine. It's time for you to lock up and go home to your family. Good night." He heard the front door close, and he remained transfixed, on the floor, unable to put the pieces of his life together. He had lost his sense of identity, and could not, would not, accept whom he now knew himself to be. He had always envisioned himself the product of a good mother who was forced to place him in the loving hands of Sister Patricia. There were dignity and worth in that. But, now, he knew himself to be the product of rape and incest in a family bereft of God, dignity, kindness, respect, or even the slightest tinge of love. He felt totally alone, without hope, and without meaning.

The hours passed. He looked at his watch and saw it was almost midnight. He felt hungry. As he locked the front door of the office, he glanced across the street at the abortion clinic. There on the clinic's front steps, in the middle of the night, sat a young girl, perhaps sixteen, crying. He was bone tired and emotionally exhausted, but he knew she needed help. He went over and sat next to her. Neither spoke for several minutes.

"What's up? How can I help you?" Once he had spoken those words, Yancy again knew who he was and what his life was about. He knew he was a priest. He knew he had been called by God to serve, to bring those who saw themselves as hopeless to God. Reaching out to another crushed soul, he regained his identity. He realized that God was using him to save others.

"I'm waiting for the clinic to open. My father told me I was no good and that I have to get rid of my baby or he would throw me out."

"The clinic won't be open for hours. Come with me to I-Hop and let me get you something to eat. I'm hungry, and I'll bet you are too. We can talk about your baby."

That night was the beginning of a wonderful new life for all three of them. Father Yancy now saw his priesthood more clearly as an extension of the miracle of Christ's crucifixion, a sacrifice that brought life to others. He would spend the remainder of his life witnessing to the power of God to transform that which appears hopeless into eternal happiness. The young woman gave birth to a beautiful son, married a good man, and became a devout Catholic. And her son, well, that's another story.

CHAPTER TEN

FATHER CHRISTIAN MANGAN

Albert Mangan's father Elliot was a very large fish in a rather small pond. Elliot owned five car dealerships in three counties and was the largest single landowner in Jackson County. Through the business contacts he had made, he became involved in state politics and had connections in Washington. Living in a town of only 20,000 people, he was recognized as the most influential man in town. His wife Maud saw herself as the Grand Dame of Jackson County. Elliot and Maud had five children, Albert being the youngest.

Elliot was the largest contributor to St. Michael's Catholic Church, had the pastor to dinner several times a year, and expected for him to listen to his opinions about how the parish should be run. He was able either to intimidate or manipulate the pastors with the exception of Father Joel Taylor, whom Elliot considered to be an arrogant young man and led a one man protest against him by turning off his hearing aid when he gave the homily and lessening his donations to the church. When Father Joel based one of his homilies on social justice, Elliot, who served as an usher, would lean up against the confessional in the back and loudly clip his fingernails. He could tell how much his manicure irritated the young priest which delighted him all the more.

Albert was not only the youngest of the Mangan children but also by far the brightest. He read voraciously from the time he was four and paid little attention to the antics of his older brothers and sisters. By the time he entered high school, he was an emaciated six feet four inches with a thriving case of acne. Appearing to have only disdain for his high school teachers, he was always at the top of his class throughout high school although no one ever saw him open a textbook. While his older brothers and sisters all had professional careers as their goal, Albert presented himself to Elliot one afternoon and informed him that he had decided to become a priest. While he would have preferred a more prestigious calling for his son, Elliot decided that the other four children could successfully carry on both the family businesses and name and so he gave Albert permission to enter the seminary.

Albert's seminary years were much like those that preceded them. While never appearing to break a cerebral sweat, he aced every test. His scholastic achievements seemed to mean nothing to him, but he was pleased at being chosen to study in Rome at the North American College after four years of undergraduate seminary. Rome presented him with more academic challenge from his classmates, but nothing sufficiently significant to dethrone him as the seminary's top student.

He was ordained by the bishop in 1962, returned to Rome to finish his doctorate in moral theology, and returned to the United States in 1964. Elliot was quite proud of Albert's doctorate, and from that time always referred to him as "Doc," as he considered it higher accolade than "Father." "Shows the boy has a little more on the ball than the ordinary priest." Albert seemed to like the new title.

Albert was assigned to teach at the Catholic high school and was in residence at the cathedral. He enjoyed the students who were intellectually gifted, paid little if any attention to those who were not, and made no apologies to anyone about his bias. His homilies at the cathedral would have been well-received in an environment of academia but bored the average parishioner, not a few of which found solace in counting the ceiling tiles or planning their day's recreation as Doc droned on about the intellectual niceties of the writings of the early fathers of the Church.

Five years after his ordination, Doc typed a terse letter to the bishop, informing him that he would be leaving the priesthood at the end of the scholastic year, as he found himself unchallenged and bored, at odds with the management of the diocese as well as the Church's inability to properly understand Vatican II, and, parenthetically, was in love with a former nun whom he intended to marry. He added that he would appreciate the bishop's appealing to Rome for his laicization.

The bishop sent Father Clem Donnelly to speak with Albert, imploring him to seek some counseling and renew his spiritual life. After Clem had said all he could think of to dissuade Albert from leaving the priesthood, Albert ushered him to the door without response, shook his hand, and told him where the diocese might send his final check.

Albert laid the collar aside, married the former Sister Marianne (now "Annie"), and got a job at the local junior college teaching philosophy. His high intellectual acumen along with his father's political influence proved to be a springboard in academic circles, and within a few years he was teaching at the state university. Annie bore him three children in rapid succession, two girls and a son. Christian was the delight of Albert's life, and he was determined to make his son the smartest and most revered scholar the university had ever seen.

It is not without precedent that a father's wishes for his son conflict with the son's wishes for himself. Christian was an easy-going guy who loved athletics, dramatics, and pizza in that order. He couldn't have cared less about his academic status, which was always adequate but never stellar. He was pleased that his two older sisters were both outstanding scholars, something his father never tired of pointing out, as that took the pressure off him to excel in that area. "How many brains does one family really need, Dad?"

Albert and Annie had all three children baptized into the Catholic Church but saw little need actually to rear them in the faith that they both disagreed with in so many ways. Additionally, they enjoyed an easy Sunday, reading the *New York Times* and fixing a beautiful gourmet brunch without having to rush off to Mass to listen to a predictably boring homily.

While in public high school, Christian became good friends with James Chudy. He was deeply impressed by James's goodness and the love he had for God and the Church. Christian was amazed to find that James's parents were both blind and yet obviously so very happy. He began to spend a good deal of time at their home, which was quite simple, with few things to bump into or dust. It was truly a "home," centered upon the love the family had for one another and for God. It made Christian feel good just to be with them. God was never mentioned in Christian's home, but the Chudys spoke openly of Him as if He were a good and loving friend. On Sunday morning while his own family was sleeping, he would attend early Mass with the Chudys.

Christian finally worked up the courage to make an appointment with the Chudys' pastor, Msgr. Donnelly, to tell him of his desire to go to Confession and receive the Eucharist. Clem was moved as he thought of his visit with Albert when he was preparing to leave the priesthood and the Spirit's working now to bring his son to the Church.

As his friendship with the Chudy family continued, Christian's love for the Church grew. When James told him of his plans to enter the seminary, Christian immediately knew that was what he wanted also. He had never shared with his parents that he had become active in the Church, and the thought of telling his non-practicing, former priest father and his non-practicing former nun mother that he wanted to become a priest was intimidating.

Albert was preparing a lecture in his study when he heard a knock at the door, followed by Christian walking softly towards his desk with what appeared to Albert a mixture of humor and guilt on his face.

"By the look on your face, I assume that you want to talk to me about something that is embarrassing to you. Okay, sit down. You have my attention."

"Dad, for almost two years now I've been going to the 8:00 a.m. Mass at Sacred Heart with James Chudy and his family."

"Well, you're eighteen now, and if that's what you want to do with your time, that's fine. The Chudys seem to be good people."

"There's more. I now go to Confession once a month and have been receiving the Eucharist each Sunday for almost a year and a half. It makes me very happy, and I've never felt so comfortable with God before."

"Son, as you know, your mother and I left that part of our lives behind us years ago. The idealism of youth tends to fade. If it makes you happy to believe in that at this point in your life, I guess it doesn't do you any harm. Just don't get too involved; there's too much pain and disillusionment there."

"James will be entering the seminary this fall."

"I hope it works out better for James than it did for me." Albert turned back to his computer, believing the conversation was at an end.

"James won't be going by himself, Dad. I'm going to become a priest."

The blood drained from Albert's face and he continued to look at the blank computer screen for a full five minutes before speaking.

"Why would you want to intentionally throw your life away? It brought me nothing but pain, robbed me of some of the most important years of my life, caused me to question the goodness of mankind, made me doubt the very existence of God, and sent me on a spiral of depression that, if it had not been for your mother, I would have landed in the mental ward."

"Dad, I know how you feel about the Church, and the priesthood in particular. You have reared me to be a person who questions all belief, to be slow to give assent to any established doctrine, and to prefer cynicism to gullibility. Because I love and respect you, I have attempted to do exactly that. I have viewed every person of faith as a charlatan, ridiculed those who follow any teaching or belief blindly, and have always questioned the motivation and sincerity of those who appear to possess some alleged truth.

"I built strong walls of disbelief and distrust around my mind, soul, and heart. And, guess what? I found myself lonely and discovered I had made myself the sole arbiter of truth and goodness. I had become a prisoner, a victim, of my own cynicism. But, then, God sent someone to rescue me. In fact, He sent an entire family who gave me a vision of the joy that can come from faith, hope, and love. The belief they hold is something outside their capacity to discover or even totally comprehend, but it has transformed their family into something beyond any beauty I've ever experienced. That blind couple have been able to see more than I could have ever envisioned in my prison of doubt. I want to have that too, and I want to help others have that beauty."

"You're a damn fool, but you do deliver a good speech. You've given me something to think about; in the old days, I would have said 'pray about.' You need to give me time to digest what you've said. We'll talk about this tomorrow."

"Dad, you can think—or pray—about this all you want, but it won't change anything. I'm going to become a priest if God will have me."

"I think it was the great modern day philosopher Yogi Berra who first said, 'It's déjà vu, all over again.' I can't believe it's happening. It's a nightmare. We'll talk in the morning."

Christian knew that he had pushed his father as far as was wise. He nodded and left the room. Once the door closed, Albert shook his head in dismay; he hadn't seen this coming. "Isn't it enough, God, that I tried? Do you have to screw with my only son's heart too? Are you punishing me for leaving the priesthood? For marrying Annie? As hard as I've tried to shut you out of my life and that of my family, you found an unlocked door, my only son. Am I Abraham that you are now asking me to deliver my Isaac to you? I don't have Abraham's faith, and I won't sacrifice my son on the altar of God's service. I'll fight you on this. Damn it. I will fight you every inch of the way."

Neither Christian nor his father got much sleep that night. After breakfast, Albert motioned to Christian to follow him to his office. They faced one another across the desk. "I want you to at least postpone your entrance into the seminary long enough to be able to approach this decision with a more mature mind. Go to college. Date some pretty girls. Think of the options that life offers you. If, after four years, you still wish to pursue the priesthood, I will reluctantly not stand in your way. If you insist on entering now, I wash my hands of you, which will be the most difficult thing I've ever done. I love you and I can't let you throw your life away based upon a hurried, highly idealistic decision."

"I'm not sure that it is really love that makes you stand in the way of my following the call of Jesus Christ, but maybe it is. Maybe you are trying to protect me in your own way. But if waiting four years will prove to you that I'm serious, I'll do as you ask. But I want your promise."

"You have it."

So James Chudy went to the seminary alone. Christian found out what courses he should take in college that would be accepted when he entered the seminary four years later. He met with the director of vocations for the diocese, without his father's knowledge, explained his desire and his problems with Albert, and the director formed a plan that would keep him on the road to the priesthood.

During his college years, Christian made decent grades, joined a fraternity, dated several different girls without becoming too involved but always kept his eyes on his goal and availed himself of every opportunity to stay close to the Church. His fraternity brothers admired him and were impressed by his being a regular guy with outstanding moral values.

Graduation day arrived. Christian crossed the stage, received his diploma, paused, looked at his dad seated on the stage in his doctoral robes, smiled, and made the sign of the cross, and raised both arms in triumph. Albert shook his head in defeat, sighed monumentally, and resigned himself to the inevitable.

Five years later, on May 30, 1996, Christian was ordained a priest. He was vested by Father James Chudy. His rather sheepish-looking father barely made it through the ceremony without showing signs of the cynicism and condescension he felt. It added to Albert's discomfort that Christian had chosen Msgr. Clement Donnelley to deliver the homily at his First Mass. The irony of having the very priest to whom he had delivered his letter of resignation from the priesthood deliver his son's First Mass homily was just a bit much for Albert to swallow. His mother never had much trouble with Christian becoming a priest as her life primarily revolved around his two older sisters who had now provided Annie with three grandchildren. Additionally, Annie felt some satisfaction that the nuns who had disapproved of her leaving the convent would see that she had produced a priest. Several of Christian's college fraternity brothers were present, two of whom would remain close friends throughout his priesthood.

Christian's greatest asset as a priest was his sense of identity and his joy. Albert may have lost his way and regretted his priesthood, but his son relished his. Christian's unvarnished enthusiasm and gratitude were so obvious that he became a virtual poster boy for vocations. The bishop recognized his potential to draw others to the priesthood and assigned him to teach at the Catholic high school for boys. Within two years he formed an organization for boys who were genuinely interested in their faith; he called it the Chesterton Club, which would later become a constant source of vocations.

Just as Elliot had gradually become proud of his priest son Albert, the years also softened Albert's heart toward Christian. Many approached Albert to tell him how his son's ministry had changed their lives, how they admired his fervor, and how his joy had altered their entire perspective of the liturgy. Albert began to suspect that there was more to his son than he had ever seen—and more to the priesthood than he had personally experienced. He pondered how he might have lived his life as a priest if his spiritual efforts had been more sincere, more energetic, or if the cynicism in his personality had been replaced with joy of his son.

Whether it was the newfound admiration for his son, the prodding of the Holy Spirit, or simply a guilty conscience, Albert finally found himself at the door of his nemesis Clement Donnelly asking to have his Confession heard. All the pride, distrust, anger, and hurt began to disperse as he knelt before the priest whom he once dismissed summarily from his presence. Returning home, he shared the happiness he had found with Annie. Together they cried. It had been a long and painful journey for them, one that for years they could handle only by consciously avoiding any contact with the Church they had both sought to serve in the acceptance of a religious vocation. Finally, they recognized that they no longer needed to justify themselves or whatever mistakes they had made in their lives but needed rather to humble themselves before an understanding, loving, and merciful God. The flight from God's presence was over and they were home.

CHAPTER ELEVEN

FATHER LUKE SMITH

Luke was the fourth son born to Estelle and Robert Smith. In all, Luke had six brothers and eight sisters. Robert worked for the postal service delivering mail, and Estelle cleaned motel rooms at the local Holiday Inn. Robert was black and Estelle Hispanic. They had met in El Paso, Texas, when Robert was in the Army. Their courtship was difficult as both their families were opposed due to their racial difference. Robert was very strong-willed and Estelle was very much in love. They were both Catholic and were finally married by the Catholic chaplain at the base chapel.

When Robert had served his term in the Army, he became a postman. Estelle delivered their first baby ten months after their marriage. They purchased a small, three bedroom, one bath home in a decent but slowly deteriorating section of the city. They would rear all fifteen of their children in that home. Discipline and schedules were very important in their well-ordered home. Needless to say, the children learned the value of bladder control early in life, but the boys found the abundance of trees in the backyard helpful.

Robert was an extremely intelligent man who could have achieved success in any profession but had been limited by his lack of formal education. He placed great value upon education for his children and insisted that they all attend Catholic grade and high schools. Estelle's income helped make their children's education possible, counting on the older children to care for the younger during her work hours. The children started working at about twelve years of age, babysitting, delivering newspapers, cutting grass, running errands, or whatever jobs they could find. Robert made them aware that a good work ethic establishes personal dignity. The children took pride in being able to contribute to the welfare of the family.

Robert and Estelle never missed taking their children to church on Sunday and filled two pews. The boys and girls were always dressed in clean clothes and all looked as if they had just stepped out of the shower. Robert took up the collection and never failed to be the first to contribute. The congregation was amazed at how well-trained and well-behaved the children were.

The nuns who taught the children were equally amazed at their neat appearance, their respectful and cheerful conduct, their intelligence, and their scholastic drive. No family was more highly regarded in the convent. Sister Aloysius, Mother Superior, was quick to assign the Smith boys to altar serving as she knew they would be prompt and would perform perfectly, and that she would not have to worry about Father Coors sending her an angry note about the misconduct of the servers.

In February of 1985, Luke and his younger brother Peter appeared in the sacristy at ten minutes 'til eight to serve Mass and found Father Coors incoherent, slurring his speech, and weaving when he attempted to walk. Luke had heard the rumors about Father Coors' "trouble with the bottle" and had once overheard his mother and dad expressing their suspicions about the conduct of their pastor.

"Father, you look sick. Let Pete and me help you to the rectory, and we'll tell the people you're sick."

"Well, aren't you a smart little darkie. You think the padre's had a snootful, don't you?"

The comment both hurt Luke and made him angry, but his parents had warned him that he must always be respectful to the priest. "Come on, Father, put your arms on our shoulders. We'll get you out the back way to the rectory."

Father Coors tried to focus. He'd been drinking all night. Maybe this was the way out anyway. He didn't want the parishioners to know; they might go to the bishop. "Okay, boys, saddle me up and lead me to the barn."

Two very frightened, humiliated boys supported their drunken pastor to his rectory and led him to his bedroom, where he dropped unconscious on his bed. They returned to the church. Luke, trembling, entered the sanctuary and told the congregation that Father seemed ill and would not be able to celebrate Mass. The parishioners looked at one another knowingly. It wasn't the first time. Within the hour, Msgr. Clement's phone would be ringing.

Robert had made it abundantly clear to his children that bigotry against anyone due to race, color, or creed was wrong and sinful. He had pointed out to them that they might well be the objects of prejudice due to their color, being both black and Hispanic, as well as being Catholics in the South. "While you have three strikes against you in the minds of bigoted people, you must always walk with pride and dignity, knowing that you are God's children, have good parents, and are wonderful people. Always stand up for your rights."

That a priest whom he had been taught to respect and admire would refer to him as a "darkie" bothered Luke so deeply that he told Sister Aloysius that he could not stay in school that day and would never serve Mass again. She tried to calm him down but was unsuccessful. She had never seen any of the Smith children act that way and wondered what Father Coors had done now. Pete seemed to let the incident roll off his back and went to class.

When Estelle came home from her job at 2 p.m., she found Luke sitting on the porch. "Well, Luke, what are you doing home? Why aren't you in school?"

He couldn't look at his mother and did not immediately respond to her questions. He looked down at the porch steps. Estelle placed her purse down and sat beside her son. She knew him well enough to feel how deeply he was hurting. She placed her arm on his thin shoulders, "It'll be all right, Son. Whatever it is, it'll be all right."

The minutes passed with mother and son sitting quietly. Finally, "I can't go back there, Mama. It's all been a lie; they don't love us there. They think we're just 'darkies,' that we don't amount to anything. As hard as you and Daddy work, as hard as we all try, to them we're just 'darkies.'" And then the event before Mass unfolded.

"I want you to understand something, Son: Father Coors was drunk. He's got a sickness. He wasn't speaking for the Church. Always remember that priests are human; they make mistakes. They say things that shouldn't be said. They have to deal with their own personal problems. Your daddy's always made all you children aware that some people inherit prejudice and that they have to fight it all their lives. Father Coors must come from some very ignorant people who planted those ideas in his head. You need to pray for him. He needs help.

"Now, I want you to go to Sister Aloysius tomorrow morning, tell her what happened in the sacristy, tell her you're sorry if you showed her any disrespect, and then be man enough to go on with your life. You know you're as good as anybody else, and better than a lot, particularly those filled with prejudice and hatred. I'll tell you father what happened, and he'll deal with Father Coors."

That night in bed Estelle told Robert about the incident. Her timing might have been better. Robert was furious and got little sleep. The next morning he contacted Msgr. Clement Donnelly, and Father Joel Taylor replaced Father Coors two weeks later. When Adam heard what he had said to Luke, he felt genuine embarrassment and regret that he could have been so insensitive even when drunk. He had never thought of himself as prejudiced, and he realized that there must be some feelings buried within his subconscious that needed attention. The hurt he had caused also helped him see the wisdom involved in his being sent away for treatment for his alcoholism. He was not a mean man but he had suffered at the hands of a mean father, and he never wanted anyone to be afflicted with the feeling of worthlessness that had plagued him throughout his life and that he eventually attempted to drown in vodka. He wrote Luke a letter from the treatment center, apologizing for what he had said and how he had acted, begging for Luke's forgiveness, and even explaining similar injustices he had suffered at Luke's age.

Luke was touched by Father Coors's letter. While he would never forget the sacristy event, he could sense the agony and contrition in the letter. He showed the letter to his father, who read it aloud to all the children at the dinner table. "Children, I don't want you to ever forget what has happened here. Father Coors has written a letter of apology to our family. He was right in doing that; we deserved that apology. And it is right that we all forgive him for what he said to Luke in his drunkenness. Alcohol makes men say strange, stupid, and hurtful things. We will offer our family rosary tonight for Father Coors, that God will make him a good priest.

"I want you all to learn three things from what has happened: One, you are black because God made you black, just as He made trees green and the sea blue. God does not make mistakes, and you are beautiful. You are His creation. Two, you are a Catholic, a follower of Jesus Christ, living your life in the Church that He gave to us. You are a part of that Church with every black, white, yellow, and red person that makes up this living body of Jesus. Three, you must know that being a black Catholic will make many people prejudiced against you because they are not blessed to know what we know. Never look down on those people, but do everything in your power to change their minds and hearts and to correct injustice."

Estelle rose from her seat, walked up behind her husband's chair, bent over, kissed the top of his head, and smiled: "You sure are wise . . . for a darkie." There was a shared, stunned moment by all at the table before Estelle broke into loud laughter, which was followed by all in the room. She knew how to defuse a tense situation. A good sense of humor is required to survive as one of seventeen people in a small house with one bathroom. Both Robert's wisdom and Estelle's sense of humor that evening would warm the hearts of their children for the remainder of their lives.

Luke took his father's sage words to heart. He became so comfortable with his blackness that he was no longer personally sensitive to the ignorance of others who might gauge a person's worth by his color. And the love that he had for being a Catholic grew as he learned more of his faith and saw how desperately the world needed exactly what his father had stressed, to have their hearts and minds changed and injustices corrected.

He became close to Father Joel but had enough of his father's wisdom to recognize that all priests were human and had faults like everyone else. He could see that Father Joel had an inflated idea of his own importance but that he was a good priest intent upon serving his parish. He also admired his intelligence and would verbally spar with him prior to serving his Masses. And Father Joel loved knowing this unassuming but obviously intensely bright kid, who had potential coming out of both ears, who came from an amazing Catholic family, and whose personal goodness was refreshing.

During the spring of Luke's junior year in high school, Father Joel made an appointment with Robert and Estelle to come by their house to visit with them on a Sunday afternoon. They imagined that Father might want help from their family on one of his projects. "Robert and Estelle, in the few years that I've been your pastor, I've found you and your children to be absolutely amazing. You are a prayerful and loving family whose life has revolved around your Church. It is no surprise to me that God may have rewarded your goodness with at least one vocation to the religious life. I've spoken with Luke about the possibility of his going to the seminary to become a priest. He seems open to that possibility. Would you encourage his doing that?"

Sitting next to her husband on the couch, Estelle placed her hand on Robert's knee and squeezed it gently. He took her hand and raised it to his lips and kissed it. "Father, every night before we go to sleep, Estelle and I pray that some of our children will be called to serve God as priests or nuns. We've both thought for a long time that Luke should be a priest, but we never mentioned it to him. Of course, we will encourage his going to the seminary. I don't know how we'll afford it, but God will take care of that as He has all our other needs."

"God has already taken care of it. You leave the money part to me. I'll talk with Luke after Mass and we'll get things started."

Luke was the valedictorian and, therefore, spoke at his high school graduation. He surprised his 273 classmates by revealing that he would be going to the seminary and by giving such a stirring speech on his love for God and the Church that the bishop, present to hand out diplomas, whispered to the high school rector, during the standing ovation that followed the speech: "I wish I could ordain that kid tomorrow; he's the best I've ever heard."

The eight years of seminary training passed with Luke always at the head of his class academically. He spent the last four years at the North American College in Rome, where his zeal for the faith and his facility in apologetics won him the respect and admiration of fellow students and faculty alike. He challenged the other students' sense of social justice and racial equality to the extent that several later became activists for change within their own dioceses.

Luke's first assignment was as an associate to a pastor who had experienced little contact with blacks and certainly had never lived or worked with one. Msgr. Clement Donnelly suggested to the bishop that his friend Father Greg Owens needed a new assistant and that he would give Luke a good start in parish life. The bishop had seen a steady improvement in Greg's priestly life in the last six years since his mother's death and accepted Clem's suggestion.

As Clem had envisioned, Greg and Luke were really fond of one another from the beginning. Greg was absolutely astounded when he heard Luke's first Sunday homily. He couldn't believe that a newly ordained priest could handle himself with such finesse and deliver a flawless and moving homily on the presence of Jesus in the heart of the believer. There was a time in Greg's life that jealousy would have stopped him from giving Luke a hug after Mass and telling him how proud he was of him, but the curse of Marlene's venom had died with her and Greg was free to be the loving person he was meant to be.

As Greg watched Luke mature in his priesthood over the next three years, he felt the pride a father would feel towards a son. Almost every priest would like to have a son of his own, but no father could have taken greater pleasure over his son than Greg did over Luke. He recognized that Luke was superior to him in intelligence and innate goodness, but that knowledge made him happy for Luke, a true sign of unselfish love. Whenever Luke needed guidance or correction in small matters, it was both given and received in humility and mutual respect.

Greg's parish had only a smattering of black parishioners and only a few other minorities represented. The largely white congregation was quick to accept Luke; with only a few exceptions, Luke's personal sanctity, sincerity, intelligence, and charm went a long way to dispel any prejudice or bigotry which might have existed. Whenever he sensed someone who might be uncomfortable with him due to racial difference, Luke went out his way to tear down any misconceptions that person might have, but it was his reverence at Mass and the superior qualities of his homilies that put the last nail in the coffin of prejudice.

Luke's love for the underdog caused him to befriend any person or group he thought might be marginalized. Finding that there were no activities in the parish for young adults, he formed a social-educational group which became the avenue for strengthening the participants' faith, which resulted in a number of Catholic marriages. The program was so successful that it became citywide and the model for similar organizations throughout the diocese. He helped establish the Order of St. Peter Claver in the parish, giving fellow blacks an organization of their own in which to take pride. With the help of retired people, he instituted an educational mentoring program, and children were bused from disadvantaged areas to be fed a good meal and helped with their homework.

Luke's most effective work was among the poor. He met with the ministerial alliance for the city and helped create an expansive program that delivered meals to the indigent in their homes, alleys, under bridges, wherever they could be found. He never took a managerial or hands-off position, but rather was a part of the delivery process. He always seemed to find the time to visit with each indigent person to impart some sense of dignity and worth.

The bishop took note of all that Luke was doing. He remembered the kid who had delivered the knock-out speech at his high school graduation, the seminarian who never made a false step and set the curve for everyone else, and the young man he had ordained just three years prior. He knew that he had to give Luke wings so that the Spirit could continue to work through him. On Luke's twenty-ninth birthday, he was given his own parish and appointed chancellor for the diocese.

Luke's appointment as chancellor was not met with immediate approval by the majority of the established priests of the diocese, who simply thought him too young to be given such authority and resented his being advanced before one of the elder priests. (The ones who objected the most were those who had envisioned themselves in that position). Luke was blessed to work with Vicar General Msgr. Clement Donnelley for the next five years, until Clem's death. Clem knew the negative scuttlebutt from his fellow clergy about Luke's appointment and set about trying to convince them that Luke was an extraordinary priest and they needed to get to know him better. He made suggestions to Luke about how to handle the more sensitive cases the bishop gave him to handle.

Luke had three powerful diocesan advocates pulling for him: the bishop, Clem Donnelly, and Greg Owens. But it was Luke himself who changed the opinion of the diocesan priests, and he did so simply by being Luke, with his love for the underdog. Whenever a priest was depressed, lonely, or sick, or when he had lost a family member, needed a little break or just someone to talk with, Luke seemed to show up. Luke didn't do this to win a popularity contest; he did it because he genuinely loved to help people who were down and out, particularly his brother priests.

Luke's own parish thrived. People would hear of Luke's homilies, or his insight as a confessor, or his love for "the little guy," and they would cross parish lines throughout the city to be with this dynamic young priest. Luke's color had become irrelevant. He was loved by all because of the manner in which he lived his priesthood.

On March 28, 2013, Holy Thursday, Luke received a call on his cell while he was preparing the servers for the evening liturgy. His secretary informed him that it was necessary for him to come to the office immediately. She smiled as he entered the office and followed him to his private office, where she informed him that he was to return a call from the apostolic nuncio.

"Father Luke, His Holiness Pope Francis, has appointed you as a bishop. Will you accept this appointment?"

"Archbishop, are you sure you have the right priest? 'Smith' is such a common name. I've just been a priest for fifteen years and I'm only forty years old."

"Father Smith, I have the right priest. I repeat, 'Will you accept the appointment from His Holiness Francis as bishop?'"

"Domine, non sum dignus."

"I'm not your 'Domine,' and none of us are 'dignus,'" the archbishop said with a chuckle. "Do I have to ask the third time?"

Luke accepted. He slumped down in his chair and buried his head in his arms. "Oh, Jesus, are YOU sure you have the right 'Smith'?" He really had not thought such an appointment was a possibility and had hoped to spend his priestly years taking care of those who most needed help.

Luke remembered that the altar servers were waiting for him to finish their Holy Thursday practice. He darted back to church and tried to keep his mind on what was he was doing. That evening the liturgy took on ramifications that he had never fully understood before. He was about to be made "a successor of the apostles," that group gathered around the Last Supper table. He would be like one of those whose feet Jesus washed. Not knowing his mind, the parishioners wondered at his tears and trembling during the Eucharist; they presumed they were witnessing a mystical experience.

When he arrived at the rectory a little after ten, he saw a familiar car in the driveway. It belonged to the bishop. They got out of their cars simultaneously. The bishop embraced him: "Congratulations, my brother bishop." And then he quoted

Zechariah's prophecy to his son: "You shall be called the prophet of the Most High for you go before the Lord to prepare His way, to give his people knowledge of salvation by the forgiveness of sin." As often as Luke had prayed those words, they now took on new meaning . . . and provoked a new sense of responsibility.

Luke was ordained a bishop in the cathedral of his new diocese, now "his" cathedral. In attendance were his parents, Robert and Estelle, all his siblings with their spouses, his now fifty-eight nieces and nephews, over forty priests from his previous diocese, almost all the priests from his new diocese, seven bishops from the region, and the apostolic nuncio.

The music was a combination of traditional, Gospel, and Hispanic. Luke's father shed tears of pride during most of the ceremony, but his mother beamed in wonder that God could have blessed her family so deeply. At the end of the Mass, Bishop Luke spoke of the gratitude he felt to God, his parents, his former bishop, Msgr. Donnelly, Father Owens, Sister Aloysius, and all the priests and nuns who had been a part of his spiritual journey. He pledged to be a bishop who would serve all within the diocese, particularly those who were most in need.

The reception following lasted several hours as everyone wanted an opportunity to speak with the new bishop. Finally even Luke's family had parted, and only a few stragglers and servers remained. One priest had waited until the end to approach the bishop. He looked older than his years and was gaunt and a bit jittery. He knelt down before Luke, head bowed, and asked for a blessing. Luke helped him up and looked into the teary eyes of Father Adam Coors. Both were remembering the incident in the sacristy almost thirty years before.

"Father Adam, I can't begin to tell you how glad I am that you're here. There was one person I forgot to thank in the cathedral, you. The word that you let slip that morning in the sacristy changed my life. It led me to question who I was, how I viewed myself, and what I wanted to do with my life. Out of that moment, hurtful to both of us, my vocation as a priest took shape.

"I've seen you struggle with your addiction, and I've seen you work so hard to be a good priest, and I know that the journey has been particularly difficult for you. I've enjoyed the luxury of having been supported by family and friends all my life; you haven't had that. And, yet, you continued on. You fought the good fight. I can't tell you how much I admire you."

Adam couldn't believe what he was hearing. Here was this newly ordained bishop, admired and loved by all, telling Adam how much he meant to him. As always in his life, Adam had difficulty in accepting unconditional love and forgiveness—this time from Bishop Luke. He felt so unworthy. After a life of rejection and failure, he found it difficult to trust or to hope that either he or his future might improve. He also failed to see how much the effort he had made to come to Luke's ordination as bishop meant to Luke, who was genuinely moved by Adam's humility and the guilt that he had carried for three decades.

"Father Adam, I want you to promise me something."

"Anything."

"I want you to come visit me for a few days once a year. I need a friend like you, and I think that we can learn from one another." Luke sensed how deeply Adam needed a real friend, someone in whom to confide. Even on the day of his ordination to the episcopacy, he wanted to help his brother priest and care for still another underdog.

"If you will have me, I'll do that, Bishop."

"My name is Luke, Adam."

CHAPTER TWELVE

FATHER STANISLAW JANOSKI

Jerzy and Ilona Janoski took life very seriously. It was no wonder as they were born in Poland in 1955, when even the basics of life were difficult to come by. They both came from Catholic families. They met their first year in college and fell in love. As they were devout Catholics and had a strong sexual attraction to one another, they married three months after they met in 1975 to avoid falling into an immoral relationship. Ten months later they were blessed with the birth of their son on April 11, the feast of St. Stanislaw. They had absolutely nothing and lived with Jerzy's parents in a small apartment with two bedrooms.

The priest who both married them and baptized their son was Father Jerzy Popieluszko, an anti-Communist affiliated with the Solidarity movement. The Communist party did all it could in a largely Catholic country to suppress religion, intimidate the clergy, and make it dangerous to practice the faith. While many priests kept their views to themselves, Father Popieluszko continued to denounce the Communist regime from the pulpit. Even after intimidation and arrest, he sought to serve the will of God rather than that of the state. He was assassinated by three agents of the Polish Communist Internal Intelligence Agency on October 19, 1984, and his body dumped in the Vistula Water Reservoir.

Jerzy and Ilona Janoski had become close to Fr. Popieluszko, had arranged places for him to celebrate Mass, and were vocal in support of his political views. They realized that their friendship with the priest was common knowledge and that their own lives and that of their son might well be in danger. With the help of anti-Communist sympathizers, they made their way into West Germany, where they found a Polish priest who helped arrange passage to the United States.

They arrived in Chicago, where they were embraced by the large Polish Catholic community. Although both Jerzy and Ilona were intellectually gifted, Jerzy having a degree in architecture and Ilona in biochemistry, neither could speak English. Jerzy found a job in a bakery in the mornings and a small factory in the afternoons. Ilona, who had made her own clothes from the time she was a child, went to work altering clothes in the shop of a fashion designer. Both worked hard from early morning until evening, at which time they studied English.

Their son Stanislaw was approaching his ninth birthday and was enrolled in a Catholic school in the heart of a thriving Polish neighborhood. The nuns delighted in helping him learn to speak English for which he seemed to have a facility. In a short time, he became his parents' tutor. His name was anglicized to "Stan." He was strong, possessing a stocky build, intent on learning everything, rarely speaking and almost never laughing. He had learned from his parents that life was a serious matter, that one was to work hard and long, that education was the key to success, that standing up for one's belief was a sign of integrity, and that his faith must be the center of his life.

Within a year, Jerzy and Ilona had become proficient in English, had jobs in their chosen fields, and were buying a modest home. The nuns encouraged Stan's parents to let him skip two grades as he was bored with the simplicity of his subjects and irritated that his classmates showed so little desire to learn. He needed to be challenged and was impatient with his own inability to progress more rapidly. At age ten he was placed in the seventh grade, where he was happier and had no problem with mastering the subject material. Stan became the youngest student ever to enter Loyola Academy and the youngest ever to graduate at the age of fifteen. He missed being the valedictorian by three-tenths of a percent, largely attributable to his having always opted to take the most advanced classes. He accepted a full scholarship to Loyola University, graduating summa cum laude in three years with degrees in both philosophy and political science.

During his junior year in college, he decided to become a priest and was accepted as a seminarian upon leaving Loyola. He entered Mundelein Seminary, where he was mistakenly placed in the freshman year. As canon law required that a man be twenty-five years old to be ordained to the priesthood, the director of vocations thought it best that he begin with those his own age. It didn't take long for his professors to find that Stan's knowledge and previous college education placed him so far above the other students that it was detrimental to the class for him to remain at that level. They suggested that he be placed in theology and that the age requirement be addressed later.

For the next five years, Stan delighted in the study of dogmatic, moral, and aesthetic theology. He developed a particular love and knowledge of the writings of the fathers of the church, and his patrology professor thought he was the most gifted student he had ever taught. Stan was ordained, with a special dispensation from Rome, at the age of twenty-three.

As he had progressed through the years at Mundelein, there was never concern among the faculty concerning Stan's intellectual abilities, his academic accomplishments, or his personal spirituality. There was concern, however, about his relational skills. Comments included "too intense," "never seems at ease," "inflexible," "no sense of humor," "lacks the common touch," "little acceptance by his peers," etc. Their concerns, however, were deemed not of sufficient merit to prohibit recommending him for ordination.

Shortly before Stan's ordination, a bishop from the South had visited with the cardinal archbishop of Chicago and told of the dire need his diocese had for clergy. He explained that with the influx of Hispanics, there simply were not enough priests to care for the spiritual needs of the people. The cardinal was moved by his brother bishop's predicament and promised to supply him with at least one priest per year for the next five years. The names of several ordinandi surfaced as possibilities. The cardinal thought it might be a good idea to have a newly ordained priest begin his ministry in the diocese he would continue to serve rather than to assign one who was already established in his archdiocese.

Stan was known to be conservative and the Southern diocese had that same reputation. The chair of the Clergy Personnel Board for the archdiocese made a trip out to Mundelein and approached Stan concerning the possibility of his being ordained for the Southern diocese. Stan had established no close friends among his classmates or the priests of the archdiocese, and he felt a challenging sense of mission in joining the work of Christ in a diocese so in need of priests. Father Stanislaw Janoski was ordained a priest on June 11, 2001. Two weeks later he arrived at his new diocese and received his appointment as associate to Father Joel Taylor.

Joel had been delighted when the bishop called and told him he was to receive a newly ordained priest from Chicago. He had been holding down a good sized parish and two missions on his own and knew that he had stretched himself too thin both for the good of the parishes involved and for his own good as a priest. He was not getting enough sleep and found little time for prayer or R & R. It had been over a month since his last day off.

Joel's hopes were high when the doorbell rang on the day that Father Stan was to arrive. He was surprised to find an extremely young priest dressed in a cassock. Joel opened his arms and greeted him with a huge smile. Stan did not respond to the offered embrace, nor did he smile. He extended his right hand to shake Joel's hand.

"My name is Father Stan Janoski. The bishop has sent me to you to serve as your associate."

Joel felt his exuberance fading. "Well, Stan, my name is Joel, and I want you to know how happy I am to have you here, my brother. Let me help with your bags."

"I have only these two bags, and I am capable of carrying them myself. My books will arrive later. If you will show me to my room, it's been a long drive from Chicago and I will rest before dinner."

Joel imagined that the cassock must have been quite a hit in the filling stations and fast food restaurants as Stan drove from Chicago to his new rural, largely non-Catholic diocese. "Fine, then, Stan, get some rest. I'll call you when I get dinner ready and perhaps I can show you around the parish plant after that."

Joel was a good cook but had little time to spend in the kitchen. He prepared a salad, baked potato, a smothered chicken breast, and purchased a dessert. He called Stan to the table and found him to still be dressed in his cassock. Joel wore the clergy shirt and black slacks he had worked in all day.

"Stan, this is our home. I want you to be comfortable here. You'll find your cassock a bit formal in your new diocese, and you certainly don't need to wear it around the rectory. You'll rarely see me in anything more formal than what you see now."

Stan's face reddened a little. "Thank you for your concern, Father, but I'm very comfortable in my cassock. I consider it a sign of who and what I am to others and a reminder to myself."

"Well, suit yourself, and good luck with that. Help yourself to the salad, and I'll get the rest from the kitchen."

"You do not have a cook?"

"No, that would be a rarity in our diocese. Our priests are so busy that a regular meal time is difficult to predict, and so we pretty much fend for ourselves, cooking a little, getting a bite out, grabbing what we find in the fridge, or having an occasional meal at a parishioner's home."

"But, Father Joel, I do not cook."

"Well, Stan, maybe you'd better learn." Stan's face reddened a bit more. It was obvious that things were not getting off to a good start. Joel attempted to lessen the tension. "Look, it's really good to have you here. I know that you must be tired from your long drive. Why don't you just turn in early this evening, and I'll give you that tour I promised in the morning."

"You will find that I'm never too tired to perform my duties. I also need to find the chapel to make my holy hour, so I will appreciate your showing me around."

Stan ate most of the dinner Joel had cooked but offered no word of appreciation or comment other than the dessert's being too rich for him. Nor did he offer to help clear the table or clean up the kitchen. It was obvious to Joel that some of the social skills that had always been a part of his upbringing were lacking in Stan's background.

During the tour of the parish plant, Joel also felt the lack of any compliments from Stan. Joel had worked really hard to fashion what he considered to be an ideal parish plant with a beautiful church, Eucharistic chapel, large elementary school, inviting parish hall, and well-landscaped grounds. It hurt that his new assistant seemed to just take it all for granted. What Joel did not know is that Stan was doing his best to hold his tongue and not point out all the flaws he noted. As was his custom, when he had nothing positive to say, he said nothing.

The Eucharistic chapel was the last stop on the tour. There both priests knelt in prayer before the Lord they both loved and sought to serve. Jesus must have chuckled as He heard his two priests.

"Lord, why did you send me this arrogant, thick-headed Polack from Chicago? Was it to show me how arrogant I was as young priest, how unkind I was to Msgr. Dumbarski? Is this a case of the chickens coming home to roost? You really had to send your Holy Spirit to show me how filled I was with myself. You had the bishop send me away to deal with my anger and arrogance. Please give me the grace now to swallow my own pride and help this young priest see in himself what I failed to see in myself when I was starting out. Help me to help him be a good priest. And, dear Lord, give me the grace to turn the other cheek. Help me to love Stan as You must love him."

"Oh, most Sacred Heart of Jesus, why have you put me in this godless place with a priest who doesn't even love you enough to wear a cassock? Isn't he proud of being your priest? He spends his time cooking instead of taking care of his flock. The church looks like a factory and has almost no statues honoring your friends. There is nothing honoring Our Lady of Czestochowa, only saccharine images of pale-faced madonnas. Even the vigil light in this chapel is the wrong color; he must know nothing of the liturgy. He treats me with no dignity and expects me to dress the way he does and spend my time cooking! Lord, give me the patience to put up with this wretched excuse for a priest and do your work in spite of him. Amen."

Well, maybe Jesus wasn't amused all that much after all.

On Saturday both Joel and Stan heard confessions. While Joel's waiting line moved both smoothly and rapidly, the penitents in Stan's line moved only occasionally. Most of the penitents in Stan's line exited the reconciliation room with rather stunned looks on their faces and then stayed in the church saying their penance for a considerable length of time. After the first half hour, most of those waiting shifted to Joel's line, recognizing that they could be there all evening otherwise.

Mrs. Lorenzo approached Joel outside the church after all the confessions were heard. "Father Joel, I am a lifelong Catholic. As you know, I go to confession at least once a month. The sacrament always brought me much peace and hope. Today your new associate changed all that. I was lectured, made to feel cheap and ignorant, and given a penance that will take me a week to fulfill. I did not confess knocking over any Seven-Elevens, murdering my husband (although I may have to confess that sometime in the future if the old goat doesn't change his ways), or committing adultery. Please speak to that boy and tell him the confessional should bring peace, not despondence."

"As you noted, he is young, newly ordained, and this is probably the first time he has heard confessions. Give him a little time and pray for him. I'm sure he'll be a fine priest. And, by the way, give 'the old goat' a break too." Mrs. Lorenzo rolled her eyes, huffed, winked, and strolled away.

Stan's initial Sunday homily to the parish was on mortal sin and the reality of hell. He spared the congregation no detail of the horror of each and his examples were graphic. He made a point that those present who were in marriages unrecognized by the Church, those engaged in pre-marital intercourse, and those who were homosexual were wallowing in mortal sin and would suffer eternal punishment. The picture he painted of the last judgment surpassed even the goriest of the medieval artists' depictions. One could almost hear the jaws dropping in the congregation. Red faces and teary eyes were scattered throughout the church, some angry, some just mad as hell.

The telephone calls to the parish office began Monday morning and continued throughout the week. Joel found himself in the position of trying to defend his brother priest who he thought was a first-class jerk. He was determined, however, to cool down himself before approaching Stan, as he was certain his advice would be not well received.

On Thursday, Joel told Stan that he would like to speak with him after dinner. Stan indicated that he, too, would like to have an opportunity to speak with Joel. Both spent some time in sincere prayer prior to the meeting.

Joel and Stan were both smart men and both realized the meeting was not likely to be a pleasant one. Joel intentionally had the meeting in the living room of the rectory rather than his office to dismiss a sense of formality or of Stan's being called in by the pastor for a dressing down.

"Stan, I've noticed how very hard you've been working ever since you arrived. You obviously meant what you said about never being too tired to do your duty. I've noticed your excellent care of the elderly and sick, your visits to the hospital, your counseling sessions, your visits to vacation Bible school, your promptness at daily Mass, and that you never shirk an opportunity to serve. I want you to know that I'm appreciative of that."

"I'm a priest. That's what a good priest does; he cares for his people. You do not need to thank me; those things are done for Our Lord, not for you. And I wish you would call me FATHER Stan; I've worked hard and long to earn that title and do not take it for granted."

Joel swallowed . . . hard. "Okay, FATHER Stan, I had hoped for a more brotherly relationship with you, but if that's the way you want it, Amen. Now I want to counsel you on a few matters you need to address. Firstly, your homily on Sunday while theologically correct was overly harsh and left people feeling without hope. We are not selling despondency here, but rather resurrection and hope."

Joel noticed the veins in Stan's neck tightening. "I didn't know we were SELLING anything here, Father Joel. I rather thought we were preaching the Gospel of Jesus Christ . . . in its entirety. I don't feed adults baby food. Exactly what part of my homily did you find 'overly harsh'?"

Joel was prepared and ticked off several examples and then mentioned the embarrassment that couples who were dealing with moral problems felt.

"Nothing I said was without Scriptural or dogmatic basis. I would not change a word; in fact, I felt inspired by the Holy Spirit. As regards the 'embarrassment' your parishioners may have felt, let the chips fall where they may. There is a condemnation in the Scripture for watch dogs who do not bark. It is obvious that in this parish there has been precious little barking for a long time."

Joel chose to ignore the insult and saw that he was getting nowhere on the subject of homilies. He heaved a sigh, bowed his head momentarily, and looked Stan squarely in the eyes. "There is another matter. Last Saturday you had penitents leaving your confessional in tears, and they did not appear to be expressions of relief. You spent so long with each penitent that I was forced to hear confessions rapidly so that all who came could be heard."

"So now I am to be lectured upon my conduct in the confessional. How are you to know what happened within the sacred confines of that confessional? But, for your information, without revealing anything under the seal, I spent most of the time cleaning up from the poor counsel they have obviously been receiving over the last few years."

Joel swallowed again . . . even harder. He didn't want to release the fury he felt in his heart against this brash, newly-ordained priest. He was determined not to endanger Stan's promise as a priest of the diocese.   When Joel finally spoke, he words were measured and so quietly delivered that Stan had to strain to hear them.

"Father, you are a very bright young priest with much promise. You have received excellent seminary formation and education by people better educated than I. It is my prayer that we will be able to work together in the vineyard of the Lord we both love. That will not be possible, however, if you will not accept the counsel that I am supposed to give you at this juncture in your priesthood. You must realize that the oils are still fresh on your hands and that I have been a priest now for almost twenty-five years. Don't you think it possible that I learned a few things that would benefit you?

And don't you think that I've met a few dangers in my priesthood that I could warn you to avoid on your journey?"

Stan responded in an almost bored tone. "Thus far, I've seen nothing in your ministry that I would care to learn from. And as regards the dangers you may have encountered, it appears to me that you must have come out the loser in all of them. Would you like me to tell you what I see in you and your parish? In you I see a priest who has become lax in his priestly vocation, barely even dressing as one; a priest who is afraid to teach the realities of God's truths lest he offend some of his parishioners, who are mired in mediocrity and sin; a priest who substitutes busyness for true ministry; a priest who obviously fails to comprehend the intricacies of the liturgy and has replaced prayerful reverence with empty, feel-good showmanship."

Joel rested his head against the chair's back and stared at the ceiling for a few moments before responding. "Thanks for your honesty, Father. If there is any truth in your perception of me, I ask God's forgiveness. Should it not be true, I'm sure you will eventually ask God's forgiveness for your rash judgment. Have a good night."

As the next few months passed, there was a slight lessening of the tension between the two priests. Joel realized that his own actions as a newly-ordained priest probably caused Msgr. Dumbarski much pain, and it was only just that now he would partake of a taste of what he had so generously dispensed. As he did not want Stan stigmatized in the diocese as being uncooperative and inflexible, he did not report Stan's problems to the chancery office or speak disrespectfully of him to parishioners or his fellow priests. In fact, he took every opportunity to make excuses for him, which may have been a considerable injustice to the young priest who probably needed an entire pack of barking guard dogs to warn congregations he might serve in his priestly life.

Stan, for his part, probably mellowed a little after recognizing a few mistakes of his own, learning of the respect the parishioners had for Joel and of the many kind and priestly acts he had performed for them over the years, and for Joel's continued attempts at kindness toward him. It didn't hurt that he overheard Joel defending him one day to a parishioner whom he had verbally assaulted over being habitually late for daily Mass. Stan knew he had been abusive and recognized that Joel comforted the parishioner without saying anything negative about the confrontation.

The greatest thing that Stan had going for him was his prayer life. It gave the Holy Spirit an avenue to enter his personality and make Stan aware of his deficiencies. A day never passed without Stan's being on his knees for an hour before the Blessed Sacrament. His devotion to Our Lady of Czestochowa and the admiration he had for the now Blessed Jerzy Popielusko also made him strive to imitate the virtues he found in them both.

When Stan's first anniversary as a priest approached, Joel saw it as an opportunity to make another attempt to tear down the philosophical walls that existed between them. He located a large icon of Our Lady of Czestochowa and placed in the Eucharistic Chapel, along with a kneeler and vigil lights, to surprise Stan on his anniversary. It had cost Joel a month's salary, but he thought it would be a good investment in the future of a priest. When Stan first entered the chapel, he was speechless and wondered if he were seeing a vision. As he knelt before the icon, he realized what must have happened. He spent a long time in prayer that day, trying to unravel his feelings about Joel and the parish he served.

That evening when Joel entered the rectory, the odor of sausage and cabbage filled the air. During all that year, Stan had never cooked dinner. Now he was in the kitchen filling their plates and dishing up the pierogies. He brought the plates to the dining table and set them before Joel with even a hint of a smile. And, wonder of wonders, he was in a tee shirt, his cassock nowhere in sight. "There is apple kuchen for dessert." Stan led the grace, but Joel kept praying in his heart: "Oh, Lady of Czestochowa, thank you, thank you, thank you." Stan never mentioned the icon to Joel; he thought the pierogies said it all . . . and he was right.

Stan and Joel would never see eye to eye on homilies, sacramental administration, clerical conduct or dress, or relations with parishioners, but they finally came to respect each other regardless of their differences. Stan would become a pastor, continue being Stan, and his inflexibility would cause hurt and dissatisfaction. He and the bishop would have meaningful conversations, sometimes heated. But Stan would always be a prayerful priest, would always do his duty, and would appeal to some whom other priests with a more gentle touch could never reach.

The oil of ordination did not change Stan. The personality defects that professors noticed at Mundelein did not evaporate in the heat of parish life. But some of the rough edges did get smoothed along the way through age, grace, and the intercession of Our Lady of Czestochowa and Blessed Jerzy Popieluszko.

CHAPTER THIRTEEN

FATHERS PETER, JAMES, AND JOHN CHAMBERS

A triple-header is a rare event. Nel and Ernest Chambers were farm folks. Ernest had almost three hundred acres, which he planted primarily in soy beans and milo, and he and Nel also ran a small hardware store in the town of a little less than two thousand people. They had eight children, all of whom worked in either the fields or the store as soon as they were physically able. The Chambers were thrifty people who knew that hard work and careful spending normally resulted in a full larder, peace, and security. When the children started arriving in 1930, Nel and Ernest were both twenty-five and had enough faith to leave the size of their family in the hands of divine providence. The first three children were girls, and Ernest was beginning to wonder if he would ever have boys who could help him with the farming. The boys started coming in 1936 with Peter; 1938 with James, and 1939 with John. The last two children, a boy and a girl, were born in 1942 and 1943.

Peter was large for his age and by the time he was eight he was driving his dad's tractor and pulling his weight with the farm duties. He was constantly on the go, loved farming, and idolized Ernest. James was good natured, loved everybody, laughed a lot, and did his share of the farm work with a little prodding from his dad and Peter. John was hyper and generally too busy making life miserable for his siblings to be of a great deal of help on the farm. While John was definitely the runt of the litter, he made up in impishness what he lacked in size. His sisters were always a little uneasy when they saw a sly smile creep across John's face.

Sunday lunch was a huge affair at the Chambers house. It started about 2 p.m. and always included the parish priest, who was genuinely loved by the whole family. He had served the parish for decades, married Nel and Ernest, and baptized all their children. He was as much an uncle to the children as he was their pastor. There was never a reason for family celebration or grief that did not include the easy-going Father Jonathan. His ever expanding waistline was testimony that Nel and her daughters were the best cooks in the county. Peter and James both ate like ranch hands and eyed their sisters' plates to see if they could forage any leftovers. John was a little picky and was more interested in kicking his sisters under the table when his parents were talking with Father Jonathan.

All the boys in the family took turns at serving Father Jonathan's daily Mass at the church, only two blocks from their home. Their parents had made them aware that it was a privilege to do so and that nothing else was as important as the Mass. The nuns at the small school were all friends of the Chambers family and were understanding if the boys needed to serve a funeral or help Father. Peter and James served well and took pride in doing so. Father had to keep an eye on John as he would normally fidget during most the Mass. If his impish ways got out of line, John would be counseled by his pastor, scolded by the nuns, and spanked by his mother.

As each of the three older girls graduated from high school, one by one they entered the convent to become nuns. Nel and Ernest were delighted to see such devotion in their children and encouraged them in their choice, even though it would mean waiting for one of the younger children to present them with grandchildren and less help in the store and kitchen for Nel.

The parents were more surprised when Peter and then James declared their intentions to enter the seminary. Neither had excelled in their studies and both were just easy-going, good-hearted country boys. Ernest was shocked with the realization that sharing the workload on the farm with his sons as he had always envisioned might well not be what the future would hold at all. And, then, there was the matter of grandchildren to carry on the family name and traditions. But if they felt called to follow in the footsteps of Jesus, Ernest knew that he should be proud and supportive. Besides, there were always John and little Stephen, the baby of the family.

In the spring of his senior year in high school, John was helping Ernest plant soy beans. They stopped to eat the lunch that Nel had prepared. "You know, Dad, I've been thinking as we planted these seeds that I might be better off planting the seeds of Christ by becoming a priest like Peter and James are trying to do."

Ernest laughed so hard that he started to choke on his ham sandwich. "Oh, come on, Son. You never had a serious thought in your life. You're more likely to end up in prison than in a collar."

John joined in his father's laughter for a moment, but then that impish twinkle in his eye, always a prelude to impending trouble, settled upon his father, who recognized John was serious.

That night Ernest knelt down by his bed and prayed. "Jesus, you know I named those three boys after the apostles you chose to be closest to you. I wanted them all to be like you, but I really didn't expect you to take them all from me, as well as my three daughters. I don't know if I should feel blessed or like Job. I don't know how I'm going to do all this farming without the boys to help me. Don't you want me to have grandchildren and rear more good Catholic children to praise you? I've always tried to leave everything in your hands. Just help me to see what you're doing, Lord. Amen."

As unlikely as it might seem, Peter, James, and even John made it through the seminary and were ordained to the priesthood. Peter had to special order his religious garb. He was six feet, ten inches and weighed over three hundred pounds. Genetics, hard work on the farm, and Nel Chambers' abundant table had conspired to make a colossus of a priest. But for all his imposing stature, he was as gentle, soft-spoken, and kind as any human could be. He was never adverse to hard work as a priest, and, therefore, was loved by every pastor he was assigned to as an associate. He loved being a priest and being around other priests. He had an infectious laugh and lifted the spirits of priests with endless family stories.

When Peter was given a day off, he generally headed to the farm to help his dad out. He was proud of his family roots, his ability to farm, and that his family's gift to the Church of three nuns and three priests. Every Catholic in the diocese knew the Chambers name and the majority had been ministered to by at least one of them. Throughout his priesthood, Peter always asked his bishop to assign him to country parishes as he understood farmers and even loved to help out on their farms during the stressful times of spring planting and fall harvesting. Peter would never be remembered for any extraordinary acts as priest, but he was solid as a rock and deeply loved by the people he served.

Father James was so much like his brother that people often confused them. They were close to one another in affection and personality and were often seen in one another's parishes. Deer and duck seasons found them together in the woods or in a duck blind. They filled the freezers of their parishioners as well as their own with venison, quail, and duck. They fished every lake in the diocese and held fish fries for family, parishioners, and brother priests.

James was a bit more introverted than Peter, and his flock at times misread his shyness as grumpiness, which provoked occasional letters to the bishop from those easily offended. James never understood how to handle those who were provoked by his manner and would do whatever necessary to avoid confrontation, which simply aggravated the situation rather than solved it.

While he was not as revered as Peter, James was a fine priest who had a slight personality quirk which some of his parishioners misinterpreted. James was aware that some of his flock really didn't care for him, and it was a cross that he carried to the altar at each Mass he celebrated. The occasional hard stare that met his attempts to preach his homilies would disturb his self-confidence and diminish his effectiveness. To his credit, he never retaliated against those who showed him disdain; in fact, he tried even harder to please them.

Peter and James often wondered if their dad had found John in their turnip patch, left carelessly behind by a pair of jackals. They both loved him but rolled their eyes at one another over the antics of their little brother when he joined their priestly ranks. Neither of them had ever entertained a liberal thought; both were conservative religiously and politically and would no more have disrespected their bishop than they would God.

No longer having sisters to annoy, within a year after his ordination, John took it upon himself to become a burr under his bishop's episcopal throne. He objected to the bishop's stance on religious and social issues, his assignments, and imputed unworthy motivations on those rare occasions when he did something that John begrudgingly liked. He became cynical and sarcastic and generally looked as if he had just consumed something that disagreed with him. Peter and James attempted to talk with John about his attitude with the result of John's distancing himself from his family.

John attempted to ingratiate himself with other priests by telling inappropriate, off-color jokes. Most of his comrades responded with an internal wince and an external pro-forma muted chuckle. He spoke with a high pitched, nervous voice and seemed unable to make eye contact for more than a second or two. He smoked heavily and generally smelled like an ash tray.

It would not be accurate to say that John had troubles with the priesthood; he had troubles with himself. He had always felt overshadowed by his older brothers both physically and emotionally, unappreciated by his parents, and unnoticed by the rest of humanity. Although he was of average height, next to Peter and James, he appeared small, and he probably suffered from "small man syndrome." His impish behavior was endured by others when he was young, but as he grew into a middle-aged priest and seemed unable to mature emotionally, he was generally avoided by other priests as well as his own parishioners, and, finally, even by his own siblings.

Ernest died at the age of seventy-five, in 1980, followed by Nel, two years later. By then the farm that he had labored on so hard throughout his life had appreciated in value to the extent that each of the children inherited over a half million dollars. Their hopes for grandchildren had not been realized as their last two children never married and seemed happy living in the old family home and operating the general store. They took pleasure in providing a home for their brothers' and sisters' vacations and family celebrations.

The sisters who had entered the convent had taken vows of poverty, and their inheritance went to their religious order and into a fund that helped provide for the sisters in their advanced age. Their parents' hard work and thrifty ways aided not only their own religious daughters but also some of the nuns who had taught their daughters and encouraged them in their vocations.

Neither Peter nor James knew what to do with all the money they inherited. Each began by giving their sisters' religious order $100,000, and donating $50,000 to the diocesan seminary fund. Peter's only change in personal lifestyle was that he drove a luxury car for the remainder of his life. He rationalized the expense by deciding that a large car would help him get to his missions more safely and that he needed a larger car due to his size and some signs of arthritis, but his choice still bothered him as he had been reared frugally and was taught that a priest should live a simple life.

James convinced Peter to take a trip with him to Rome and some of the other major cities in Europe. While they were both impressed by St. Peter's Basilica and would talk of their general audience with Pope John Paul II for the rest of their lives, the rest of the trip was simply uncomfortable to them. They were farm boys in collars, who loved their parishes and their flocks. They were happier in a duck blind or deer camp than on the canals of Venice or the Rue de la Paix. They preferred duck gumbo, fried catfish, and grilled venison to the unfamiliar food of the fancy restaurants that had been recommended to them. And when the bills came at the end of the meals, they both felt as if they were squandering the inheritance their parents had sacrificed to provide. They agreed that living "high on the hog" was not for them and inappropriate for priests. They came home a week early, although the charge the airline levied to change their tickets made them both lose sleep. Neither would ever leave their diocese again for vacation.

John squirreled his money away more avidly than any squirrel ever collected acorns. He thought his brothers' suggestion to share it with his sisters' religious order and the seminary fund was ludicrous. "Our parents wanted us to have that money, not somebody else." "Those nuns have plenty of money that nobody knows about." "If I gave that money to the seminary fund, that bishop would get hold of it, and I wouldn't trust him for a minute."

It wasn't that John was spending it on himself. Aside from drinking too much alcohol and chain smoking, he lived a frugal life. His inheritance brought him no happiness. Perhaps he envisioned saving it for his old age, but that was not to be. Two days after his fifty-sixth birthday, John's doctor told him that he had lung cancer and that his prognosis was not hopeful.

John was extremely frightened. He knew he had led a selfish life, intent upon pleasing only himself. His prayer life had been shallow, as he did only what was required of a priest, and often skimped on even that. He felt lonely, knowing that his immaturity and self-absorption had dampened even the love of his family for him. The night of his doctor's appointment, he had gone into his darkened church and wept bitterly, feeling sorry for himself and what he had made of his life. And, then, he went back to his rectory and drank himself into a fitful sleep.

The parishioners wondered why Father John seemed even more morose than usual at Mass the next morning. He had told no one of his visit to the doctor. "Who would really care?" he thought to himself. He tried to pray the Divine Office after Mass, but was engulfed only in thoughts of self-pity. He returned to his rectory and went back to bed, hoping to escape into sleep. But then the doorbell rang. He attempted to avoid answering it, but it was persistent. "Will it never end? Quamdiu, Domine?"

He opened the door to find his two hulking brother priests. No words were spoken. Peter entered the hallway, followed by James. Peter looked directly into John's eyes, and John knew that someone had told his brothers of his condition. He had no more witty things to say, no puns, certainly no more dirty jokes. John felt emotionally naked, quite vulnerable, before his two older brothers. Without a word, Peter stepped towards John and embraced him in a bear hug that expelled whatever air he had left in his cancerous lungs. Extricating himself from Peter's clumsy attempt to show love, John experienced a fit of coughing that all three feared might be the end of him. Finally, Peter and James helped him to his bed and sat on either side.

Peter was the first to speak. "John, we've got to get you help. We've already spoken to the bishop and told him about your cancer. He's sending Adam Coors to take your place; he'll be here by the weekend. There is nothing you need to do and nothing you need to worry about. The doctor says you need to go home and let our little sister Mary Louise take care of you. She's expecting you and will have the house ready for you. You'll have Mother and Dad's old room."

Another fit of coughing. "I can't. The parish needs . . ."

It was James's turn. "Oh, shut up, John. You and I have always been straight with one another so let me lay it out for you: You don't have much time left, perhaps a few months at best. The cancer is far advanced and you waited too long for the doctor to be able to do anything for you. At this point, you are in no shape to do anything for anybody. It's time to let your family take care of you until God decides for you to join Mom and Dad."

"I'm afraid to die. I haven't been everything God wanted me to be."

James was not finished. "You sure as hell haven't been. But then, who has? You're a priest; don't you believe all those things you've been preaching for over thirty years? Hasn't it gotten through that wiseass head of yours that God loves you because He is Love, and that His son died so that poor sinners like us could be with him for eternity? Why, Pete and I have put up with your shenanigans all your life, and we still love you with all our faults. Why would you think that God doesn't? You should have been listening to your homilies all these years."

"But I haven't been to confession in over five years."

"Holy Moses," exclaimed Peter, the other part of the formidable tag team. "You mean you've been hearing your parishioners' confessions like some high and mighty sinless guru and wallowing in your own sins all those years? Get out of here, James, little brother is about to have his confession heard."

Although John made some perfunctory objections to his own brother hearing his long overdue confession, he was eager to leave all his sins behind and knew that this was no time in his life for pride or self-deception.

Stephen and Mary Louise were delighted to have John home with them. They had closed the general store two years before as all their customers went to the Wal-Mart that opened in the town several miles away. They were solid Catholics and felt that taking care of their dying priest-brother was like taking care of Jesus himself. The old house seemed to come to life once more. Realizing that John's time was limited, all the brothers and sisters visited frequently. It was almost like old times having the family back together again. Mary Louise used Nel's recipes to attempt to awaken John's appetite. Never a big eater, John's appetite ebbed as his cancer grew.

Three months after John had returned to his family home, the doctor advised Mary Louise and Stephen to gather the family and call the parish priest. They were all assembled within a few hours. Peter led the rosary as they knelt around John's bed. John drifted in and out of consciousness, occasionally calling faintly for Nel. Then, suddenly, his head rose slightly from the pillow and he looked about at his family, gave that impish little smile that had been his childhood trademark, and sank back to his pillow, exhaling his final breath.

With John's death, Peter and James seemed to lose much of their drive and gusto. They remained good, solid priests, but age and their diminishing family took its toll upon them. All three of their older sisters died within ten years of John's death. After Peter lost his younger brother James in 2012, he retired and joined Mary Louise and Stephen in the family home. Finally in the fall of 2013, Peter, that great colossus of a priest, who had been the glue of the family, died of a heart attack at deer camp with two of his priest friends at his side.

Mary Louise and Stephen continue to live in the family home. They begin each day by attending Mass and end each day by praying the rosary together for the nuns and priests that Nel and Ernest's faith-filled marriage produced.

CHAPTER FOURTEEN

FATHER JOSHUA CONSTANTINE

The nuns at Ave Maria Hospital all agreed that he was the most beautiful baby they had ever seen. He already had a shock of black, curly hair and, the nuns agreed, the disposition of an angel. Maurice and Stella could not have been more excited about the birth of their firstborn, Joshua Ignatius Constantine, on the feast of Assumption of the Blessed Mother in 1951. Stella thought that the date of his birth was surely a heavenly sign that he was destined to do great things for God. She pinned a medal of Our Lady of the Assumption on his baby blanket and vowed to place him under her protection.

Maurice and Stella made an unlikely couple. His parents were from Turkey and hers from Greece. Both sets of parents were opposed to their dating based upon a long-standing animosity between the two countries. But love knows no borders, and when the two met in high school, they both knew that they would one day marry. Since Maurice's parents were Catholic and Stella's were Greek Orthodox, religion posed still another hurdle in their relationship. Love rarely ever conquers all, regardless of what the poets may say, but Maurice and Stella were both stubborn and headstrong, so they eloped the night after their high school graduation.

After their parents' initial meltdown, the couple lived in the back bedroom of Maurice's parents' home. Maurice worked for his father selling oriental rugs, and Stella worked for her father waiting tables in his small Greek restaurant. Both Maurice and Stella were constantly reminded by both sets of parents that they were living in sin and were an embarrassment to their parents and their "people." They worked hard, saved their money, and were able to afford a small house by the time Joshua arrived two years after their marriage.

The excitement over the birth of the first grandchild on both sides of the family vitiated much of the resentment over the marriage. When the grandparents first saw that beautiful child, their hearts became putty. Joshua's premier appearance charmed his audience and would be precedent-setting for the remainder of his life. When the question of Joshua's baptism arose, the family quarrels renewed. Maurice blustered and stormed about sufficiently to quell the objections of Stella and her parents, and Joshua was baptized at St. Joseph's Catholic Church. Stella carried her son to the side altar of the Blessed Mother and asked her to protect and guide him throughout his life.

As neither Maurice nor Stella had siblings, their parents hoped that they would have many children, but that was not to be the case. Joshua then became the focus of attention and affection from both sets of grandparents. He consumed enough moussaka and baklava to fill the Acropolis, and could pinpoint the national origin of an oriental rug by the time he was eight. The charm he exhibited in the nursery grew exponentially, and he used it to manipulate parents and grandparents alike. His dark skin accentuated his deep brown, laughing eyes and radiant smile, and his enthusiasm and simple joy for life was infectious.

The beautiful boy matured into a handsome, self-assured teenager who drew the attention of every unattached girl in high school, and even some who were already going steady. He was very aware of the power of his personality and looks and often took advantage of girls sexually. He had little remorse over his escapades. He was forced to attend Sunday Mass with his parents, but his faith was shallow. His prayer life was centered upon himself: passing a difficult class, getting what he wanted out of his parents and grandparents, getting a date with a particular girl, and praying that his girlfriends did not become pregnant. He did pass all of his classes in high school and he did charm most of what he wanted out of his parents and grandparents, but in his senior year of high school he was unable to charm God into preventing one of his girlfriends from becoming pregnant.

For the first time in his life, Josh had encountered a situation that he could not charm his way around. He was genuinely frightened. As the only child and only grandchild on both sides of his family, parents and grandparents had high hopes and expectations for him, and siring a child out of wedlock was not one of them. His upbringing had been exceptional only in its permissiveness, but he knew that both Turkish and Greek, both Roman Catholic and Greek Orthodox, sides of his family would react with anger and view his conduct as an insult to his heritage. He knew that the volatile nature of their personalities could result in expulsion from the family and—even worse—disinheritance. He knew that he had to contrive a story that would either totally absolve him of guilt or mitigate it to the extent that his actions would be perceived as a mere trifling peccadillo of a hot-blooded Mediterranean youth.

Stories flashed through Joshua's mind: She was a slut who lured his virginal body into sin by ways he was too innocent to understand (He decided that his dad would never buy that one.). She had relations with many boys, any of whom could be the father (But what if it turned out to look just like him, which he was arrogant enough to assume it would?). They were deeply in love and planned to elope just as his parents had (But what if he were forced into actually marrying the girl whom he really didn't care for at all?).

He was raped. (Not even his mother would buy that one). And then he hit upon the one excuse he felt would work: He was planning to enter the seminary, but thought he should try sexual intercourse just one time to make sure he could avoid it as a priest (That, he assured himself, would play upon the faith of his parents, their pride in envisioning a future sacerdotal son, and confuse everyone sufficiently that they would feel compassion for him and distrust of the harlot who had "led him into temptation").

Strangely enough, his family actually believed him and set the wheels in motion for him to have an interview with their pastor and the diocesan vocations director. The mother of the child was sent to "visit her relatives," until the child was born and adopted. Joshua displayed little concern for the welfare of child or mother, only relief that he had escaped any major interruption to his life. He decided that he could stay in the seminary for a year or two, get some college credits, and then announce that he felt that did not have a vocation. Although he was unsure as to how he would live without female companionship, he was shaken sufficiently by the pregnancy of his girlfriend to give up even sexual activity for a limited period of time.

His charm, good looks, and ready smile made him as popular in the seminary as they always had. He was clever enough to know how to manipulate the system to his advantage even there. Those big, brown eyes could portray interest, compassion, joy, excitement, sorrow, penitence, or piety at Joshua's whim. His professors thought his eyes indicated Joshua's absolute, intense interest in their subjects, while he was actually dreaming of the day he could again be free to date as many girls as he could manage.

At the end of his first year, he began to lay the groundwork for a graceful departure from the seminary. He told his parents that he wasn't as sure as he had been before that God wanted him to be a priest, but that he was going back to the seminary and pray about it for another year. They were inspired by his seeming total abandonment to God's will and assured him of their prayers.

Upon returning to the seminary, Joel Taylor was assigned to be his roommate. He had shared some classes with Joel before but didn't really like him for he seemed to have a huge ego and to be far too sure of himself. Although Josh had to struggle to pass his subjects, Joel was always at the head of his class. Josh recognized that he might use his brainy roommate to his advantage. Joel's ego made him easy prey for Josh's manipulative charm. Additionally, Joel felt that he might be able to use Josh's popularity to improve his standing with his classmates. What began as an uneasy alliance driven by mutual advantage ripened into a respectful friendship; they recognized and used the strengths of one another.

Josh saw his college credits begin to amass. While he still had no genuine interest in becoming a priest, he reasoned that since he was well into a degree at the seminary he might as well continue until he finished his undergraduate work. With Joel's help, his grades improved, and, meanwhile, Josh's charm continued to win friends among both faculty and students. No one knew that he continued to date during his summer vacations and holiday breaks from the seminary. He had no hesitancy in lying to the young women about where he attended college and always failed to remember to mention that he was studying to be a priest. Nor did he feel compunction if he became sexually active on his dates.

After receiving his degree in philosophy, Josh decided to continue in the seminary. His friend and enabler Joel was being sent to Rome for his theological studies, and he was a little jealous, but recognized that he probably could not have managed the studies. Additionally, he had no intention of distancing himself from several young women he was dating surreptitiously. His prayer life was vague, but he made certain that it looked convincing,

There was a bump in the road for Josh in his third year of theology. An attractive woman came to the seminary one afternoon and asked to see the rector about a personal problem involving one of his students. Her name was Abby. She waited tables in a café not far from the town in which Josh and his family lived. Abby had been in a relationship with Josh for almost two years. Josh had tired of her and had begun dating another young woman from the same town. Abby caught them together, found out where Josh was really attending college and decided to ruin him. She provided enough details concerning her love affair with Josh to make the rector believe her story. The rector was furious.

Josh was in his moral theology class when the professor was given a note to have him report to the rector's office immediately. Josh knew it must be important and reasoned that the problem was either the death of a family member or trouble from one of his girl friends. On the way to the office, he began to orchestrate his response to either possibility.

The rector glared at Josh as he entered his office attired in his cassock and obviously uneasy.

"Sit down, young man. Now, I would ask that you think very carefully about your answers to my questions. Should you lie to me, you will be dismissed immediately. Do you know Abby McDonnell?"

Josh's heart was beating rapidly and he felt perspiration roll down the sides of his chest. He paused, wondering how he should play this scene. He was unsure about how much the rector knew and didn't want to overplay his hand.

"Yes, I know an Abby McDonnell. She's a friend of mine and waits tables in a restaurant where I eat on my vacations. We've talked a lot."

"And that's all you've done, 'talk'"?

"Look, Monsignor, I don't know what you've heard. Abby is a little unbalanced. She tends to confuse things and say things to get her friends in trouble just for the fun of it. Why do you ask me about her?"

"She seemed neither unbalanced nor confused when she told me a few minutes ago that you have carried on a sexual relationship with her over the past two years and are now involved with still another woman. Weigh your words, young man. Is this true?"

Josh knew that he was cornered. What now? He opted for a bold and dramatic move intended to play upon the compassionate heart of the rector. He crumpled to the floor in front of his chair, holding on tenuously to the side of the rector's desk, manufacturing enough tears to embarrass the Trevi Fountain for its relatively meager output.

"Oh, God, Monsignor, yes, I did it. She was so lost, so lonely; I tried to comfort her. She had no one. Her parents and family had turned against her. She lived in a little apartment where I would visit her after she got off work. She was so needy. And then one night, blinded by passion, my compassion turned to lust. I know that I've sinned. Please, Monsignor, help me."

"Joshua, here you are just a little over a month before your ordination to the diaconate, a little more than a year before being ordained a priest, and now I learn that you are engaged in at least one sexual relationship. How do you expect me to help you at this point? Certainly I can't recommend you to the bishop for Holy Orders. Perhaps we both need time to think and pray. Pack your bags immediately. I want you to go to St. Jerome's Benedictine Abbey for a week and give us both some time to reflect. I'll make the necessary excuses for you to the faculty."

Josh pulled himself up from the floor. "I'll do anything you ask, Monsignor. Please don't turn against me. I'll never do anything like that again. I'd never dream of embarrassing the Church. I've worked for almost seven years to become a priest; it's all I ever wanted."

"Go. Pack. Leave. I'll see you in a week's time."

As he left the rector's office, Joshua felt that his damage control had been effective. It had bought him some time. He felt sure that a week would give him more than sufficient time to justify his actions to the rector and to plan a counter-attack against Abby. She had sought to destroy him and he was not about to turn the other cheek.

When Josh arrived at St. Jerome's Abbey, he made arrangements to counsel with the abbot, whom he had known previously. The abbot had known Josh's parents and repeatedly been the guest at his mother's now famous gourmet Greek restaurant. Furthermore, the abbey had been the recipient of three large antique Iranian rugs for their sanctuary from Josh's father. Josh told the abbot of the accusations made against him and admitted that he had been guilty of several inappropriate sexual actions over the years. He felt it necessary to admit to some improprieties, knowing that the rector had probably called the abbot.

The abbot was pastoral and compassionate, seeking to assuage the manufactured tears of the apparently penitent young man, as his primary objective as a good priest was to reconcile the penitent with God. And it is entirely possible that Josh may have even experienced some true repentance, perhaps the same variety that occurs in a foxhole when a soldier is under heavy artillery.

Once the confession was over, Josh put on his most sincere face and spoke of his abject sorrow for a "few" nights when he had been unable to quell his passions. The picture he painted of an heroic, virile young man fighting temptations as he tossed upon his sleepless bed was really quite convincing. The nights in the seminary between vacations were sufficient to form a basis for Josh to counterfeit a masterpiece portraying heroic sacrifice. After over two hours, the abbot, who was normally considered a sage judge of character, bought Josh's fabrication. Not since Sotheby's auction of a bona fide Cezanne was a bidder more satisfied with the quality of his purchase.

The next day the abbot was on the phone to the rector, pleading Josh's cause. "He's a fine young man, an excellent candidate for the priesthood who went through a difficult period in his life, but has repented so deeply that it is unlikely he would ever fall in such a manner again. Additionally, your diocese needs priests so desperately that it would be a crime to pass over this man due to a short term lapse of judgment. Josh also tells me that the young woman in question was sexually abused by her father, a matter so sensitive that he withheld it even from you. She becomes delusional about men and sexuality."

The rector greatly respected the abbot's opinion and intuitive recognition of a man's worth and motives. When Josh returned to the seminary, the atmosphere in the rector's office had changed considerably from his last visit. The rector had prayed long and hard over Josh's situation. He knew that it was easy to ruin a man's reputation and his life. If the abbot was correct in his judgment, as he had always been in other sensitive cases, it would be a tragedy to lose a man who had the potential through his charming personality to do so much for the cause of Christ. He warmly greeted Josh, politely asked him to sit, and pulled up a chair in a position to look him squarely in the eye.

"Josh, it's been a rough, hard week for both of us. I slept little and I'm sure you slept less. I've spent hours before the Blessed Sacrament trying to discern God's will for you. I'm still not sure. Is there anything you can tell me so that I can make the right decision?"

Josh was keenly aware that he had arrived at the crucial play of the game and that every syllable he would utter could determine the outcome. "Monsignor, for the first few nights at the abbey, I cried myself to sleep. I know what the agony in the garden must have been for Our Lord. The Twenty-Third Psalm entered my thoughts time and again; I began to realize that the Lord really is my shepherd, and that I don't need to fear anything. Each time I became depressed about my own sinfulness, I reflected upon the forgiveness that Jesus won for me upon the cross. With that kind of loving, forgiving shepherd, I knew that whatever decision you would make would be the right one for me. And, so, I'm ready to accept whatever your decision might be."

"You will make a good priest. Those are the words I was waiting to hear, a total abandonment to God's will. In a few weeks you will be ordained a deacon. Celibacy will be an integral part of your life. I want you to look me in the eye right now and tell me that you will never violate that vow.

"With all my heart, I swear it."

As Josh left the office, he knew he had pulled it off. He knew enough moral theology to rationalize that there was no obligation to keep a promise that was coerced. He smiled as he thought of Abby and the summer vacation that would follow his ordination to the diaconate. He might wish to forgive her, for the summer at least. And, indeed, he did.

There were no more mishaps through the remainder of Josh's time in seminary. He was ordained to the diaconate as planned and spent the last year of his seminary career playing the part of the ideal seminarian. When it came time for his bishop to lay hands upon his head and anoint his hands with oil, he was glad that the formative period of his life was over and he was ready to prove his metal as a priest. His ordination ceremony was filled with the people he had charmed from his first beaming smile in the hospital nursery to his erstwhile gazes into the eyes of the abbot and the rector. No one there really knew Josh, not even Abby, who sat in the last pew–and assuredly not Josh himself.

From the viewpoint of the parishioners at St. Christopher's Catholic Church, they had the perfect young assistant priest in Father Joshua. He was energetic, dynamic, extremely good looking, capable of giving an interesting although not particularly profound homily, good with the young people of the parish (especially the girls). He was without doubt absolutely charming to everyone. Even the pastor was fond of him, although somewhat concerned about the late hours he often kept. No one ever saw him before the Blessed Sacrament, and the pastor noted that Josh's breviary remained in the same spot on the entrance hall table where he had left it several weeks before.

The parish secretary became suspicious when she kept receiving calls for Father Josh from the same young woman who didn't care to leave her name. She would often call several times a day, and there were curious calls with no one on the line. It was fortunate for Josh that before the pieces of the puzzle came together for his pastor or the parish secretary he received a change of assignment to become an assistant in a different area of the diocese. He had sensed the suspicion that was growing and determined to keep a more careful watch over those telltale signs that might unmask his true identity.

His new assignment found him in the neighboring parish where his former roommate, now Father Joel Taylor, recently returned from Rome after having received his licentiate in canon law, was assigned as an associate pastor to Monsignor Dumbarski. Joel was delighted to have Josh close as he provided an ear for him to complain about "Dumb-ass-ski" and the horrid parish practices he had to endure. Josh knew that Joel was probably on his way up in the clergy due to his intelligence and time at NAC and thought his friendship might well be useful in the future. Josh was wrong; egotists do not make strong advocates or form alliances less than personally beneficial.

Josh and Joel met once a month for dinner and a movie. Joel attempted to overlook Josh's crude remarks about women and the salacious jokes he told. Josh, for his part, tired of hearing Joel's repeated complaints about his pastor. Joel began to notice a certain evasive, secretive side to Josh, whose stories about where he had been and what he had been doing did not seem consistent. There were too many times that he called to speak with Josh, but no one in the parish seemed to have any idea as to where he was or when he would return. He realized that Josh must be up to something, and his sexual banter led Joel to think it might well be of that nature.

Just when Joel felt he was getting close to solving the riddle of the discrepancies in Josh's alibis, fate intervened with the explosion of his relationship with Msgr. Dumbarski and his reassignment across the diocese as the associate for Father Jack. As clever as Joel was and as perceptive as he prided himself upon being, he felt thwarted in unraveling the mystery of his overly charming former roommate. He soothed himself by remembering that eventually "the chickens would come home to roost."

It took the chickens another seven years to find their way home. By then Joel had been away for treatment and was dealing successfully with his ego and anger problems and had been made the pastor of the parish once held by Father Adam Coors. Joel was well-liked there and his reputation as a gifted homilist and counselor spread throughout the diocese.

Joel was in the habit of taking a short nap after lunch, which served as a welcome intermission in a day that began with early Mass and ended with late evening parish meetings. As on many other days, the nap was interrupted by the doorbell. Joel opened the door to find a nervous teenage boy of about sixteen. The boy was obviously upset and said that he needed to talk with a priest. Joel showed him to his office and offered him a seat.

"Father, my mother is Dora Stewart. I've never had a father. She raised me by working hard at the Westinghouse factory ever since I can remember. We have not been getting along well the past couple of years. I've missed a lot of school, done some drinking, and finally got kicked out of high school two weeks ago. Mom and I had a huge argument, and we both said some things we wish we hadn't. She finally told me to go live with my father. I had no idea what she was talking about, never having had one. She showed me a newspaper with a picture of a priest blessing animals on the feast of St. Francis and told me that was my dad. I told her she was lying. Then she showed me his picture from their high school annual when he was my age. It was like looking in a mirror."

As Joel looked at the boy, he didn't have to ask the name of the priest. Josh's fear in high school that his illegitimate child might look like him had been realized.

"So, Father, what do I do? He has never contacted my mother from the time he learned she was pregnant. I hate him for that and for never seeing me. It was hell growing up without a father and being kind of poor. He just walked away; how could he do that? Excuse me, Father, but he'd have to be an asshole to do that. Is that what priests do? Is that the way they treat people? No wonder Mother left the Church and never had me baptized; I don't blame her. I want him to suffer; I want him to pay for what he did to me and my mother."

"And what would that accomplish, Son?"

"It would make me feel a hell of a lot better!"

"That has not been my experience in life. Whenever I tried to make someone else suffer, I ended up feeling worse about myself." Joel thought of his unkindness to Msgr. Dumbarski and the parish council debacle when he was first made pastor. Then Joel deftly led the boy away from his anger, confusion, and desperation. They spent the remainder of the afternoon talking over options for the boy: confronting his father, going to the bishop, filing suit for child support, or doing nothing. Joel contrived a plan that he hoped would help the boy, and simultaneously include all of the options save doing nothing.

Joel called Josh that evening and told him he was coming into town the next day and would like to treat him to dinner at a steak house they had frequented while being assigned close to one another. Josh accepted and showed up about fifteen minutes late. As he approached the leather booth where he had seen Joel sitting, he recognized that Joel was not alone. A teenage boy sat across from him, and Josh had a strange feeling that there was something familiar about him. It was as if he had seen him before somewhere, someplace. As he slid into the booth next to Joel, Josh extended his hand, "Hi, I'm Father Joshua, and I don't think we've met but you look familiar to me."

The boy's head was lowered, and he slowly raised it as he made eye contact with Josh, ignoring his extended hand. "Hello, I'm your bastard, Dora's son. You remember Dora, don't you, DAD? She's the one you saddled with me while you ran off to be a priest."

Josh's head jerked back against the booth and his eyes fixed on the ceiling. His breath came in gasps as if trying to recover from being punched in the stomach. Too many thoughts came to his mind to focus on any of them.

The boy wasn't finished. "Why, Father DAD, don't you have anything to say to your LOVING bastard son? You must have a lot stored up after sixteen years of silence. Your Jesus must be so proud of how you earned the title 'Father.' Now that you've met your little bastard boy, don't you want to give him a big hug? I've waited for that from my father all my life."

"Okay. Enough," Joel whispered across the table. He had not expected the boy to be quite so rough on Josh and began to feel that he had been part of an ambush rather than reconciliation.

Josh found himself in the men's room, not remembering how he had gotten there. He rested his forehead on the mirror over the sink, still breathing heavily. He splashed cold water on his face, knowing that he must go back to the table and face that poor boy who had obviously suffered so deeply and had become so embittered.

"Oh, God, what have I done? I've let lust rule my life from my teenage years. I used other people, rather than loved them. I've broken every vow and promise I ever made. My priesthood has been one long act of hypocrisy. That boy who hates me out there has to be my avenue back to you. Send your Holy Spirit to your unfaithful servant."

When Josh arrived back at the table, Joel was gone. The boy remained, head once more down. Josh broke the silence. "You're wrong about one thing. It's not you that's the bastard; it's me. There is nothing that I can say that can excuse what I did to you and your mother, nothing I can say or do that will make up for the pain and emptiness that I have caused. I can't even tell you that it was a single act of a sexually charged teenager and all that is in the past. Your father is not a good man. He uses people. You and your mom are not the only ones he has used and deserted, manipulated and lied to. And the now the man who has hurt you has to ask you a favor."

The boy's eyes looked resentfully at Josh, in disbelief that he would have the gall to seek a favor from the one he had harmed. "I beg you to let me spend the rest of my life trying to help you and your mother. I know you hate me, and I don't blame you.

You are the greatest thing that ever happened to me because you have opened my eyes and changed my heart. I truly believe that God sent you to me. Please do not turn your back on me, as I did on you. It's possible that I need you more than you ever needed me.

"I don't even know your name, and I'm afraid that you'd throw something at me if I called you 'Son.'"

The boy looked at his father for several moments without speaking. "I'm willing to give it a try. Why else would I have even come here? My mother loved you even after you left her; she named me after you. My name is Joshua."

The next morning, Josh went to see his bishop. He revealed all his past history, all the sexual encounters beginning in high school and continuing throughout his seminary and priesthood years. He had led a double life. He told the bishop about his son Joshua and how he wanted him to live with him in the rectory so that he could fulfill his God-given duties as a parent. He knew that he would have to address the issue from the pulpit but felt that his parishioners would understand a youthful transgression and help him love his son.

The bishop already had suspicions concerning Josh and was actually relieved when Josh honestly and contritely confessed his past. He saw this as a turning point for Josh in his priesthood and hoped he could become the instrument through which other sinners might return to the mercy of God. He told Josh to make a good confession immediately and to seek ongoing counseling to aid him in what he thought could be a sexual addiction.

After making some arrangements at the church and the bank, Josh drove Joshua to Dora's home. It hurt Josh to realize the pain he had caused her through his selfishness.

Their meeting was awkward and began with Josh's humble apology for his callous abandonment when Dora most needed him. Her lingering resentment was not so much for the pain she had endured but for what her son had suffered during his childhood and youth. The years of coping with being an unwed mother and trying to rear a boy on her own while working long shifts at the factory to provide a meager living for them had stifled whatever real love she might have had for Josh when they were teenagers. Josh was shocked at how worn she looked at only thirty-four, and he knew that his actions had caused her to turn from a vivacious, beautiful teenage girl to a woman with little hope or future.

Josh and Dora agreed that Joshua would be better with his father at this stage of his development. Joshua packed his few belongings, told his mother how much he loved her, and apologized for his teenage selfishness and moodiness of the past few years. He promised to visit often and to phone daily. Dora had asked nothing for herself and showed amazingly little resentment toward Josh. Josh asked his son to go to the car, saying he needed to talk with Dora alone.

"Dora, thank you for all these years you've loved and cared for our son. He is the sincere and good person he is because of you, and in spite of me. I can't make up for these years to either of you, but there is something I can do for you. As their only heir, both sets of my grandparents have set up a very generous trust fund for me. I have arranged for you to receive an initial check for $200,000, and you will receive an additional $5,000 a month for the rest of your life."

"I don't want your money, Josh. I've made it on my own so far, and I'll continue to do so. Don't take away my pride and my son at the same time."

"This is not charity, Dora; it's justice. The initial gift is a kind of overdue child support, amounting to a thousand dollars a month for Joshua's sixteen years. And, if we had married and I left you, I'd be paying alimony. I did leave you, and there is a court beyond that of the world that will one day demand justice of me. Please don't let me stand before God's judgment seat, knowing how I ruined your chances in life without trying to do what little I can to make things better for you."

"I don't think much of God or his justice anymore," she said softly.

"That's another thing I need to attend to in justice. I robbed you of your faith by running away from you into the arms of the Church. You must have seen God as 'the other woman' who took me away from you and our son. The truth is that I was a scared kid who used the Church as a convenient excuse not to accept responsibility. I had no intention of actually becoming a priest. Once I got into the seminary, I just went along with the flow. God and His Church didn't take me away; my pride, selfishness, and immaturity did.

"Our son has awakened within me the recognition of how much the priesthood means to me. I've used people even as a priest. The priesthood gave me power over people, and I used it in terrible ways, just as I used my good looks and charm over you when we were kids. Joshua let me know how wrong I've been all these years. The rest of my priesthood will be spent as it all should have been: trying to bring people to Christ and trying to serve them as Jesus would have me do. I doubt that I'm the right guy to bring you back to Christ, but please let me ask Father Joel to speak with you."

With some reluctance Dora agreed to accept both the financial arrangements and the spiritual guidance. She was able to quit her job and live comfortably. Father Joel was successful in getting her to come to his church. After Mass one Sunday, Dora met Charlie Drane, a farmer and strong Catholic, whom she married three years later. God used Charlie to nourish Dora in the faith and bring her back to the sacraments.

It took the better part of the next two years for Josh to earn the respect and trust of Joshua. There were heated arguments; Josh came away always a little bloodied emotionally from his son's honesty but better, as a priest and man, for it. Through counseling, Josh was learning to substitute sincerity for charm, and the parishioners noted a marked and welcome change.

Josh arranged for Joshua to enter the local Catholic high school. At first, Joshua objected to the stronger disciplinary code, the required white shirt and tie for classes, the stress on religion, and the absence of girls. As time passed, he made friends and began to take pride that the school always expected the best he could give. Seeing other guys he respected go to confession and communion tweaked his interest in God, the Church, and the sacraments. In the spring of his senior year, Josh had the thrill of baptizing his own son with Maurice and Stella serving as godparents. Joshua's great-grandparents, who were inordinately proud of the one who would carry on their line, created another trust fund in his name, agreed to pay for his college education, and gave him a new convertible for his senior graduation. Needless to say, life had taken a turn for the better for Joshua.

Josh became an increasingly devout priest. As with all priests, he fought temptations, and–like most of them–he fought successfully. He had known the pleasures of the flesh, but he had seen the pain that sin can cause and wanted no part of it. He always looked at Joshua as a gift from God that drove him to the priesthood and later helped him to realize what the priesthood was all about. It all seemed to come together when he witnessed the marriage of Joshua to a beautiful Irish girl, who Josh recognized would encourage and support him in his faith. Nothing ever made Josh happier when he baptized their first child, his own grandchild, whom they named Joshua III.

CHAPTER FIFTEEN

FATHER CARLTON GREENE

His Holiness was radiant, joyfully beaming. The roar of the crowd was deafening. It appeared that every teenager in the United States had joined those from around the globe, all shouting "JOHN PAUL II, WE LOVE YOU! JOHN PAUL II, WE LOVE YOU!" The pope rose from his chair and extended his arms, as if to embrace the hundreds of thousands assembled for the concluding Mass of World Youth Day in Denver. The electricity of the moment charged every heart present, making it beat more rapidly in the cool air of the high altitude.

No one was more excited than Carlton Greene as he stood among his high school buddies, arms around one another's shoulders, joining in the jubilant shouts. He had fallen in love with the pope, the Church, the crowd, the day, his friends, and most importantly with Jesus Christ. He knew that it was a moment he would remember for the rest of his life and that he had never been so happy before and wanted it to last forever.

Father Joshua Constantine had brought twenty-eight teenagers from his parish along with several volunteer chaperones. He had chosen Carlton because he felt the boy needed something good to happen in his life.

Carlton was the younger of two sons born to Marge and Anthony Greene, and his conception might well have been the last activity in which they were mutually cooperative. Marge had developed into a first class nag, intent upon sharing her unhappiness with all who dared enter the perimeter of her dreary existence. She blamed her wretchedness upon Anthony's alcoholism. Anthony conversely blamed his drinking upon Marge's constant nagging. Carlton was not able to discern which came first, the nagging or the drinking, nor did it make a great deal of difference to him. His older brother Jake dealt with the constant family turmoil by smoking pot and taking prescription drugs he had stolen from his mother's medicine cabinet. Jake grew progressively more distant from all his family and was rarely at home.

Marge and Anthony had given up going to Mass shortly after Carlton's baptism and left it up to the boys as to whether or not they would attend. During his years at St. Joseph's Catholic School, Carlton learned to love the Mass. He began serving in the fourth grade, continued through high school, and took pride in helping the priest prepare the sanctuary. Father Josh noted his eager capability and asked him to serve weddings and funerals. Members of the congregation were impressed with this good-looking kid who served both often and well. He received many compliments almost every time he served. Receiving the validation from parishioners that he lacked at home from his parents prompted Carlton to look upon the Church as his family.

By the time Carlton was seventeen, both his parents were totally self-absorbed. Marge spent her days in an aura of self-pity, playing bridge to pass the time and using her female friends as a forum for parading her woes. Anthony ran his insurance agency, inherited from his father, and began drinking at lunch, continuing until he fell asleep in front of the television in the evening. There was absolutely no communication between the parents and only perfunctory communications with their sons. Jake had escaped to college, where he would spend four years partying much and learning little. Carlton fixed his own meals, did his own laundry, and, for all practical purposes, lived an independent life devoid of parental care, guidance, or love. The only thing he shared with his parents was a common address.

Carlton was always flattered by Father Josh's attention. They would joke before Mass, and Father had begun calling him "Bishop," telling him that he was going to shanghai him into the seminary. Carlton laughed while thinking to himself that the seminary didn't sound all that bad. He was thrilled when Father told him he wanted him to join the group going to World Youth Day in Denver. He knew his parents wouldn't care, really would not care one way or the other.

As he stood with his buddies, chanting, swaying, singing, laughing, praying, crying with joy, he knew that God was inside him and that was all he would ever want. As he looked at John Paul II, he wanted desperately to be just like him, so close to God, so filled with purpose, so in sync with all that was right and good. It's doubtful that even St. Paul's conversion had a more dynamic impact. It was as if the sky had opened and from the clouds, Carlton had heard a voice inviting: "Come, follow me." From that moment, Carlton knew he would be a priest.

It wasn't easy for Carlton to bring news of his determination to become a priest into a house shrouded with despair. He decided it would be best to tell his parents separately, which wouldn't prove difficult as they were rarely in the same room. His mother seemed stunned for a moment, as if recognizing for the first time his existence as a person with ideas separate from her own. She was, however, not impressed for long. "Oh, you just saw the big man in Denver and were impressed. It'll pass. I don't much like priests anyway. You've got one more year in high school; fall in love, get married, have kids. Maybe you'll be luckier than I was with your father."

Carlton waited to speak with his dad until the next morning, before he had his first drink of the day. "Well, kid, do what you want to. I even thought about being a priest once, but then I fell in love with your mother… On second thought, if I were you, I'd go to the seminary today and never look back. I sure as hell wish I had."

With those "ringing endorsements" from his parents, he spoke with Father Josh, and they made plans for him to enter the seminary after his graduation from high school. When he phoned his brother to tell him of his decision, Jake seemed unimpressed and suggested to him that he come experience the fun at the university for a few years. He further implied that Carlton would forget his desire to be a priest once he had tasted the pleasures of the flesh and the good life away from Marge and Anthony. Carlton told Jake that he loved Jesus Christ and was determined to serve him as his priest.

During the eight years of his seminary formation, he experienced periods of great spiritual elation but also periods of emptiness and temptation. Carlton loved being with men who had the same values and the same drive to serve God. He formed close friendships with classmates from different sections of the country and benefited from sharing their particular views on life and the Church. On holidays he would normally visit one of his friends' families. It was eye-opening for him to see how members of a loving, faith-filled family related to one another. He felt more accepted and loved in those homes than he had ever felt in his own.

Within his first year in the seminary, Carlton's parents divorced on the grounds of incompatibility. Marge explained to all who would listen that she had suffered long enough and had stayed with Anthony only to provide a "loving home" for her sons. She was adept at playing the martyr. Within a few months she was seeing one of her "friend's" husbands, who later divorced and married her. Anthony continued to drink heavily but found a female drinking partner at a local tavern he had begun frequenting. Carlton was embarrassed by his parents' actions but had emotionally distanced himself from them years before.

He spent his holidays either visiting a fellow seminarian's home or helping at one of the rectories in the diocese. The priests were always glad to have him, both for the real help he was able to give them and for the genial companionship he offered. These visits enabled Carlton to see how a number of the priests lived out their vocations and served their parishes. He discovered how very different priests were from one another. There was something about being with Carlton that made each of the priests with whom he stayed want to be a better priest, and they were always on their best behavior around him for fear of sullying the purity of his idealism about the priesthood.

Carlton was most impressed with Father Luke Smith, who seemed to have such clarity about what it meant to be a priest. No one had ever been as kind to him as Luke. They had long talks in the evening, and Luke shared with Carlton the joys and challenges of the priesthood. He enjoyed accompanying Luke on sick calls, and was amazed at the profound quality of his homilies, the reverent manner in which he celebrated Mass, and the genuine kindness he showed to each parishioner as he greeted them before and after each weekend liturgy. Carlton could see in the eyes of the parishioners how much they admired and even reverenced Luke as he spoke with them. The appointment of Luke as bishop affirmed what Carlton felt about the beauty of the priesthood of Jesus Christ he had witnessed in Luke's daily life, and he promised God and himself that he too would be such a priest.

On May 26, 2001, Carlton became Father Carlton. Marge attended the ordination with her new husband. Marge looked troubled, and her husband looked embarrassed. Anthony was present physically, but as he had now started drinking earlier in the day, it would be difficult to say where he was mentally. He was accompanied by his female drinking buddy who viewed the proceedings through glassy eyes. Jake's new significant other, a nice-looking young man, convinced him to attend the ordination, which would mark the first time Jake had entered a church since the tenth grade. The Greens were not the model Catholic family filled with pride and support for their son and brother; they were all fulfilling what they thought to be their social obligation.

But the cathedral was filled with the love of Catholics who looked upon Father Carlton as part of their own families. These were people who had gotten to know him as he served Mass for Father Josh as a teenager, close friends with whom he had shared the joy of World Youth Day in Denver, members of the parishes in which he had served as a seminarian on his holidays and vacations, and priests with whom he had lived and developed close friendships, now his brother priests. Carlton had instinctively understood from childhood on that these were his real family, people who loved him unselfishly, people with whom he shared in the life of Jesus Christ. These were the people who had supported him with their love and their prayers; these were his family.

When the priests of the diocese came before him during the ceremony and imposed their hands on his head, Carlton deeply felt the bond of the priesthood that united them as one. From the older priests to those ordained only one year, he recognized Christ, and his heart reeled in wonder and appreciation of what God was doing in his life. After Father Josh took his hands from Carlton's head, he smiled and said, "Just as I told you almost fifteen years ago in the sacristy, 'Bishop,' you were born to be a priest." And, with all his heart, Carlton knew that Joshua was right. When Bishop Luke stepped back from the imposition, it was Carlton who spoke: "With God's help, I will be the kind of priest that you are." Luke replied: "Better!"

Both Joshua and Luke were right about Carlton. He was not the brightest priest in the diocese, or the best homilist, or the most charismatic. He did not receive the best or most prestigious appointments. But, like the seed that must fall to the ground in order to bear fruit, he died to any selfishness at all. He served with all that he had to give and he did so with unlimited joy. He made no distinction between the young or old, the wealthy or the poor, the esteemed or humble; to him they were all his family and he loved them all. He was genuinely interested in all their joys or sorrows; he rejoiced with them and grieved with them.

Carlton's parishioners knew they came first in his life. None felt unloved in his presence. None felt they had anything less than his undivided attention. They would often find him before the Blessed Sacrament on his knees; there he received his strength, there that he felt perfectly at peace. When he celebrated Mass, he did so deliberately, attentively, and piously. His homilies were simple and sincere, generally hitting right in the center of the listener's soul. There was no affectation, no planned dramatic effect, just the Gospel of Jesus Christ delivered lovingly by a holy priest. Most importantly, he lived what he preached.

Carlton never stopped loving Marge, Anthony, or Jake. They were still his parents and his brother. He prayed for them daily and would have loved for them to be closer to Jesus and the Church, but they weren't and he had moved on spiritually. He

196

recognized that they had made their choices as to how to live their lives and his attempts to bring them closer to Jesus had failed. He was happier than he had ever been with his real family, the Church, and celebrated his life with his brothers and sisters in Christ every day of his priesthood.

CHAPTER SIXTEEN

FATHER JASON ARNOLD

It is always difficult to follow a priest who has been a beloved father to the parish for decades. When Msgr. Clement Donnelly died, his parish went into deep mourning. He had truly been their spiritual father and created the kind of bond that can be forged only through compassionate care, baptisms of children, First Communions, funerals of loved ones, counseling, attention to school children, thousands of Masses and homilies, unrelenting kindness in confession, and meeting whatever the spiritual needs of the congregation might be.

After Father Alain found Msgr. Clement dead in his chair one evening, it became his duty to prepare the parish to welcome a new pastor. Alain did a superb job of caring for the people for the next five months and preparing them with the diplomatic finesse proper to the French. He did cringe a bit when told the name of the new pastor. He only knew Father Jason Arnold in passing, but he could sense his coldness across a crowded room. Alain thought that all Jason needed to fit perfectly into the condescending foppery of the court of Louis XIV was a powdered wig and binocles-ciseaux. Nor was Jason lacking the political sarcasm rampant in the court.

Alain did the best he could to put a happy face on a dismal appointment. He had heard that Jason was an excellent administrator, known for his ability to turn a parish around financially, and a gifted, if somewhat dramatic, homilist. Alain was careful to stress those qualities when he spoke of the incoming pastor to the congregation, although his inability to disclose his reservations about Jason made him feel unfaithful to the parishioners and his own conscience. Yet he could hardly mount his charger like Paul Revere and ride through the flock warning them of what he felt would surely lead to the destruction of much of what Msgr. Donnelly had worked so hard to establish. Besides, Alain thought, he had been ordained only a short time, and the bishop must know what he was doing. If the bishop thought that priest and parish were a good fit, who was he to object?

Jason Arnold was born on September 15, 1960, the Feast of Our Lady of Sorrows. His parents were both conscientious teachers, his father a high school history teacher and his mother a special education teacher at the grade school level. They were devoted to their four children and determined they would all be highly educated professionals. Fortunately, God cooperated by giving all four sufficient gray matter to make this goal achievable. Hedda and Garfield demanded that the children did their absolute best at all they did.

George was the eldest, extremely smart, handsome, and athletically gifted. He set the bar for the others. His bedroom wall covered with football and track trophies and academic awards stretching from grade school throughout high school. Following him was Samantha, fiery red hair and flashing blue eyes that melted every schoolboy's heart; she was a match for all three of her brothers, who recognized her as a worthy opponent in any contest be it athletic or academic. Next came Jason, who was small-boned, guarded, introverted, had overly large ears, shifty eyes, but was intellectually very quick. The baby of the family was Barrett, a huge, affable oaf who brought joy to the Arnold home. Barrett was smart but didn't care and never made a point of it.

The competition within the Arnold home was intense, and Hedda and Garfield did all in their power to foment it. Upon completion of homework, the parents devised stratagems to pit the children against one another in games that would test their knowledge, with high praise and acknowledgement given to the victor, generally good-natured ribbing to those who performed not quite as well, and open ridicule for those who performed poorly. Being the eldest, George was the most frequent winner; Samantha and Jason split second place honors, and Barrett simply laughed off the negative comments heaped upon him by parents and siblings alike–particularly Jason, who loved having someone to look down upon–what else are little brothers good for?

On Sundays the Arnolds always attended the 10:30 a.m. Mass. They arrived ten minutes early, never tardy, and always sat in the third pew from the back. All wore the best clothes that teachers' salaries could provide. They knelt devoutly upon arriving and remained so until the beginning of Mass. The children never served Mass as Garfield did not see the necessity of his gifted children having to attend practices when they could be doing something more productive; furthermore, he preferred to have the family together for Mass. Jason felt he would like to serve but was not ready to face his father's ridicule to do so.

When the family arrived home from Mass, Garfield would sit with his children and quiz them on the meaning and quality of the homily and the liturgy while Hedda prepared lunch. He was quick to criticize any mistakes the priest had made, both in content and grammar. He pointed out how a better-educated man might have used additional or preferable references, analogies, or metaphors. The children were learning to become critics of the liturgy, the homily, and the priest—lessons that became a habit for them all, but particularly for Jason.

George was the first to leave the nest, heading for Harvard to major in chemistry and finally to become a neurosurgeon. He had both a full academic scholarship and a scholarship to play football. While Samantha had her choice of a number of scholarship offers, she chose to attend the University of California at Berkeley, pursuing a double major in anthropology and archaeology. When it came time for Barrett to make his choice, while he also had multiple scholarship opportunities, he enthusiastically chose to play football for the state university and major in drama, an odd combination that fit his personality perfectly. Only Jason chose to attend a Catholic university, receiving a full scholarship to Notre Dame, majoring in philosophy.

Jason was stimulated by the academic excellence in the classroom and the provocative homilies of the priests at the university church. He was socially inept and had difficulty in making friends, unlike his siblings. Jason felt particularly alone when in crowds, where he felt he was surrounded by people with whom he had nothing in common and who were generally inferior to him intellectually as well as socially. Away from the structure and companionship of his family life, he became a loner and preferred it that way. He attended Mass daily which may have served to temporarily dampen his caustic attitude. Eighteen years of Garfield's lessons on critiquing the actions, words, and characters of others had made an indelible impression upon Jason's psyche and he was on duty 24/7.

As he progressed through his college years at Notre Dame, Jason became increasingly aware of the need for others to reform. He viewed most of his fellow students as immature, unable to grasp the realities of life and their need to come closer to Christ. The priesthood seemed a legitimate avenue to awaken his fellow man to the need for reformation and salvation.

Armed with a philosophy degree and a sense of moral righteousness, he entered the diocesan seminary at the age of 22. His reactions to seminary life were mixed. He found the large majority of his teachers inferior to those at Notre Dame but enjoyed baiting them when they came to class improperly prepared. He found most of his classmates spiritually sincere, intellectually mediocre, socially backward, and only marginally more mature than those at Notre Dame.

A small coterie of students formed around Jason who enjoyed his biting wit and sharp comments about faculty and students. After reading Alexander Pope, they dubbed Jason the new "Wasp of Twickenham." Jason found himself kneeling in the confessional each week confessing the same sin of uncharitable conversation, but he did enjoy the popularity he achieved through the use of his rapier wit. He had pet names for each of the faculty, which, if they had known, would have landed him on his rear outside the seminary gates. He was able to render a seminarian speechless by insightful ridicule in the company of his friends, delighting in his ability to zero in on the more vulnerable areas of his victim's personality or appearance. Jason always felt remorse after using his intelligence to bully those less gifted, but not enough to change.

Jason's ordination and First Mass were planned with extraordinary care for detail. The charming and well-liked Father Joshua Constantine would vest him in his priestly robes at the ordination. Msgr. Clement Donnelly was asked to preach at his First Mass; he was a good speaker and his position as vicar general would add additional prestige to the occasion. Little did Jason imagine that he would one day follow the beloved monsignor as pastor. Hedda had attended Mass throughout the city to determine what choir might best add its musical talents to the day. This was the opportunity for the family of critics to plan the perfect First Mass, and they knew that Father Jason would have some choice words to say if it were not up to his standards. Both the ordination and the First Mass were successful, and they got by with only a slight look of derision and a subtly raised eyebrow from Father Jason for a Responsorial Psalm that meandered on for over ten minutes.

Father Jason's first two assignments as associate pastor went reasonably well, with Jason silently suffering the incompetence he perceived in his pastors. He was smart enough to know that he should not get a reputation as a malcontent, as had his mentor Father Joel Taylor when he had begun his priesthood. Joel had seen some of the same qualities in Jason that had marred the first eight years of his priesthood and had only been remedied through in-house counseling. He shared those things with Jason in an open and kind manner, and they became fast friends for the remainder of their lives. They enjoyed verbally sparring with one another and only occasionally unintentionally stepped over the line and bruised one another's egos. Jason decided it was best to hide his superior intellect until he was no longer merely an associate pastor but would be in a position to exert some real authority.

Jason received his first pastorate six years after ordination. The bishop recognized Jason's intellectual strengths and named him pastor of the university parish so that he might minister to others academically inclined. It marked the first assignment he had been given where he felt free to give homilies that might prove too deep or provocative for the average congregation. His acumen was recognized by the professors in his congregation, and he was soon being invited to speak to college classes on the intermarriage of philosophy and theology. He received invitations to speak at the more liberal Protestant and Jewish campus ministry centers and became rather celebrated for his well-researched and precise presentations. No one enjoyed his presentations more than he did, and he was beginning to neglect his priestly duties in favor of his academic pursuits among the university cognoscenti. The bishop decided that Jason was becoming an intellectual snob and drifting from his vocation as a humble follower and advocate of Christ and reassigned him to a working class parish with the hopes of reconnecting him to the realities of what the priesthood was really about.

As Jason saw himself as highly successful in his university parish, he deeply resented being reassigned and became increasingly vindictive in his attitude toward the bishop. His priest friends were the recipients of lengthy and often witty diatribes portraying the bishop as a buffoon. In actuality, the assignment was good for Jason and did end up teaching him some humility, which rubbed off from the loving service of the parishioners that even he could not overlook.

Jason was celebrating his twentieth anniversary as a priest when news arrived of Msgr. Donnelly's death. Every priest recognized that Clem's parish was the plum of the diocese, and it took the better part of the ten minutes for Jason to begin thinking about the possibilities of succeeding Clem. He naturally felt he would be the logical choice for the best parish in the diocese. There was not a great deal of grief in Jason's heart for the priest who had spoken at his First Mass.

Alain outdid himself to welcome Jason. He had used his culinary skills to prepare a beautiful dinner for him; had the pastor's quarters repainted, newly carpeted and furnished; and had a written report prepared on the financial status of the parish as well as an outline of all the parish activities, upcoming agenda for the pastor, and possible problems. Jason received this thoughtfulness as his due and without any expression of gratitude. He grilled Alain on how he had used his time since Clem's death and what deficiencies Clem may have had in running the parish. Alain was hurt and angered by Jason's coldness but squelched any sign of displeasure, remembering that he was to leave the parish the following week.

That weekend Jason spoke at all the Masses. He was cordial from the pulpit, even cracking a little joke, complimented Clem's work as pastor, and expressed his gratitude to Alain for caring for the parish over the last five months. The manner in which he recognized Clem's and Alain's work could only be considered perfunctory; the real message of his talk was: Now that these men have laid some groundwork he would get down to making some needed substantial changes. That message did not go down well with the congregation, who glanced at one another with meaningful consternation. After the Masses he received the welcome normal when greeting a new pastor, but several people at each Mass stopped to praise the work of Msgr. Donnelly and express their desire that the parish continue on the course he had set. The suggestion that the parish maintain the status quo was received with a noncommittal smirk, and the praise of his predecessor with a blank stare.

After the last Mass, Jason returned to his rooms in the rectory, abruptly dismissing Alain's invitation to lunch, and collapsed in his arm chair. He stared glumly at the ceiling, wondering if he had made a mistake in asking for the parish; perhaps he had underestimated Clem's enduring influence. He was depressed that the parishioners failed to recognize that his arrival would surely signal a better day for all. It never dawned on him that his words to the people were less than inspired and inspiring. Perhaps it would take a month or two for them to recognize the quality of the gift the bishop had given them.

Several months passed and the general reluctance of the parish to change anything only heightened, while their reverence for Msgr. Donnelly fell only a little short of calling for his canonization. Jason thought that if he heard Clem's name or wisdom referred to once more he would implode. The parish council seemed to be composed of no one but ardent Donnellyites who formed a Greek chorus chanting Clem's praises.

Some say, "When all else fails, fall to your knees and pray," and pray is exactly what Jason did. He prayed that God would allow him to serve the parish and lead it according to His will, rather than his own. Perhaps God had gotten what he wanted from Jason because within the next six months, people began to warm up to Jason and to accept him as their pastor. While they would always remember Clem with fondness and respect, they mentioned him less and became open to the idea that some of the changes Jason mentioned might actually benefit the parish. The parish secretary told him that the number of families leaving the parish, which had been considerable during Jason's first few months, was now exceeded by those joining. Newly elected parish council members did not feel unfaithful to Clem by supporting changes, as had their predecessors. It was new day for the parish and for Jason.

If Jason had only stayed on his knees and kept his sharp tongue in check, all would have been copacetic, but his old ways returned and he began to sharpen his tongue on his parishioners. He developed distinct tastes as to whom he liked and whom he did not, almost always determined by those who danced to his tune and those who did not. He devised pet names for those he did not care for and used them freely with his associate, the parish staff, and even his favored parishioners.

It was just a matter of time until the loquacious lady found that he referred to her as La Boca Grande; the stern-looking couple was not delighted to have been named the Munsters; and the obese parish council president failed to be amused when he learned that the pastor's nickname for him was the Elephant Man. All were hurt that their own pastor was making fun of them, particularly since they had gone to some length to make certain he was well-received in the parish. When they confronted him, rather than being angry with himself he became angry at his accusers and felt betrayed by whoever had told them they were the constant butt of his sardonic mind and tongue. He actually cast himself in the role of a martyr and became paranoid that the parish was "out to get him." His homilies became strange, defensive, and condemnatory, provoking some parishioners to voice concern about Jason's mental health.

Word of this discontent reached Msgr. Gregory Owens, who was distressed that the accomplishments of his friend Clem were being undermined and that his brother priest Jason might be having troubles. Greg invited Jason to lunch so that he might see if he could be of any help. As Jason was aware that Clem and Greg had been close, he was initially guarded in his comments to Greg, and the conversation was awkward.

"Jason, I want you to know that I've asked you out because I've heard you may be under some stress. I once lived under Clem's shadow and had some difficulty personally in accepting that. It created distance between me and this priest who would never have harmed me in any way. I let jealousy and my personal ambitions create a wall between myself and my best friend for decades. From some things I've heard, I think it's possible that you may be dealing with the same problem in working under the shadow of Clem's memory."

"Exactly what have you heard, from whom, and what do you think gives you the right to interfere with me or my parish?"

"Look, Jason, I'm not here to hurt you or confront you or accuse you of anything. I'm here out of love for a brother priest, period. I don't want you or your parish to suffer. I do not wish to interfere. Certainly you know that it would have been easier for me to disregard what you probably already know is a problem and let you dangle in the wind. I did not think that was the honorable thing to do, nor what Christ would want me to do.

"As to what I've heard, I've heard that your sermons show you are under considerable pressure, that you are defensive, perhaps even a little paranoid, and that you are lacking in charity for those in your parish who you feel are not supportive. As to who told me about these problems, if you find any truth in what they say, would that be important?"

Jason took a long sip of his iced tea while considering his options. Was he to leave the restaurant abruptly, hurl insults at Greg, defend himself righteously, or was it possible that Greg really was trying to help him? He decided to give Greg the benefit of the doubt and presume that his intentions really were honorable, even kind. "I . . . I'm sorry. I haven't been sleeping much lately, and the parish is a greater challenge than I had anticipated. I've got to admit that the ghost of Msgr. Donnelly parades around the parish more actively than that of Hamlet's father flitting about Elsinore. I've been really uptight and almost anything a person says or does that relates to the good monsignor sets me off. It has been an unfortunate family trait that we tend to verbally attack when cornered. You just felt a bit of it yourself. Again, I'm sorry."

"You know that Clem and I were very close at the end of his life. We had been like brothers when we were young. There were a lot of wasted years when we could have shared in one another's lives if I had not been such a dope. It was my entire fault, not his. I know that Clem would have tried to help you if he were alive. Maybe I can make up for some of my mistakes by giving you the help that he would have. Will you let me do that?"

Jason knew that the priest sitting across from him had humbly made himself vulnerable out of sheer kindness and generosity. He'd been ordained over twenty-five years longer than he had, had nothing to gain personally, and was simply trying to help him. What did he have to lose by trusting Greg? "You are a very kind man, Monsignor. If you can help, I'd be eternally grateful."

"My name is Greg; let's drop the 'Monsignor.'"

Throughout his life, Jason would always have to battle temptations to use his superior intelligence for belittling those whom he did not care for, but from the day of his luncheon with Greg, his life as a priest took a positive turn. He recognized in Greg the possibility of personal change and the love of a brother priest. Greg became not only his advisor but also his spiritual director, who taught him to love Jesus in the people he served . . . and even in himself.

CHAPTER SEVENTEEN

PADRE JUAN ROMERO-MARTINEZ

Beginning in the 1990s, large numbers of Mexicans came across the border into the United States both legally and illegally to find jobs and better the lives of their families. At first they found work in the fields, cleaning houses and performing other menial labor; but as time passed, large corporations found the immigrants to be industrious workers and employed them in factories, merchandising, and even, finally, administration. As the large majority of the immigrants were Catholic, particularly the dioceses located in the southern part of the United States found that they had insufficient clergy to minister to their growing Hispanic congregation, particularly clergy who were fluent in Spanish. Bishops scurried to find ways to educate their native clergy in the Spanish language and to seek priests from Mexico and South America who were willing to minister in the United States.

Father James Chudy's bishop became aware of the extraordinary job that he was doing among the Latino community and of his facility with Spanish. James was young and energetic, and the bishop saw him as a natural leader. Although he had only been ordained a few years, James was asked by the bishop to travel with him to visit several bishops in Mexico, asking them to provide his diocese with as many as ten Mexican priests. The bishop would provide the authority while Father Chudy would provide the charm and hurdle possible language barriers. The Mexican bishops were cordial but explained to the bishop and Father Chudy that they also had a priest shortage and were, sadly, unable to provide for the needs of the United States.

After James and his bishop had made their third unsuccessful plea, the archbishop of Chihuahua invited them to stay at his home and enjoy dinner with him and his young priest secretary.   James had not been aware that a good friend of his in the seminary at Santa Fe, New Mexico, had been named the archbishop's secretary.   During the meal, the secretary listened closely to James as he told of the Mexican Catholics leaving the faith and joining evangelical churches due to the lack of priests to care for their needs.   It was easy to see the empathy in his face as he listened; he asked question after question about the living conditions of the Mexicans, how they were treated by the Americans, and the reason for their leaving the Catholic Church.   James was close to tears as he told of stories of the sheep that had no shepherd and had strayed.

Juan Romero-Martinez was born in Chihuahua, Mexico, in 1970, to Jose Romero and Maria Martinez.   He was the third boy in a family of ten children.   Jose had a ranch in the Rio Grande Valley where he raised cattle and horses.   Maria ran a well-ordered ranch home, cooked for the caballeros that worked for Jose, and reared her children.   Jose rarely went to church, but Maria was a daily communicant and insisted that all her children attend Mass with her each Sunday.

All the children attended school faithfully through high school.   After school the boys would help on the ranch, and the girls would help Maria with the cooking.   By the time of his First Communion, Maria noticed that her son Juan seemed to have a special love for the Church.   Each day she offered her rosary to Our Lady of Guadalupe that Juan would be given a vocation to the priesthood.

Our Lady did not disappoint her namesake; when Juan graduated from high school, he was accepted by the archbishop as a seminarian and sent to the seminary in

Santa Fe, New Mexico. Jose was not particularly pleased with his son's decision, but he knew better than to argue with Maria, who insisted it was work of the Blessed Mother. Juan's teachers in the seminary, who noted that he possessed not only an exceptional spiritual life but also an excellent mind, praised him highly to the archbishop when it was time for his ordination to the priesthood. When the appointments were made at the reception following the ordination, Father Juan learned to his surprise that he was to become the secretary to the archbishop, a highly-prized position in the diocese. It was neither what he expected nor wanted.

For the next two years, Juan assisted the archbishop, arranging his schedule, making his appointments, doing his clerical work, acting as his master of ceremonies, being a buffer to fend off unwanted calls and troublesome people (both clergy and laity), and being his chauffeur.

Juan slept little following the dinner with Father Chudy and his bishop. He was not pleased with his position as the archbishop's secretary and yearned to minister directly to the people. He prayed throughout the night to the Holy Spirit for the words to say to the archbishop to accomplish what he felt was God's Will. After celebrating Mass, he knocked timidly at the archbishop's office door and entered as he did each morning.

"Your Excellency, I have a personal matter that I must ask you about."

"Juan, do you not think that after being with you every day for the last two years I don't know what is on your mind? Your questions last evening betrayed your personal interest. You have come to ask me to let you return with Father Chudy and his bishop to minister in the United States, and the answer is "NO!""

"But, Archbishop, those are OUR people, YOUR people who are leaving the Church because they have no shepherd to care for them. Please . . . ."

"You are the brightest and most promising young priest in the archdiocese, and you expect me to let you go? I depend upon you. You are my right hand. The work of the archdiocese would suffer without you now and in the years that lie ahead of us. Frankly, here you have a place of power and prestige, and you live with me in the archbishop's residence. They will place you in some insignificant little town to take care of migrant farmers. Is that what you want?"

"Nazareth was also an insignificant little town filled with poor people, but it was there Jesus chose to be born and begin his ministry. I was not ordained for power and prestige; you ordained me as a priest to serve the people. Won't you let me do that? What I do for you here could be done just as well or better by one of the laity. Please do not stop me from ministering to our people as the priest you ordained me to be."

"Juan, I knew I would lose this argument when I heard your tentative knock on my door. When I saw the hunger in your eyes last evening as Father Chudy described the needs of our people, I anticipated this visit and your request. I even thought of the arguments you might give me to obtain my permission and, for the life of me, I could not form an adequate rebuttal. But I did think that I would test your metal and the firmness of your intent by providing some minimal resistance; I would have been deeply disappointed in you if you had not pressed your request. Well done.

"We belong to a universal Church, and we must care for the needs of our people regardless of where they may be. It is also imperative that we do not turn our backs on those who beg of us. You will report back to me each year to determine the plausibility of your continued ministry in the United States. I will loan you to their diocese for five years, and at the end of that time, you will return to Chihuahua. You will find this in your letter of appointment, which you may obtain from my new secretary Senora Montez, located in your former office."

"You mean, Archbishop, you had all this planned, a secretary already hired, the letter of appointment already written, and intended to let me go all the time?"

The archbishop took a long draw on his cigar. "Don't look so surprised, Padre Juan. You've never been a match for me. I may be old, but I'm not stupid." He smiled and winked. "God bless you. Go and pack."

Due to the time that Juan had spent in the seminary at Santa Fe, New Mexico, his arrival in the United States did not pose a culture shock for him. Within a few weeks, he had been assigned to a small parish with a mission. He was the first priest from Mexico to be assigned a pastorate in the diocese. Due to his excellent command of English as well as Spanish, he was well received by both the Anglo and Spanish members of his congregation.

His reception in his mission, however, was a bit different. The mission was centered in a large agricultural area, and the majority of the flock were Mexican migrant laborers who were ecstatic to receive one of their own as their priest. The same could not be said of Julius Broussard, the major contributor of the parish and the owner of a massive farm where most of the migrants were employed. Julius paid the laborers considerably less than the going wage and housed them in rundown shacks without running water. He did not welcome the arrival of an intelligent Mexican priest, who might well upset the status quo, an arrangement which had enabled him to reap a handsome income from his crops when harvested by migrants whom he paid slave wages. Julius had written a strong letter to the bishop, detailing his contributions to the parish and diocese over the decades and objecting to the assignment of Father Juan as someone who would cause trouble; the letter went unanswered, further infuriating Julius.

Father Juan's first homily primarily introduced himself to the congregation but also touched on the dignity of every individual as the beloved of God. He sensed that the workers needed to have their spirits and self-respect raised. Throughout the homily, Julius fidgeted and his face grew increasingly red. His wife Naomi tried to calm her husband by patting him on the thigh, but he swatted her hand away as he would a pesky fly. Father Juan was startled when a man received communion from him with an openly angry stare, which he realized was in all likelihood a prelude to something unpleasant.

After Mass, the migrants greeted Juan with enthusiasm and joy, expressing their gratitude for his presence and asking him for his blessing. Julius hung back until the last worker had left. "Padre, I'm Julius Broussard. My family built this mission church. We own all the land around it as far as you can see. Almost all of the people at Mass this morning work either for me or one of my family. They have food on their tables and clothes on their backs because of me. I don't want you upsettin' the apple cart while you're here. Do you understand me, Padre?"

Juan had been ordained for just a little over two years and was only 27 years old, but he was not intimidated; and his face was now becoming a bit red. "Mr. Broussard, I also come from a family with a great deal of land. My father hires men to help with the cattle and the horses. Those men are also our friends and our brothers in Christ. They eat at our family table and are all paid just wages to provide for their families. I assume that is also your custom."

"Look here, you smart-ass little tamale—if you cause me any trouble or rile up my workers by puttin' fancy ideas in their dumb heads, I'll send you back to taco land in a box, and you can tell your damn bishop that too. I'll close this church and burn it down before I let you put ideas in these people's heads. I own the county and every lawman in it, so tow the line." With that Julius grabbed the hand of his bewildered wife, yanked her down the sidewalk, and shoved her into his Cadillac.

Father Juan's knees were so weak that he could hardly make it back to the sanctuary. And he was angry, angry to the point of tears. Was this what he had left his diocese, his family, and his country for? To be threatened and demeaned by this nut? He had come to minister to the flock in the name of Jesus, not to begin a Mexican-American War. He had never looked into the face of prejudice and greed before, and it was scary.

That afternoon he called Father Chudy and asked if he could meet with him. The next morning James Chudy greeted his shaken brother priest with warmth and understanding. When he heard Juan's story of his experience with Julius Broussard, he felt shame that Juan should have been treated in such a fashion by a Catholic in his diocese. James knew that prejudice existed, but he had never had to deal with it. He was filled with justifiable anger and assured Father Juan that he would take care of the problem, although he had absolutely no idea what he would do.

The next morning James felt both fear and anger as he drove up the tree-lined driveway to the Broussard mansion. He still had no idea what he would say or do, but knew he had to confront Julius Broussard. The home was built to intimidate; it was an imposing structure looking much like Tara in *Gone with the Wind*. He almost expected Hattie McDaniel to open the front door. Instead, Naomi opened the door, looking perplexed to see this young, thin priest whom she had never known.

"Yes, Father, what can I do for you?"

"Mrs. Broussard, I need to see your husband."

"He's in his office. May I tell him your name and the nature of your business?" She flushed when he told her that he needed to discuss her husband's conversation on Sunday with Father Juan. Without comment, Naomi showed James to the lion's den where they found Julius examining the accounts of enterprises. She introduced James and quickly left the room. Julius did not rise from his chair nor offer one to James.

"I presume that you have come here to tell me what a terrible Catholic I have been by speaking to that new Mexicali priest in such a harsh manner. Save your breath. As long as that man we call a bishop continues to send his trouble-making imports here as pastor, I'll do exactly as I please. You can tell your boss that. You might also mention that he will not get one more dollar from me or my family for this mission or any of his diocesan projects until he rectifies this situation; perhaps that will get his attention since he does not deign to answer my letters or return my phone calls."

James felt like a school boy being scolded by his teacher. He lowered his head and shifted his weight from one foot to another as he carefully chose the words he would use to reply to Julius.

"I spoke with my boss, as you refer to our bishop, about the incident on Sunday this morning. He asked that I come here and deliver a personal message to you. He took great effort to obtain Father Juan from the Archdiocese of Chihuahua, where he held a prestigious position as personal secretary to the archbishop. He did this so that the Mexicans that work for you as well as others could be properly cared for as Catholics. The bishop is very pleased and honored to have Father Juan working for our diocese.

"The bishop would be happy for you to voice any specific problems that Father has caused. Should there be no such problems, he wishes to remind you that prejudice is a sin and disrespect to a priest of God is not something he takes lightly. Should you stand in the way of Father Juan's ministering to his people, as well as to you and your family, he is prepared to excommunicate you."

Julius was aghast that this young priest would dare threaten him and was surprised at the firmness with which he delivered the bishop's message. "Get the hell out of my home. I don't need to be lectured by you or your boss."

"I'll be most happy to leave this house built on the sweat of those whom you would deny the spiritual guidance of their pastor. But, first, I have a little something of my own to say to you. I have served the good people who have made your lifestyle possible. I know enough people in the diocese to get them all jobs right away, jobs that will pay them a living wage. They trust me. If you do not apologize to Father Juan and support his mission, I will see that no Mexican laborer works for you now or ever. I believe it is about your harvest time; I do hope you and your wife have strong backs.

"Just try me. And what a shame it would be if the immigration people were to learn that you have been hiring illegals. I wonder how they might get that word. Oh, I think I failed to mention that the president of my parish council is the regional head of the Immigration and Naturalization Service."

"That's blackmail!"

"Here is my card. You have twenty-four hours to call me with your decision. Have a blessed day." With that he turned and left Julius, still seated, but with an astonished look on his face.

Naomi was waiting in the hall and showed James to the front door. She followed him onto the porch where she grasped the sleeve of his clergy shirt and looked into his eyes with a strange smile. "Congratulations, young man. Finally someone put that bastard in his place. Amen and Alleluia!"

As James drove down the shady lane leaving the Broussard home, he glanced in his rear view mirror to see Naomi smiling broadly and waving good-bye.

When Father Juan had finished Mass the next morning, he walked into his rectory to find that the secretary had seated Julius and Naomi Broussard in his office. His stomach became weak, as he expected another deluge of prejudice and threats. The Broussards rose from their chairs and extended their hands. While Julius' face was glum, there was no sign of anger or hostility.

Julius had spent most of the day after James left checking Father Juan's background. He was surprised at the results of his inquiries. He had learned that Juan's father was one of the wealthiest ranchers in the Mexican Rio Grande Valley, having introduced Santa Gertrudis cattle from the King Ranch in Texas to the area and owning the largest herd in Mexico. He was impressed to find that both Juan's mother and father were well-connected politically, and that their families were highly respected throughout the state of Chihuahua. The initial impression that Julius had held of Juan as being unimportant and having no influence was obviously mistaken; Julius had insulted a man not only of the cloth (a matter of little importance to him) but also of a wealthy and well-connected family (a potential mistake as there were possibilities of his profiting from a pleasant relationship with such a family).

After they were all seated, Julius handed a check to Father Juan for $5,000. "I wanted you to have this to help with your work in our mission. Use it in whatever way you see fit."

"And . . . ?" Naomi coached.

"And . . . I'm sorry for the things I said Sunday after Mass."

Naomi opened her purse, smiled benignly at Julius and took out another check. "Father, I wish to match the gift my husband made. I would like you to send this check to your archbishop in gratitude for sending you to minister in our diocese."

Julius' eyes widened at Naomi's little surprise burst of generosity which she had neglected to mention to him. He knew there was nothing he could do; his rash words on Sunday had cost him his pride and $10,000. He had no idea that Naomi could possibly have anything more to say, but she did.

"Father Juan, Julius and I were talking yesterday about how deeply touched we were by your homily about the dignity of each person. We got to thinking that it was high time we recognized that in the wages we pay. We would like to sit down with you and Father James Chudy and a few of the workers to negotiate a new pay scale that will better recognize their dignity and the enormous help they have been to us throughout the years." Naomi did not look at Julius as she made her proposal, but she knew that he must be on the verge of blowing his top. She didn't care; at last, after all those years of marriage, she had him where she wanted him. "Just give us a ring when you can arrange the meeting. We have to be going now and thank you for your time, Father." This time it was Naomi who led a bewildered spouse to their Cadillac and slammed the door behind him.

Father Juan didn't understand exactly what had changed Julius' attitude so abruptly. He knew that the mild mannered Father Chudy had paid the Broussards a visit but could not imagine anyone as kind and gentle as James being able to change Julius' mind. The wage meeting was held, and the laborers' salaries AND benefits were increased dramatically. All the Hispanics thought that both Father James and Father Juan were living saints who performed miracles, even changing Julius Broussard.

The bishop became increasingly aware of the impact the Latinos were having upon the Church. He was impressed by the vitality of their faith, the beauty of their devotion to the values of family life, their humility, and their love for the Blessed Mother. He looked forward to his visits with Father Juan and noticed how deeply he was loved and revered by his flock. He sought Juan's guidance in how best to minister to his growing Latino congregation and was amazed by his enthusiasm, inventiveness, and intelligence.

Juan saw a need for Latino permanent deacons to minister to their people and convinced the bishop to begin a formation class to that end. It was to last for four years and the bishop asked Juan to lead the program. Juan traveled throughout the diocese speaking in churches wherever the Latino population had settled. Within a few months he had gathered forty-three applicants for the diaconate class, thirty-five of whom the bishop accepted as candidates for the permanent diaconate. Juan taught some the classes himself and enlisted other teachers from both his old seminary in Santa Fe, New Mexico, and his home in Chihuahua.

When the diaconate candidates returned to their parishes throughout the diocese after their monthly weekend formation classes, they spread the word of this dynamic young priest from Chihuahua who was doing so much for the Church. As his fame spread, so did the requests for his time.

The bishop became aware of Juan's increasing popularity and his ability to get things done in the Latino community. He knew Juan and James Chudy were close friends and that their work often found them cooperating in projects with considerable success. He asked them to form a diocesan council to address justice issues for minorities within the Church. Both the young priests loved the project and set about forming a board comprised of a mixture of Latinos, Blacks, Anglos, and Asians.

One the members Juan asked to serve on the committee was Naomi Broussard, who had become an outspoken crusader for social justice for the Latino community. Once she had established an equitable pay scale on her own farm, it was clear that she had a flair for negotiation. Ever since she led a coup against her husband Julius, she seemed to have a taste for dethroning rulers great and small. Poor Julius had lost heart in attempting to control everything and everybody and seemed quite content to drive Naomi to her next meeting.

The five years that Juan had been allotted by his archbishop came to an end in the same month that his diaconate class was ordained. The bishop went with his miter in hand to Chihuahua to plead with the archbishop to extend Juan's stay; he even pressed his luck by asking the archbishop if he had any additional priests who might serve in the States. His requests tried even the warm Mexican hospitality of the archbishop, who told him that he would pray about the matter during the night and let him know after breakfast.

After they had celebrated Mass together in the archbishop's chapel, the bishop and archbishop enjoyed a large breakfast of local fruit, chorizo and eggs, and tortillas. Finally the archbishop lit his signature cigar and fingered the pectoral cross that lay on his chest. "First we had to teach your country and your infamous Davy Crockett a little lesson at the Alamo; then you expelled us from our lands and drove us down beneath the border that now separates our two great countries. Stealing California from us was certainly not your country's finest hour. Then more recently some of our brightest and most talented young people began to leave our own country to seek their fortunes in yours. As if you had not done enough, taken enough from us, you then stole my own secretary – and now you won't give him back. And now you have the cajones to ask me for more priests, which you will also not want to give back." The bishop felt the chorizo churn within his stomach as he watched the smoke curl from the archbishop's foul-smelling cigar. But then he saw the slightest tinge of a smile beginning to make its way across the archbishop's face and a twinkle beginning in his dark eyes. Before he knew it, the bishop was listening to archbishop chortle in totally uninhibited laughter.

"Oh, my dear brother bishop, you padres in the North have so little sense of joy and humor. We archbishops must have our fun when we can. Please forgive me . . . as I assume you forgive me for the Alamo." And then he howled in laughter again. "Oh, yes, you may have Juan for two more years but then he comes back to me if I have to lead a storm of caballeros across that joke you call a border to retrieve him. And, yes, once you have returned what you borrowed, you may have another . . . in fact, take two; they're small." The archbishop laughed uproariously at his last jest, one that he would proudly tell his priests repeatedly throughout the years to come.

During the next year Juan and James worked hand in hand forming the Body of Christ within the diocese, fusing the diverse talents of immigrants and native born Americans into one loving, compassionate Church. But Juan noticed that his brother priest was losing weight and often had to stop, marshal his strength, and almost fight for breath. He asked James repeatedly if he were sick, only to be rebuffed with a jest or noncommittal response.

Finally, after the last person had left a long meeting of the social justice committee, Juan noticed that James was struggling to rise from his chair. Juan told him to sit and that he would get help. James refused and told Juan to sit next to him. "Juan, mi amigo, I'm dying. You've suspected it for a long time. I've kept it a secret; only the bishop and my mother are aware of what is happening to me. I feel that I have a very short time before I get to see Jesus and His Blessed Mother. They have been so good to me all my life; now they will welcome me to heaven."

Tears formed in Juan's eyes, and James obviously found it difficult to garner enough strength to talk; but he wasn't finished. "NO, NO! You must not grieve. You have been such a joy to me these past six years; it has been like walking beside Jesus. The greatest thing that happened to me in my priesthood was working with you. I will continue on as long as God gives me the strength. If you tell anyone of tonight, I will return on Dia de los Muertos and haunt you." Juan kissed the priestly hand of his friend and helped him to his car.

The next morning Juan received a call as he was finishing his breakfast. The bishop told him that James had collapsed at Mass and had been taken to the hospital. He was not expected to live long. Juan spread the news among the Latino community and told them to gather outside the hospital to pray for the priest who had loved them and led them from the beginning. He met them there and led them in prayer throughout the day until Msgr. Donnelly came to tell them that Padre James was in heaven. It was the hardest moment of Juan's life.

That night when Juan's head hit the pillow, he was praying for James–or maybe to James, he wasn't sure. But he was sure that he had not one ounce of energy left; he was totally spent. He drifted to sleep, to be awakened ten minutes later by the phone. It was Naomi Broussard; Julius was dying. "He's asking for you, Father Juan. Please come." In a daze, hurting emotionally, exhausted, he found his clothes, the oils, the ritual, and finally the Eucharist. He arrived at the Broussard mansion, where Naomi waited at the front door. She led him to Julius' bed, where he lay still conscious. Juan asked Naomi to leave the room so that he could hear Julius' confession. He pulled a chair beside the bed, put on his stole, sat down, and bent close to Julius so that he would not have to strain to speak.

"Father, will God forgive me for what I said to you when we first met? Will He forgive me for the hurt I've caused your people all those years? Will He forgive me for the way I treated Naomi?"

"Julius, Jesus died so that you can be forgiven all your sins. You have only to relax with faith in his love, knowing that all He wants of you is a humble and contrite heart."

Juan helped Julius make a thorough and humble confession, gave him absolution, invited Naomi and the rest of the family back into the bedroom, and administered the Sacrament of the Sick, the Eucharist, and the apostolic blessing. He knelt by Julius' bed and led the family in the rosary. He was still there when Julius died a little after midnight. God in His infinite mercy had so completely healed Juan's heart of the hurt that Julius had once inflicted upon him that he felt strangely moved at his death.

As Naomi showed Juan to the door, she told him the details of Father Chudy's visit to Julius six years earlier and how his words had changed Julius' life and their marriage. She marveled that God had seen fit to take them both within a few hours of one another and wondered if they could be rejoicing together in God's love at that very moment in heaven.

Juan continued his ministry for his remaining year in the diocese. He had mixed feelings about returning to Mexico. He was happy to return to his family, his country, and his brother priests, but sad to leave the people that he loved so deeply. His leaving was not as difficult as it would have been if James had continued to live; things had never really been the same for Juan after the death of his dear friend.

The archbishop was true to his word. He knew that the work that Juan had begun needed to continue and sent two priests from Chihuahua to take his place. They were small in neither heart nor stature.

CHAPTER EIGHTEEN
FATHER EUGENE TERRELL

Father Gene's brothers had difficulty in keeping their emotions in check as they heard the bishop give his eulogy. Gene had been the baby of the family, but they had all looked up to him and admired his decision to become a priest. Memories of their early family life kept coming to their minds and interrupting their ability to concentrate on the bishop's words.

Their dad, Phil, had been a truck driver and was often absent from their home as he drove on long hauls across the country. Their mom, Rose, was both strict and loving. She worked in the school cafeteria at Saint Rita's and was loved by all the children for her warm personality and her hot yeast rolls. Phil and Rose were strong Catholics and had five sons in rapid succession following their wedding. Finances were always tight, but the home was a happy one, filled with the rough-housing and laughter of normal boys.

The boys loved sports and their backyard became the neighborhood arena for football, baseball, and basketball. Each of the four elder boys joined the school teams beginning in the sixth grade, and as the years progressed the bookshelves in the living room were crowded with their sports trophies.

When the fifth son was born in the sixth year of their marriage, Phil was certain that he would be able to have his own basketball team. He was wrong. Whatever attempts the older brothers might make to draw him in, Eugene had showed absolutely no interest in anything that involved a ball of any shape, size, or color. Even in his crib when they would roll a ball to him expecting some response, he would just look at them with a questioning gaze. As a toddler, he had an amazing lack of hand-eye coordination. Throughout his grade school years, when he was forced into team sports, he was invariably the absolute last child to be chosen by the team captain who had lost the toss. By his high school years, parents, brothers, friends, and even usually persistent physical education teachers had all abandoned the notion that they could ever convince Eugene that any form of sports was anything but a huge waste of his time.

Eugene did enjoy reading; in fact, he would read when walking to and from school (falling on uneven sidewalks or stepping into dog dirt or having near collisions with cars driven by angered motorists only made him lose his place for a moment or two). While reading, he mechanically ate his school lunch, giving his older brothers and mischievous friends the opportunity to place unappetizing items in his already unappealing lunch—in addition to stealing Rose's hot yeast roll. While forced to attend his brothers' endless school games (although it was difficult with all those fans yelling and jumping up and down around him) and even during Father's homily at Mass (until Rose hit him on the back of his head with a missalette), he read.

With four older brothers, a working mother, an often absent father, and limited family finances, Eugene's social life even in high school was largely limited to his family. All the boys were expected to get jobs to pay for their Catholic school tuition and books, their clothes, and spending money. It was not only a natural fit for Eugene to work in the public library, but that soon became the best part of his day. He worked as hard and fast as he could so that he might also have time to peruse one book after another. By the time he was in the eleventh grade, library patrons depended upon him for both information and suggestions for their reading.

Divine providence had to have something to do with Eugene's being assigned to Father Joseph Mulalley's English class. It took Father Joe less than a week to discover that Rose Terrell's fifth son Eugene actually had read extensively and even comprehended what he read. Having taught Eugene's older brothers with limited success, he was amazed to unearth this gem from the Terrell mine which he had before always found devoid of anything but athletic equipment.

Eugene relished finally finding a teacher who had something important to say and who recognized that he had a mind and soul hungry for nourishment. Father Joe made Shakespeare come alive. Gene had never known anyone who was obviously as excited by skillfully written words as he was. He was mesmerized by Joe's elegance and good breeding. Joe interjected the teachings of Jesus Christ into the writings of the great English authors and by doing so gave Gene a deep appreciation for both. Gene was feeling the excitement that his brothers had experienced on the football field, the baseball diamond, and the basketball court. At last he felt the surge of adrenalin that came with belonging and excelling.

None of Gene's brothers had attended college after high school. Each got a job and learned a trade and was happy in his occupation. Gene wanted desperately to continue his education beyond high school but knew that it was not what the men in his family did and that it was unlikely that he could afford to go to the college. As he was talking with Father Joe after class one afternoon, Joe asked him about his future plans.

Gene told him of his situation and said he would probably try to get a permanent job at the library.

In early April, Gene received a letter from the dean of admissions of the state university informing him that an anonymous donor had paid his full tuition, including room, board, and books for four years. Gene knew that there was only one person who both cared enough about him and had the means to make this happen. The next day he stayed after class to speak with Father Joe.

"I don't know how to thank you, Father. It's a dream that I never thought could come true."

"Gene, I'm a priest and, therefore, will never have my own children. The most I can hope for is meeting a fine young man like you to help along the way. You are worth helping; you have both a beautiful mind and heart. Someday you will find how God wants you to use those gifts. I have only one stipulation attached to the gift, that you pray to God every day that He gives you that insight. Is it a deal?"

"Deal! Is it okay if I also pray that I become like you?"

"Set your aim higher. Now, hurry along or you'll be late for your job at the library."

Eugene aced college. He saw his presence there as a gift from God, and he was not about to let Father Joe down. In fact, he decided that he did want to be just like Father Joe: he wanted to be a priest. He attended the seminary and was ordained in 1998. By then Father Joe had taught at the Catholic high school for ten years while working as an associate priest in parishes and was now ready to become a full time pastor. He recommended that the newly ordained Father Eugene take his place teaching English.

Eugene could not have been more pleased than to be assigned to follow his mentor's example and found himself standing in front of a classroom only three months after his ordination. He was to find that his students were no more interested in fine literature than his own brothers had been. There was that occasional student who made teaching exciting, when Gene could see a light of recognition suddenly ignite in the eyes and know that somehow the mind of the author had connected with the mind of the student.

Gene yearned to see that same light of recognition appear in the eyes of the congregation when he celebrated Mass and gave a homily. He prepared his homilies carefully and was genuinely concerned when he saw people who were obviously in another world, saying their rosaries, admiring children in the congregation, or taking a little nap. He wanted so much to connect the mind of Jesus Christ with those of the parishioners. Why could they not comprehend how important the word of God was for them? There appeared to Eugene to be little real hunger in the hearts of average Catholics to really know Jesus better or to grow in their faith.

The respect that Gene had for Joe Mulalley only grew. Joe took an older brother's interest in Gene and was eager to see him do well in the priesthood. He was also eager to share with Gene some of the worldly advantages that his parents had not been equipped either financially or educationally to give him. Gene was soon to learn that Joe's paying for his higher education was only the tip of the iceberg of his generosity. As Gene had never had much materially, he was awed when Joe bought him expensive clothes and art work, introduced him to opera and the theatre, invited him to dine at the finest gourmet restaurants in town, and took him on short but elegant vacations. Because he held Joe in such high esteem as a priest, educator, and friend, Gene became used to all these kindnesses almost as one becomes accustomed to the generosity of God.

What Gene did not see in himself is that he had begun to pattern his own life and priesthood upon Joe's rather than Christ's. He was becoming too comfortable with "the good life." He began to pull away from his own family, subconsciously viewing his parents as uncultured, uneducated, and unrefined. He rarely answered his brothers' calls to come to visit their families, as he felt he had outgrown their manner of living and disdained still another evening of noisy ill-mannered children, meatloaf and mashed potato dinners, followed by "watching the game" on television.

Ivory towers are rarely built quickly or even intentionally, but Gene was well on his way to becoming a tenant. He had largely dismissed the parishioners where he served as apathetic towards the faith, his parents and brothers as past history which he did not intend to revisit, and his students as troglodytes unworthy of the pearls he spread before them. He had imitated the externals of Joe without perceiving his underlying love of God and people—the motivation for Joe's phenomenal generosity.

Gene tried desperately to ape Joe's refined and expensive tastes. He became a regular at every place that sold works of art and decorated the associate's quarters elaborately in stark contrast to the simplicity of the remainder of the rectory. His paycheck was always spent shortly after he received it. Father Christian Mangan was becoming increasingly concerned about Gene and sensed that his priesthood was going in the wrong direction; he tried to speak with him about it but was rebuffed. Some of the less charitable priests simply made fun of Gene and began to speak of him as "Little

Monsignor Lord Fauntleroy." Sensing the attitude of his brother priests, he became increasingly distant even from them. It seemed to him that only Joe appreciated him and understood who he really was.

Joe had heard that his former student, now Father Gene, was becoming withdrawn and the butt of cruel jokes by his brother priests. He knew a former classmate in New York City who had a good reputation for turning around young priests who were experiencing trouble acclimating to priesthood. He phoned Gene and told him he had arranged a short vacation for him to New York where he was to stay with a priest friend of his stationed in the lower part of the city. Gene would never have denied Joe anything he asked, and, as he had never seen NYC before, he was eager to accept what he thought was a short vacation.

Joe's friend had been assigned to a rather poor parish and the accommodations there were clean but simple. Within a couple of days, Gene had opened up to this priest to the extent that Gene was beginning to see the false steps he was making in his priesthood and personal life. After he had concelebrated Mass on Wednesday morning, Gene decided to walk around the area and soak in a little of the Big Apple. It was a beautiful morning, and Gene was feeling really good about himself and the priesthood. He was oblivious to his surroundings and the people walking hurriedly past him on their way to work. Someone bumped against him, and he fell to the sidewalk. He became aware that the people were now running and screaming. He grabbed the arm of a young man and asked what was happening.

"Don't you know, Father? Planes have hit the World Trade Center, and it's burning. The smoke is terrific down there. Hurry, run; God knows what will happen." With that he pulled free of Gene's grasp and continued to run away.

Whatever may have been his faults, Gene knew what he must do as a priest. He started running against the crowd. The image came to him that he was at last like his older brothers running skillfully against the opposition's tackles to make a touchdown. As he came nearer the scene, he became increasingly afraid of what he might do and how he might act, whether he would have the courage and wisdom to do the right thing. He prayed to the Holy Spirit to supply the virtues he would need. He was within two blocks. The air was filled with dust and smoke. People's cries surrounded him. The police attempted to stop him until they saw his collar and motioned him on. There were people dying all around, some bodies burned, some gasping for air, some in intense pain. Gene knelt over one after another, gave them absolution, prayed with them, and told them of God's love amid all the horrendous tragedy.

It is doubtful that in all the turmoil, the blinding dust and smoke, the cacophony of cries and sirens, his desire to bring Jesus to still more of the suffering and dying, that Father Gene ever knew the first tower was collapsing.

It took some weeks to determine that Gene had been a heroic priest at one of the greatest tragedies the United States had ever known. Information was pieced together from the young man Gene had stopped on the street, the policemen who had seen the young priest, and others who had escaped alive to tell of how Gene had ministered to them and others.

Now the bishop was ending his eulogy and the brothers no longer even attempted to restrain their tears for their strange little brother whom they loved but never understood. All they knew is that they had a brother who was a priest and a hero, and that they had loved and lost him.

CHAPTER NINETEEN

FATHER PATRICK GRAY

He had it all. It seemed that God had outdone himself in generosity when he formed Patrick in the womb: smart, handsome, agile, kind, compassionate, thoughtful, and immanently lovable. Pat's father was a pediatrician, and his mother a neo-natal intensive care nurse; they had met during his dad's internship at Barnes Hospital in St. Louis, fallen in love and never really recovered. Both coming from long established Catholic families, they were married in the cathedral with eight priests in the sanctuary.

Nine months and three days later, Dr. and Mrs. Thomas Gray became the parents of Patrick Thomas Gray, who from the beginning showed every sign of being a phenomenal child. Fourteen months later, they became the parents of another son, Edwin Andrew Gray, who had severe cerebral palsy. Their final child was delivered four years after their marriage, Annette Marie Gray, who showed signs of slight mental retardation but was absolutely beautiful physically and loved everyone.

Patrick, as the eldest child, was taught to help care for Edwin's needs and to watch over his sister. He connected emotionally with them both and took delight in making Edwin happy. While it was difficult even for his parents always to know what Edwin needed, Patrick seemed to have a special gift for understanding him. Pat was the first to notice that Edwin was extremely intelligent and helped him to find ways to communicate and utilize that gift. The two grew up not only as brothers but also as best friends. Edwin knew that while others, even his parents, might not understand him or his needs, he could always count on Pat and his face would light up whenever he entered the room.

By the time Pat reached junior high school, he was being pursued both by girls for his good looks and personality and by coaches who had noticed his extraordinary physique and agility in physical education classes. Pat took it all in stride, loved being with the girls, and became the quarterback of the football team. He possessed a simple straightforward approach and had little difficulty in telling both the girls and the coaches that his family was his first priority and that he needed to spend most of his free time with them. Both the girls and the coaches were a bit perturbed that neither was in the driver's seat when it came to Pat, but he was important enough to both that they were willing to take the back seat to his family.

Pat considered Edwin his student as well as brother and friend. From the first grade through high school, Patrick would share whatever he had learned each day with Edwin, who then progressed educationally along with his teacher. Annette was placed in a special education section which allowed her to progress at whatever speed she was capable. She had little interest in books but loved people and tried to please her parents by learning what she could.

As Pat approached graduation from high school, he asked the principal that Edwin be given the opportunity to be tested in the same subjects that Pat had taken and also receive a diploma at graduation if he passed them all. The principal was aware of Edwin as he had attended all of Pat's football and basketball games in a wheelchair, accompanied by his parents. He was guarded in his response and told Pat that he would have to check with the state department of education as Edwin had never attended classes but that he would consider the request.

At graduation Pat received as valedictorian the honor of giving the commencement address. He praised his school, his parents, and his sister, but told the audience that the real hero in his life and the one he wished most to imitate was his brother Edwin. He then motioned to his parents to bring Edwin to the stage. They pushed his wheelchair next to where Patrick stood. Patrick took off his graduation gown and cap and placed them on Edwin, who was amazed but smiled broadly. Patrick was not finished: "Our state now wishes to confer upon you a diploma, recognizing that you have fulfilled the scholastic requirements for graduation, the first such diploma awarded to someone who never attended a single class." At that, the entire graduation class rose and cheered for Edwin.

The scholarships announced at graduation included several for Pat, even a couple from Ivy League universities. Against his parents' wishes, Pat chose to stay at home and attend a local college so that he could continue to be with his family and help with Edwin and Annette. His freshman year was the most difficult of his life, not because of the studies but due to the tragedies within the family he loved so deeply.

In January Edwin was diagnosed with pneumonia. He had always had difficulty with his lungs, and the new stress upon his frail body was more than it could withstand. With his family at his bedside and Pat holding Edwin's hand, they looked at one another with the love they had shared throughout their lives, and Edwin died. Father Mark Sanders, who had just finished anointing Edwin, stood by his parents and began the prayers for the dead. Pat placed his arms around the body of his brother and hugged him tightly, not wishing to let him go. After a few minutes, the burly former Marine, now priest, helped Pat release his brother. "You have all taken care of Edwin all his life. God loved him through you. Now you must trust God to care for him and give him a fullness of life."

Pat lost a lot of his enthusiasm for life when Edwin died. He seemed disoriented without Edwin. But there was still another tragedy to befall the Gray family which would further cause Pat to question his values and even his faith.

Annette in her sophomore year of high school stayed after school for much-needed tutoring. Following the session but before she left the school building, she was beaten and raped. In her innocence, she had always trusted everyone and had been easy prey for the janitor, who had lured her into an empty classroom with promises of a surprise. Prior to the days of background checks for school employees, the administration established only after the attack that the janitor had an extensive record of sexual misconduct with minors. As a result of this experience, Annette became withdrawn and mistrusting. She was not emotionally capable of returning to school that year and required prolonged counseling.

Pat was the first in the family to see Annette when she entered the house following the rape. Her formerly beautiful face was now swollen, with one eye practically closed. She was crying inconsolably. She was not able to tell Pat what had happened and only her mother, Emily, was finally able to put Annette's story together. When Pat understood what had happened, he tore out of the house in absolute rage and ran to the high school. There he found the janitor emptying the trash into the dumpster in the back of the school. Pat leapt upon his back, knocking him to the ground. With his knee on his chest, he struck the janitor over and over again with his fists. The janitor had lost consciousness when the police lifted Pat from his body. Emily had called them, warning them as to what she feared Pat might do.

The janitor was taken to the hospital with a broken nose and jaw and multiple lacerations while Pat was taken the police station and put in a cell until he could regain his composure. He was released that evening into the custody of his parents. Once the police were able to reconstruct the entire story, no charges were pressed against him. The janitor was tried and convicted for rape and received a life sentence.

Pat did not return to classes at the college for several weeks following the rape. He stayed in his room, took long walks, and spent hours in an empty church. He had lost his brother, and now his sister was like a zombie. He had loved them both so deeply, and they had depended upon him to protect them. He felt he had let them down and was a failure. This young man who had been given everything by God now felt that he was totally abandoned and had no reason to live.

Two weeks after the rape Father Mark Sanders went to the darkened church to lock it up for the night and was startled to see movement in the back pew. It was Pat. He took him over to the rectory, and they began to talk. At first Pat was reluctant, guarded, and seemed almost angry with Father Mark. Finally Mark was able to break through the barrier, and Pat let all his feelings about Edwin and Annette and God's injustice spill out with such force and fury that the priest was startled. It was past midnight when they stopped talking, and Pat promised to return the next evening.

Pat continued to meet with Father Mark almost every day for several weeks. Mark shared his stories of Vietnam and the miraculous way that God had worked in his own life through tragedy. Gradually Pat began to trust God once again and to steady his tottering faith. As the months progressed and their friendship grew, Mark suggested to Pat that he might have a vocation. He perceived in Pat's innate desire to help others, as he had Edwin and Annette, the possibility of his using that to address people's hunger for God. Pat had to admit that the greatest happiness he had ever experienced was in the love and support he had given to Edwin, Annette, and others and that gift might well be used within the priesthood.

After Pat graduated from college, he entered the seminary. He had never been happier. He made friends with James Chudy, Christian Mangan, and Juan Romero-Martinez. He was impressed with James, especially the devotion he had for his blind parents and the strength with which he accepted his beloved father's death. He admired Christian for the faith that impelled him to study for the priesthood despite his own father's objections and personal failure as a priest. He saw Juan as the most driven man he had ever known, leaving his country and the parents he loved so deeply to come to another country to study for the priesthood. In truth, all three of them admired Pat, whose obvious gifts could have made him successful in any walk of life, and yet chose to become a priest so he could help people spiritually. They became close friends as seminarians and would remain so as priests.

No one was happier at Pat's ordination than Annette. She had always loved the priests assigned to her parents' church, frequent guests for dinner in their home. She looked upon them as an extension of her family. She was radiant as she sat with her parents in the first row of the cathedral and watched the bishop as he placed his hands upon her brother's head. At his First Mass the following day, Father Pat praised the exceptional manner in which his parents had lived their faith and the way God had used them to heal the sick. He then spoke of the inner beauty of his sister, which far exceeded her startling exterior beauty which others seem to recognize initially. Annette seemed confused and embarrassed by his remarks. But Pat's comments about Edwin were the most touching; he expressed his undying love for his brother and a desire to achieve the holiness and gentleness that he had seen in Edwin. He also spoke of Father Mark Sanders, who had died two years before in a tragic automobile wreck as he drove through the night to minister to his parish. Pat attributed his priesthood to the example of Mark and told of how he had brought him from the brink of despair to the joy of rediscovering his faith and wishing to serve God in the priesthood.

Father Pat was assigned as associate pastor in three parishes over the first six years of his priesthood. It would have been difficult to find fault in his ministry; difficult, but not impossible. His first pastor was Father Jason Arnold, who had been ordained ten years before Pat and thought he knew everything there was to know about . . . well, about everything. He couldn't believe that Pat was as amiable and open as he appeared to be and thought he must be trying to undermine his authority as pastor by capturing the affection of the people. He resented Pat's intelligence, good looks, and amiability which won the admiration of the congregation.

Whenever Jason heard Pat praised by parishioners, he found himself becoming angry. Jason would not have been able to identify his jealousy of his brother priest, but most of the parishioners noticed it in Jason's eyes and demeanor whenever Pat entered the scene. Pat was too open and young to identify Jason's coldness, even rudeness, towards him, but he knew that his pastor definitely did not like him. Jason spoke to Pat only when necessary and shared few meals with his associate. When they were alone, Pat received the cold shoulder, icy glances, and abrupt instructions regarding his duties.

Jason was a master of passive aggressive personality traits. When they were with others, Jason's disposition changed so as not to appear to others as unchristian.

As a newly ordained priest, Pat was hurt that his first pastor would treat him in such demeaning manner and decided to confront Jason.

"Father Jason, you seem to be displeased or angry with me. If I have done something wrong, I'm really sorry. I'm new at being a priest, and I don't want to offend you. Please let me know what I can change or what I need to do differently."

Pat's humility and vulnerability irritated Jason, who recognized that his unwarranted apology had proven him to again be the better man, adding further coal to the fire of his jealousy. He wanted to hurt Pat as he turned to look at him coldly: "Why, what could you have possibly done? You, the fair-haired boy wonder priest of the diocese? When the bishop assigned you to my parish, he informed me that he was sending me a great gift; I'm still wondering when it will arrive. Now I believe you have some work to do if it is not too much trouble." With that, Jason turned on his heel, leaving Pat stunned but now more aware of the root of the problem.

It was an unfortunate first assignment for Pat, one that lasted for two years. Recognizing the problem with Jason was not something he had caused or could do anything to remedy, he poured himself into parish work, earning the respect and friendship of most of the parish. The secretary became accustomed to parishioners trying to find a diplomatic way to request that Pat take care of their spiritual needs rather than their pastor. Although Jason was the pastor and had been in the parish for some years,

Pat had the majority of the weddings and funerals and his appointment calendar was filled with counseling sessions. Pat was invited to dinner at the homes of the parishioners almost every night, diversions he welcomed rather than sharing a meal with Jason, certain of either no conversation or monosyllabic responses to whatever conversation he initiated. When he was reassigned, Pat was given a reception by the parish; Jason's absence was noted by all as was his lack of praise or good wishes for Pat at the weekend Masses.

Pat's second assignment was as an associate to Father Josh Constantine and, happily, could not have been more different from his experience with Jason. Father Josh's son, Joshua, was still living in the rectory with his father, and Pat and Joshua immediately became close friends. Josh was delighted as he recognized that Pat could be a strong positive influence in the life of his son. He also saw the extraordinary gifts Pat had as a priest and made certain those gifts were utilized within the parish. Within a few months, Josh began to look upon Pat not only as his brother priest but as another son and a friend. Pat could not have been happier; he had a pastor whom he respected, a friend in Joshua, and sufficient latitude and even generous encouragement to use his talents.

Father Joel Taylor was the pastor of the church to which Pat was assigned for the third and final time as an associate. Joel had experienced difficulty with arrogance in the early years of his priesthood; but through professional help and counseling from his brother priests, he had become an extraordinarily compassionate, kind priest and an excellent mentor for young associates. He and Father Josh were close friends, and Josh had told him how much he hated losing Pat. Josh had also mentioned that Pat endured the same ill treatment from Father Jason that he meted out to all his young associates.

Joel was determined to make whatever time Pat might spend as his associate one that would help him along in his priesthood. He realized that it was almost time for Pat to receive his own parish, and he made certain that Pat became familiar with all the administrative responsibilities that are part of being a pastor.

Pat was in the parish for only three months when Annette showed up in his office accompanied by a young man from Nebraska. They sat on the couch holding hands, and Annette told Pat that Carl had asked her to marry him. She had met him at the church bingo, where he distributed bingo cards for the Knights of Columbus. He was from a Nebraska farm family of eight. They were both twenty-seven years old, and Pat could hardly contain his joy as he saw the love they shared. Carl's simple goodness was as obvious as Annette's beauty. They began marriage instructions that day and were married six months later. Pat felt that he could now rest assured that his little sister had a protector who would care and love her all their married life.

Pat was nearing the end of his two years with Joel when a highly agitated woman in her early forties whom he had never met or seen in church asked to see him on a personal matter. She sat across the desk from Pat and for several minutes said nothing. There was something about her manner that told Pat he should not initiate the conversation; so he waited. She glanced around the room nervously, stared at the carpet, and picked at her finger nails.

"I don't like being here. I'm also not sure that I can go through with this; perhaps I should not have come at all."

"If you would rather leave and come back at another time, I'll be happy to reschedule your appointment. You might be more at peace later."

"Putting this off would just make it more difficult. I've got to tell someone so that they can stop him. I hope you will understand. You seem nice, but you're very young."

"Who needs to be stopped and why?"

"It's Father Jason Arnold. He has had sexual relations with my eleven-year-old son."

Pat involuntarily gasped and felt his stomach turn cold. The news of priests involved in pedophilia had just broken in the country, and Pat had difficulty in even comprehending how a priest could possibly be guilty of such a heinous betrayal of trust. "When, how did this happen?"

"My son Rex is an altar server in Father Jason's parish. Rex served morning Mass last Saturday, and Father invited him over to the rectory for breakfast afterwards. Father told him he had something to show him in his bedroom. There were pictures of naked boys and . . . I can't say anymore . . . It's too painful." She started to leave.

"Please, sit down; we need to get to the bottom of this." She resumed her seat, and Pat buried his head in his hands as he thought about what he should do. After a few minutes he said, "I'm going to need to talk with Rex, you, and your husband together."

"My husband left shortly after Rex was born, and I have no idea where he is. I'm not sure that Rex could talk with any priest right now."

Pat convinced her to come back the following day and to bring Rex with her.

As soon as she left, he went to the Blessed Sacrament to pray about Rex, his mother, and Father Jason. He was there for over an hour. As he prayed he thought of the poor boy, the agony of his mother, the harm that could happen to the Church, and the future of Father Jason. His own painful experience with Jason's coldness made it difficult for Pat to imagine him being involved in any crime of passion. But if this were really happening, Pat knew that the bishop would need to be informed and that Jason needed to be gone from the parish; he could not remain in a position where he could molest other boys.

And then Pat remembered Annette's rape and realized the boy must be experiencing the same hell that she lived through. The memory rekindled Pat's anger, and he was tempted to deal with Jason in the same manner he employed with the janitor. As he prayed, he found that he had a great deal of unresolved issues with Jason. He had simply bowed his head and kept going while he lived with Jason, accepting anything that Jason heaped upon him, knowing that his position as his associate would not last too long. When Pat recognized deep resentment still lingered in his heart towards Jason, he resolved that this would not enter into his handling of this scandal. The anger blazed again when he considered the harm that such an act could inflict not only upon the boy but also upon the Church that he had given his life to serve. Kneeling, he begged the Holy Spirit to give him the wisdom he needed after having found himself in the middle of a crisis that frightened, angered, and disgusted him.

Rex and his mother arrived fifteen uncomfortable minutes late for their appointment. The boy was large for his age and appeared both beaten down and nervous. He did not shake Pat's hand when it was offered but looked away. Pat began their meeting with a prayer, asking the Holy Spirit to heal those who were hurting and to guide their meeting. Neither mother nor son responded in any manner to the prayer.

"Rex, I know this is very difficult for you. I want you to know that I'm here to help you. I need to hear what happened between you and Father Jason so that I will know what I need to do. I can't tell you how important what you say is for everyone involved."

The boy did not take his eyes off the floor except to glance at his mother from time to time as if for approbation. "Mother told you. Why do I need to say anything? It hurts too much."

"I need to hear you tell me, Son."

The room was quiet for several minutes. "He took me to the rectory. He gave me some donuts and funny-tasting soda pop. I didn't feel so good and was sleepy and wanted to go home, but he told me that he had something he wanted to show me in his bedroom. He had me sit on the bed next to him, and he showed me some pictures of some native boys on some islands without any clothes on. I was becoming more and more sleepy and couldn't keep my eyes open. I must have gone to sleep. When I woke up, I didn't have any clothes on either, and my butt was sore. Father wasn't around anywhere. I got dressed and went home and told Mom what had happened." Rex glanced at his mother again, and she patted him gently on the back.

After they left, Pat thought about what had been said. In the two years that he had lived with Jason, he had never seen any sweets in the house as Jason was a diabetic. He had never seen any kind of soda in the refrigerator. Somehow the story wasn't gelling for Pat; he just couldn't imagine the fastidious Jason doing the things that Rex had related. Additionally, he knew that Jason was too smart to commit an act which would almost certainly come to light later and ruin his life.

Pat had never remembered to return the key to Jason's rectory when he had been reassigned. He decided that an unannounced visit was called for. Neither Jason's car nor his present associate's car was in the driveway. He let himself in by the kitchen door. As he had suspected, he found no traces of donuts or of any kind of soda, funny-tasting or not. He then went to Jason's bedroom and hunted for any kind of inappropriate reading material. He looked under the bed, through the closet, through the medicine chest, even in the dirty clothes hamper; there was nothing incriminating, nothing suspicious at all. He went to Jason's office and found nothing.

Pat then sat down in the office and waited for Jason's return. It was almost an hour later when Jason returned from his hospital call. He was startled to find Pat sitting in his office. "And what would you be doing in my office, Father Patrick? I do not remember extending any invitation."

"The invitation came indirectly through Rex Wilson and his mother, who said that you raped the boy."

"WHAT? I did WHAT? You sure as hell can't believe that?"

"Actually, you know, I don't. I don't think a cold fish like you would have sufficient passion for anyone besides yourself to risk any kind of relationship, immoral or not. I'm not sure that I care enough about you to care what might happen to you, but I do care enough about the Church and the grave scandal she would suffer if this were true. So you and I have to figure out what is going on and try to stop a great deal of suffering."

In the following hours Jason and Pat hatched a plan which involved both the bishop and the police. The police found that Mrs. Wilson had a criminal record for extortion, had read the newspaper stories of the pedophilia scandals in other dioceses, and had decided to set up Jason and the diocese for lawsuits. She did have a husband who helped coach Rex on the details of the alleged rape, promising him a handsome reward for a good performance. They had even gone to the trouble to have Rex join the altar servers three months before. What they had not counted on was Pat's knowledge of Jason and of the rectory. It also helped that Jason had attended a deanery meeting on that fateful Saturday morning.

Jason knew that Pat had saved him from grave scandal and perhaps even the loss of his priesthood. While the words Pat had spoken to him in the office that day hurt his pride deeply, he also recognized some truth in them. The letter of apology to Pat was probably the most difficult thing Jason had done in years, but also probably one of the most beneficial both for himself and for Pat. From that incident on, Jason adopted a kinder, more understanding attitude towards his associates. It would be stretching the truth to state that Jason and Pat became great friends, but they both became better priests through the incident.

The bishop finally assigned Pat as a pastor to a community that had endured a string of elderly priests who lacked sufficient energy or desire to inspire much activity in the parish. He delighted in accepting the challenge to breathe new life into the listless community, and it was a tribute to them that they responded so rapidly and wholeheartedly to his efforts. Father Mark Sanders could not have been more perceptive in foreseeing Pat's desire to help others as being beneficial to them both spiritually and physically. Within two years Pat had enlivened the hearts of his flock to the extent that they became one of the model parishes of the diocese. Pat had found them hungry for the life of Christ and hurting from being neglected spiritually.

During his priesthood, Pat would serve as pastor in a series of parishes that needed rejuvenation. He seemed to take the same joy in helping them that he had experienced in teaching Edwin or protecting Annette. The people always saw a real hunger in Pat to help them come closer to Jesus Christ. It was a hunger that would never be satiated but would serve to make him an extraordinary priest.

CHAPTER TWENTY

AVE ATQUE VALE

Father Adam Coors had mixed feelings as he drove through the countryside towards the annual priests' retreat at St. Dominic Monastery. He had now been ordained for 39 years, had been in and out of treatment for his alcoholism three times, struggled with sobriety every day, attended daily AA meetings, and still loved the priesthood. He often reflected upon his life as a boy: his mother disappearing, his irresponsible and unloving father, the kindness of Father Smith, the older couple who had taken him into their home, and his siblings disappearing from his life. He had long since stopped being sorry for himself and still wanted to become a truly holy priest.

He looked forward to seeing some of his brother priests but dreaded seeing others. He continued to feel embarrassed around priests who had witnessed his periodic drunkenness and felt particularly awkward around those who had attempted to cover for him. He anticipated the struggle he would experience as the priests met before dinner for cocktails and decided that it might be best for him to take a short walk at that time to avoid both the temptation and the feelings of unworthiness.

Adam's mother, Ferris, had surfaced ten years into his priesthood. He had not seen or heard from her since the day he returned home from school twenty-seven years before to find that she had left. He was making calls in a convalescent home when his attention was drawn to a lone woman in a wheelchair mindlessly singing songs to herself, which for some reason unknown to him sounded familiar. Feeling sorry for the lone woman, he went over to greet her. She stopped singing abruptly and looked at him vacantly. Once he saw her eyes, he knew it was his mother; and the songs were those he remembered her singing during his childhood. He knelt beside her and told her who he was. Ferris appeared to struggle to understand, then gave up and returned to her singing.

Adam returned to the convalescent home weekly for almost two years. His mother never displayed any sign of recognition. One night he was called to anoint her. She was barely conscious, but opened her eyes for a moment and looked at him. She appeared to be trying to say something before she died; he felt sure it was "Adam." Adam said a funeral Mass with only his brother Jake present; his other siblings expressed little sorrow and said they had no intention of mourning the mother who had abandoned them.

Twenty-seven years had passed since then, and Adam didn't like all those memories that had haunted him throughout the years returning as he drove toward the retreat. He felt depression taking hold of him. He knew Jesus was the only answer for him and that with all the sadness in his life he was called to be a priest. He knew life was difficult for everyone at times and he just had to keep going—and keep sober.

As Adam drove onto the monastery grounds, he saw from the number of cars that most of the priests had already arrived. He thought to himself how the make and model of the cars so often spoke to the character and personality of the priests who owned them. There were a couple of Cadillacs, a Lexus, a few Ford Focuses, several rather worn Chevrolet compacts, a number of pickup trucks, a Jeep, and a large number of Japanese-made inexpensive cars. Pope Francis was still relatively new in his papacy but had already made comments about the need for simplicity and poverty among the clergy and had specifically mentioned how inappropriate it was for them to own expensive cars. Adam wondered if those comments would change the look of the parking lot during priest retreats in the future but rather doubted that it would. Priests are not immune from the process of rationalization to justify what they want in life.

Father Josh Constantine was unpacking his Cadillac when Adam drove up. He had stopped to visit his son Joshua's family in a small town where he worked as a forest ranger. Josh made any excuses he could to visit Joshua's home, primarily because of the pride he had in his son and the grandson who also bore his name. Joshua had become a fine man and had married a devout Catholic girl, Marilyn, who had given him four children. Marilyn had prepared a huge dinner for Father Josh as she shared the love Joshua had for his father.

Life had been good to Father Josh. He was now sixty-three years old and loved the priesthood more than ever. God had used his son Joshua to open the gates of Josh's heart, and no one, including Josh, had ever imagined so much love was there. As he had worked to gain the trust and love of his son, he learned to place himself and his desires second to others. His parishioners were the recipients of his growth. No one in his parishes was ever scandalized by the son he had. In fact, as a teenager Joshua had become the "adopted son" of all the parishioners. When Father Pat Gray had joined Josh and Joshua in the rectory as the parish assistant, he brought an added dimension of family.

As Adam and Josh reached the registration desk, they ran into Father Stan Janoski. Stan was as intense as ever. He wore his cassock, while the other priests wore casual clothes, relaxed around their brother priests. Stan also wore his customary grim expression and was quick to let Adam and Joshua know that the first conference would begin in only a half hour and that they might hurry lest they be late. As both had been

255

ordained more than twenty years longer than Stan, they simply nodded their agreement while thinking to themselves what an uptight little twit he was.

Stan was always the first to arrive at the retreat. He took a good deal of pride in the precise manner in which he lived his life. He ran his parish like a concentration camp, and his parishioners referred to him as "the commandant." Stan would spend much of his retreat in fervent prayer before the Blessed Sacrament. He shied away from too much contact with the other priests as he knew he was never really accepted by them. He was a good priest, but he would go to his grave without being emotionally connected to those whom he served or those with whom he served. If it is possible to love through service and hard work, he loved. He loved dispassionately.

Patrick Gray, Yancy Trotter, and Christian Mangan had arrived earlier in the afternoon as their parishes were not far distant from the monastery. They were in the recreation room, trying to recover from a busy weekend in their parishes. The bonds they had formed as seminarians almost twenty years before had only grown stronger. They had formed a support group and met once a month to encourage one another in their priesthood.

Patrick was still the guy who had to help everybody. He defined his priesthood by trying to find out what each person needed, either spiritually or physically, and meeting those needs. His early training with Edwin and Annette had honed an aptitude for anticipating the needs of others, and he received his own joy in life by fulfilling those needs. He was often swept up in the compassionate love he had for others, and he empathized with their problems and pains as well as their joys. His love for Annette and her husband was a constant in his life, and he took his position as uncle to their children very seriously.

Edwin's death had left a real hole in Patrick's life as he deeply wanted a brother with whom to share his priesthood. As Yancy had no siblings (as well as he could ascertain), he and Patrick became as close as any two brothers could be. Again, Pat saw that Yancy needed a family beyond that of the Church and he sought to supply it. When Christian was a seminarian his parents had been cool to his becoming a priest. Christian then turned to his two classmates, Pat and Yancy, for the encouragement that he needed. Christian and James Chudy had been close; but with James's death, Pat and Yancy became his closest friends.

Priests do not always have the satisfaction of seeing the result of their labors. Yancy would be an exception in that area. His work in pro-life causes often brought tangible results in the form of healthy babies and happy mothers. One of the most gratifying experiences resulted from the young woman he found of the steps of the abortion clinic the evening he discovered his personal background. Peggy was the girl's name, and she gave birth to Joseph Ryan six months after she met Yancy. She married Russ Dempsey, the father of her child, a year later. They joined Yancy's parish and he baptized Joseph Ryan. By the time he was eight, Joseph began to serve daily Mass for Yancy. Joseph never understood why Yancy took him to breakfast at I-Hop each year on his birthday; Peggy knew. Joseph was blessed with an extraordinary musical talent; he could play both the piano and the violin with equal dexterity by the time he was eight. At midnight Mass on Christmas, he had brought the congregation to tears as he stood before the ambo in his red altar server cassock and starched white surplice with violin in hand and played the "Ave Maria" as a communion hymn.

By noon of the second day of the retreat, some of the priests who were always late for the required retreats came drifting in. Those same priests would also find excuses to leave the retreat at least a day early and would miss the afternoon conference each day to take advantage of a nearby golf course. They would invariably have negative things to say about the theme of the retreat and ridicule the presentations of the retreat master. Jason Arnold was the leader of this group and took delight in mimicking the retreat master's delivery. He had natural abilities to mimic others, a talent he had perfected over years by ridiculing his bishops and brother priests. This year was a little different as the priests had voted to ask the highly regarded Bishop Luke Smith to return to the diocese to lead the retreat. Everyone was so eager to hear the new bishop that attendance at the conferences was at record level.

Bishop Luke did not disappoint. He knew his brother priests well and understood that no priest ever faces a more critical audience. They have all been well educated in aesthetical theology, have attended multiple retreats and religious conferences, have prepared hundreds or even thousands of homilies themselves, have read a ton and half of spiritual books, and can catch the scent of a phony three counties away. They all want the speaker to do well but have grave doubts that he will. Luke knew that he had to speak from the heart of a priest to the hearts of other priests with no frills, no smoke and mirrors. He spoke of living the priesthood of Jesus Christ while burdened with individual eccentricities and sinfulness. He was open about his own sinfulness, his own sensitivity regarding racial prejudice towards him, and his own failures in attempting to become the holy priest he still desired to be. He was successful in placing all the priests in the same storm-tossed boat as he and rowed them word by word to the peaceful harbor that living in Christ can bring. He renewed within them the hope that is sometimes dimmed through sin, disappointments, discouragements, personal failure, fatigue, or even plain ennui. By the end of the initial conference, he had captured the trust and interest of almost every priest present and would build on that through each talk.

On the last day of the retreat, the priests had already loaded their cars with their belongings, ready to make a hasty getaway back to their parishes as soon as the last Mass was celebrated. Bishop Luke seemed a bit somber when he came to the ambo to deliver his last homily to the group.

"A few minutes ago, Father Owens, not having seen our senior priest in the diocese this morning, went to Msgr. Lillis's room to check on him. He found that this man who had been a mentor to many of us had died in his sleep. Charlie Lillis was eighty-eight years old, had been a priest for sixty-three years, and continued as pastor of his little church in Prairieville. None of us ever heard Charlie say an unkind word about another priest or any of his parishioners. All of us loved his almost ever-present smile and the way he seemed to genuinely care for each of us, even when we didn't deserve it. We loved his hearty laughter and even his corny jokes which he seemed to enjoy telling far more than we enjoyed hearing.

"I had prepared a closing homily for this retreat, but I would suggest that Charlie's life is a better homily for all of us than I would ever be able to give. He was a priest to the core. He loved being a priest, loved saying Mass, loved proclaiming Christ and giving hope to others. While the majority of priests find it necessary to retire from parish life as they near seventy, Charlie could never understand how they could voluntarily leave a life filled with so much love and joy. We all knew him as a man of prayer, simplicity, humility, and service. That is the life that all of us were called to, but few of us seem to totally embrace.

"You will forget much of what I have said during the retreat these last few days, but I doubt that any of us will ever forget the lesson that Charlie taught by the Christ-like manner in which he lived out his priesthood. It would be my prayer that Charlie will live in our hearts every day and that his memory will help us all be better priests of Our Lord Jesus Christ. That is who and what we are; that is our identity: We are priests of God."

There was little conversation among the priests after Mass as they left to return to their parishes. They were all thinking of Charlie, the kind of priest he was and kind of priests they must strive to become. A few pulled their cars over to the shoulder of the highway and stopped to say a prayer for Charlie and for their brother priests with their human flaws who somehow find the faith and courage to answer Christ's call. All the problems they had left behind in their parishes seemed quite small now. They were priests, and God would find a way to level the mountains and fill in the valleys.

> To the higher shrine of love divine
> My lowly feet have trod.
> I want no other name, nor fame,
> Than this, a priest of God.
>
> Father Abram Ryan (1839-1886)
> Poet Laureate of the Confederacy